MODERN PHYSICS

AND OTHER TALES

Purnell Christian [signature]

MODERN PHYSICS
AND OTHER TALES

PURNELL CHRISTIAN

WATERMARK PRESS

WATERMARK PRESS, INC.
149 North Broadway, Suite 201
Wichita, Kansas 67202

Copyright 1991 by Purnell Christian
All rights reserved

No part of this work may be copied by any means — including electronic, mechanical or photocopying — except with express written permission of the publisher and copyright holder.

Library of Congress Cataloging-in-Publication Data

Christian, Purnell, 1950–
   Modern physics and other tales / by Purnell Christian.
      p. cm.
   ISBN 0-922820-16-3 (hard cover)
   I. Title.
   PS3553.H7275M63 1991
    813'.54—dc20   91-13017
                                CIP

Cover and interior design: John Baxter

Cover art: Tate Gallery, London / Art Resource, New York
Gherardo Dottori, *Explosion of Red on Green*, dated 1910.

FIRST PRINTING

TABLE OF CONTENTS

HEAL THE SICK	3
RASPUTIN	21
TOWN	37
DOGGED	67
MODERN PHYSICS I	79
MODERN PHYSICS II	89
MODERN PHYSICS III	99
APES	105
THE MOWER	119
THE MOBILE	127
AN EVENING WITH THE PROFESSOR	139
THE ICE CREAM MAN	163
69FFF	171
THE CRICKET	181
ANOTHER STUPID WEEKEND	183
FUN WITH DICK AND JANE	221
IN THOSE DAYS	227
BUMS	233
A KILLING	241
BUGMAN	251

MODERN PHYSICS AND OTHER TALES

I'd see them walking on the sidewalks, driving cars, going into supermarkets, laundromats, restaurants. Hanging around in bars. Women. They ignored me. I was unemployed. My clothes were worn out, my car was torn up, and I was drinking heavily. The drought had lasted almost a year.

HEAL THE SICK

One day in a bar I ran into this guy I sort of knew. I thought he was a dork but he had a reputation for being a lady's man. We talked. I mentioned my problem. He suggested personal ads.

"Almost as good as a church group. A veritable rain of pussy," he said.

"Forget church groups. Are you talking about ads in the newspaper?" I asked.

"Oh hell no. They've got these single swinger rags now. That's all that's in them. Ads. I guess some people find all their meat in the things."

"That sounds a little kinky. I could get a disease. Amoebic dysentery. Typhoid. Who knows what those people do? Hog cholera."

"Suit yourself," he replied. He returned to his drink.

I went down and bought one of the rags and took it back to my vermin ridden crib. I pushed a week's worth of fast food wrappers off the kitchen table and sat down to study the thing. After awhile the dull repetitiveness got to me and I stopped. In spite of the authors' intentions the desperation leaked out around the periods and commas and dribbled down the page. They were stupid. I didn't fit any of the male self-descriptions which could be roughly classified as "successful executive," "fun loving party animal," or "sincere." The sincere really bugged me. Describing oneself as sincere showed a dangerous lack of self-knowledge. The whole

concept was degrading. A heavy ennui settled upon me. I got up and kicked the newspapers off the couch and laid down. I dozed. I was in a department store or some place. On display was successful executive with three piece suit and razor cut hair. A face like a moray eel. Next was party animal. Dumb and greasy. Finally we had sincere. Desert boots, jeans, flannel shirt. Soulful eyes like a cocker spaniel. Maybe a guitar.
    I woke up. The traffic noise outside had increased so it must be five o'clock. That was something about being unemployed. You lost track of time. Hours, weeks, months. It was much better than working. I poured a shot of tequila and drank it. Then I poured another and sat down at the kitchen table and composed my ad.

WM SEEKS F NIHILIST
AGE/RACE UNIMPORTANT
NO PHOTOS BOX 931F

    I called the rag office. They were open. I went by my mother's house and told her I needed ten dollars for a date. Then I went to the rag office. It was some kind of boutique-like setting. Loud music played. Evidently, this was what swingers preferred. The girl behind the desk took my money and ad, read it, and looked at me like I was a dog turd. I would have bet she didn't know what nihilism was. She probably thought it involved animals or rubber toys or something. It was humiliating. I went home and drank four more tequilas and went to bed.
    I waited. I fiddled with the car until it more or less ran again and spent the rest of my time sleeping 12 hours a day and sitting on the couch reading back issues of *National*

Geographic. The post office didn't call so apparently they weren't swamped with letters.

After two weeks had passed I went to my box. Inside were two thin envelopes. I took them home and opened the first one.

> Sinner! How dare you solicit yourself with such a shameful and Godless statement. Yours is a voice crying out in the wilderness. Call me. I can help.
> —D

This was puzzling. I guess I didn't think a Christian would be reading the rag in the first place. I threw the letter on the table and opened my second and last chance.

> I don't care what you are.
> Let's get together.
> I'll fuck you silly.
> —D

A direct hit. I jumped up and danced a little jig, poured a shot of tequila, and put on 'White Rabbit,' loud. Man, I thought, I should have been doing this years ago.

I went back to the table and stuffed both letters into their envelopes. It was odd that both had signed simply with "D." I read the return address on the letter from the fanatic. Denise Johnson. I shit canned it. I pulled the other letter out and read it again. The return was Dia Smith. No address. Her number was in the book. Well, no time like the present. I dialed it.

"Hello?"

"Is this Dia Smith?"

"Yes."
"I'm the person who placed the personal ad."
"Oh?"
"Yeah. Want to get together for a drink or something?"
"Ok. When?"
"How about tonight?"
"Oh. I don't think I can do that. How about Friday?"
"How about eight o'clock Friday?"
"That would be wonderful."
"Ok. Bye."

This plan was moving like the invasion of France. Dia the nihilist. Dia the undiscovered moon of Pluto. Dia in orbit at the cold clean edge of the solar system. Dia who probably drank absinthe and had nicotine stained fingertips from smoking unfiltered cigarettes. I laid down on my bed and pictured Dia, lean and lithe, stalking my fetid room clad only in black leather bikini bottoms. Maybe with a mohawk haircut. With a purple stripe down the middle.

I daydreamed until Friday. I looked her address up in the phone book. She'd forgotten to give it to me. I didn't know where it was so I got out a city map. It was way out on the edge of town. I was mildly disappointed. I thought a nihilist would probably live in a former machine shop or warehouse, something gritty.

Friday came and I set off. I got on the freeway. I drove a long time. Finally I got there. It was terrible. A boxy cluster of crummy new apartments or condominiums or whatever they're called. The wind was hot and blew continuously from the south. Asphalt and concrete, imitation wood siding, little trees bent over in the wind, brown grass. On second thought, perhaps a nihilist didn't care where she lived. I knocked and she answered. She was wearing some kind of smocky looking dress and sandals. Maybe the leather was underneath. She had blonde hair and pale skin and green eyes. She looked about thirty. She was a good looking woman.

"Hello."

"Hello, Dia. I'm Chuck."

"Nice to meet you, Chuck. Where're we going?"

"To a quaint little bistro I'm familiar with. Let's go."

We got in my car and set off. She looked at the dust and bug splattered windshield.

"When was the last time you washed your car?" she asked.

"About five years ago."

It was true. I hadn't washed it in five years. Cars were a virtual necessity but piddling with them wasn't. I kept it outside and the rain occasionally cleaned it off. She looked at the pile of fast food wrappers and beer cans and banana peels on the floor.

"It's disgusting."

She was serious. The program had developed a small glitch.

"I thought you were a nihilist," I said.

"I never said that!" We were on the street headed downtown.

"Then why did you answer my ad?"

"Why did you call me?"

"Because you said you'd fuck me silly."

"What? No! I said I'd help you."

I pulled over to the curb. I'd committed a major blunder. Somehow I'd switched letters and names. Denise was the nihilist. Dia was the Christian. I'd thrown away the nihilist's address. Where was it? Probably ten feet under at the county landfill by now. I started laughing. Cars whizzed by on the street. I continued laughing. Dia was looking strange. I stopped laughing.

"Well, Dia. It looks like it's all a big mistake. I'll take you home. It appears I'm with the wrong woman."

"It's the way God wanted it."

"Huh?"

"Yes. He wanted you with me."

"Bullcrap. Let's forget it. I'll run you home. We've both got better things to do."

"No. Wait. I'll go with you."

I looked at her. She looked pretty good. I really had nothing better to do. I needed a drink. The ridiculous aspect of this predicament amused me.

"Ok. But put a lid on the preaching," I said. She said nothing. We started off.

I seldom went out. When I did I went to a bar that was about two blocks from my crib. It didn't have rock music, plants, or a television set. It was tolerable. I drove all the way back to my neighborhood. Rooming houses, junk shops, run down taverns. The place was almost on skid row. Maybe it was skid row. I parked and we got out. The entrance to the bar was off the back alley and down a half flight of concrete stairs.

"What's the name of this place? There's no sign," Dia asked. That was another thing I liked about it. No sign.

"It's called Elmer's."

"Ugh. What an ugly name."

We went in. I really didn't know if it had a name. Elmer had been the owner but he'd hacked up his lungs behind the bar and died and I didn't know who ran the place now. Back about 1920 it had probably been pretty swank. A place where the town movers and shakers could hang after a day in harness. It hadn't aged well. About 1950, I guess, someone had decided the tin ceiling would look better covered up with acoustical tile. Two thirds of it had fallen off leaving the original metal exposed, mottled and rusty. Pipes ran in and out of the walls and ceiling at random where various tenants had made ill-considered and doomed improvements. Water stains blotched the peeling walls. Dia sniffed the air. "I can't believe you'd bring a lady to a place like this," she said.

"Dia, as a general rule, I don't take ladies anywhere. Relax. It's quiet and the booze is cheap."

She sat down gingerly in one of the broken down naugahyde booths that lined one wall. I sat down opposite her. The place had its usual Friday night crowd of about five people. A disheveled drunken couple we'd passed on the way in. Two big Indians playing pool in the back. A wizened old fart holding forth at the bar. As usual, it looked like the waitress had decided to take the month off.

"What'll you have?" I asked.

"Oh. I don't really drink much. A wine cooler I guess."

I went to the bar and ordered two shots of tequila, a glass of water, and the wine cooler. The bartender's face looked like an alligator suitcase. He peered at me curiously when I ordered the wine cooler.

"'Bout time I sold one of them damn things," he said.

I took everything back to the booth. Dia was still there looking unamused.

"Cheers," I said.

I downed one shot and drank some water. Dia pouted and sipped at the cooler.

"So, Dia, what's your claim to fame?"

"I'm an executive secretary."

"For whom? An executive?"

"Of course. He's an important man. You wouldn't know him."

I supposed I was going to have to take this shit all night. I changed the subject.

"What was your childhood like?"

Dia started talking. She told me about her childhood. Mom, Dad, brothers, sisters, church. She was up to twelve years old when she stopped and told me she needed a refill. I went to the bar. The wizened fart was ranting.

"Goddamn spics. Goddamnit. I should round up some of my WWII unit and go down there. We'd run them communist sumbitches back to Cuba. Back to Russia, by God."

The bartender was ignoring the old crock.

"Another wine cooler, please," I said.

"Tell you what, Bud. Sell you eleven of 'em for 50 cents apiece. They ain't movin' so good in here."

I bought the eleven wine coolers and walked back to the booth. The disheveled couple was still there. The woman looked catatonic. Her shirt was open and the slob with her had his hand inside. I tried not to look and sat down with Dia.

"Let's make a long story short. Then you went to high school and then you went to college. Right?" I said.

"No. Then I found Jesus."

"Ok. Ever been in love?"

"Yes. Once. It's really none of your business. What was your childhood like?"

I made up a whopper. A father I never saw, dead in the war. Mom had to clean toilets in rich peoples houses to feed us. Her boyfriends, mostly winos and heroin addicts, used to beat me and take her money. Dia gobbled it up, hook, line, and sinker.

"Oh, that's terrible!"

"Yeah. Listen, so what are you doing with a sleazebag like me?"

"I'm an evangelical Christian. We are to go forth into the world and spread the Gospel of the Lord."

"How old are you?"

"I'm in my mid-twenties."

That probably meant she was 35. I didn't give a shit one way or the other. She was a certified nut anyway you cut it. She got up and went to the can. For someone who didn't drink much she was doing pretty well. Eight of the wine coolers were gone. I needed another shot but as usual I was flat. I opened her purse and rifled through it. A money clip contained about 15 twenties. Now this was a big point in Dia's favor. I peeled off two of them and stuffed them in my shirt pocket. What else? A driver's license. Helen Smith, age 32, contact lenses. The usual makeup and crap they all carry. At the bottom of the purse I found a tattered snapshot. It was Dia and some fat hairy guy in swimsuits. A face like a moray eel. They were sitting outside a palm thatched beach hut. A dark skinned man strummed a guitar behind them. They both looked at the camera with forced smiles of gaiety. There was writing on the back of the photo. "Helen and Frank, Cancun, 1983." I put her stuff back in the purse, closed it, and went to the bar. The fart was still ranting.

"I've thought about this for a long time. I think these UFO fellers have finally taken over the government."

I turned and looked at him. "That's correct, sir. They're usually referred to as Republicans."

He stared at me and blinked.

I got two more tequilas and returned to the booth. Dia hadn't come back. Her game was becoming a little clearer. Five to two said Frank was the executive and also her lover. I still couldn't figure the religious hysteria. Dia returned from the can. She wobbled a little as she crossed the floor. She stopped at the table and stood over me with a scowl on her face.

"Well, mister smart alecky nihilist, what's your excuse?"

"My excuse?"

"Yeah. Where do you get off criticizing decent honest people who work for a living? What makes you so superior?"

"Nothing. I just don't want any part of it."

"I'll bet you haven't done much with your life. You're lazy. And jealous. I bet you never even got out of high school."

"You're wrong there, Dia. I graduated from college."

"Oh yeah? In what?"

"Zoology. With an emphasis on entomology."

"What's that?"

"Insects."

She emitted a snide chuckle and sat down heavily in the booth. "And that's good for nothing, right?"

"Quite the contrary. I've found it invaluable in my ongoing analysis of human society."

She looked at me. I got up and went to the bar for another. I didn't like Dia. She was a mean spirited wench. I was glad I'd stolen her money. The wizened fart had passed out with his head on the bar. I ordered two more shots. Out of the corner of my eye I saw one of the Indians pull the fart's wallet. I went back to the booth. Dia was sullen. She was working on another wine cooler.

"Let me advance a hypothesis, Dia. It goes like this:

There's an executive secretary who's been carrying on for years with the executive."
She tightened. I continued. "Maybe the dude's told her he'll divorce his wife and marry her. Maybe not. Anyway, she's getting a little bored with the situation. She's going to even the score a little. So, under the self-deluding guise of spreading the Christian faith she goes out with a stranger, somebody from the seamy side of life. You know, slumming. Just to see what it's like."
She glared. "You're not fit to clean his toilet."
Well, well. Bullseye. I killed the two tequilas. "Maybe that's why you're here," I said.
"You can take me home now."
"Ok."
We walked towards the door. The catatonic woman was still sitting there with her blouse undone, staring at infinity. Her boyfriend was passed out, slumped in a corner of the booth with his mouth hanging open. We got in my junker and headed out. I was a little popped so I thought I'd avoid the freeway and take the surface streets. We drove up the old highway through the middle of town. Dia sat in icy silence, arms folded across her chest, staring straight ahead.
This street was once the major north-south seam of the prairie town. It had gotten a little rusty and the stuffing was popping out. Block after block of abandoned store fronts. Seedy used car lots hanging on for dear life. Brown grass in the fissures of the curbs and sidewalks. A brief flash of color and vitality for a couple of blocks where the Asian immigrants had taken hold and then more of the same. Traffic lights swayed in the hot wind. I drove on. Finally we were at the ragged edge of town and back at Dia's place. I was weary. I

was tired of her. Our evening together had been a mistake. I pulled up in front of her crib. She finally spoke.

"Aren't you going to walk me to my door?"

"All right."

We got out. God, this was a horrendously ugly place. Forlorn and barren on the windswept prairie. We walked up to her doorstep.

"Aren't you going to kiss me goodnight?"

After telling me what a loser and pervert I was now she wanted to kiss. I guessed I could stand it. I'd never see her again anyway. She stuck her tongue in my mouth.

"Want to come in for a while?" she asked.

"Why?"

"I'm still planning to convert you."

Like I said, I hadn't been with a woman in almost a year. She was confused and irrational but so was every third person you met these days. We went inside.

"I want to bond with you," she said.

"You mean fuck?"

"No. I mean bond. You and me and God."

"Let's leave God out of it. I don't think I could do much if He was watching."

"Oh, you're a vile man. God is always watching. I'll be back. I must prepare myself."

She trotted off to what was evidently the bedroom. I looked around. The inside of her apartment was worse than the outside. She had horrible things hung everywhere on the walls. Photographs of kittens hanging from ropes and windowsills. Paintings on black velvet of conquistadors. Deformed children with huge dark eyes watching squirrels. I felt my gorge rise. Spread on a coffee table were several glitzy magazines. *Cosmopolitan, Architectural Digest,* something called *"New Body."* She needed a new brain. The tequila had turned on me. I shouldn't be here. I found a half bath off the kitchen and stuck my finger down my throat. The tequila and the remains of dinner came up in one gush. It was clean. No dry heaves. I rinsed out my mouth and went into the kitchen. It was as crappy looking as the rest of the place. Lace curtains, more cute posters, proverbs, magnetic shit on the refrigerator. On the counter top was a church program. I read it. Sermon: "Jesus was a Businessman, Too." Rev. Frank Goodson. On the back was a list of the board of directors and church employees. "Helen Smith, executive secretary." I recognized the reverend's name. He was occasionally on local television attacking some outbreak of prurience. Ha ha ha. I found a half bottle of white wine and went back to the living room and sat down. Dia still hadn't returned. I was nervous. I could have been home now.

Dia came back into the room. She had changed into a sheer camisole thing and panties. Her breasts poked against the material. The camisole had little red hearts all over it. On the panties was printed "Take me, I'm yours." She looked good anyway.

"All right, Dia. You're getting better."

"First you have to pray with me."

"No."

"Yes."

She led me into her bedroom. I was expecting something grotesque but this was much worse. The room lights were off. Two candles burned on a small bedside table. There were more posters. Large stuffed animals occupied about a third of the narrow twin bed. A bull fighter on black velvet took up most of one wall. The room was cramped and stuffy. The windows were closed. Heat lightning flashed along the horizon. On the wall opposite the bullfighter hung a huge crucifix. It was gaudily painted. Blood dripped from the scalp and side of the Christ. Something out of a Panamanian cane cutter's shack. Dia knelt beside the small altar she'd rigged.

"Pray with me."

"No."

She commenced to mumble. I sat down on the edge of the bed. The nausea was returning. This place was foul. I reached out and stroked her hair. She shoved my hand away.

"Hands off, buster."

A massive headache was coming on. I closed my eyes and pinched the skin between them. Sometimes this worked. I opened my eyes. I was staring at the bullfighter. The artist had outlined his little buttocks with fluorescent paint. Two closed parentheses. They sneered insolently at me. I'd come to the end of the track. I got up and snapped on the overhead light.

"Time to grow up, Helen. Time to quit believing in Prince Charming and Rev. Frank."

I reached up and pulled the bullfighter off the wall, laid it across my knee and broke the frame. Then I ripped the velvet down the middle, turned it, and tore both pieces in half. Drawn and quartered. I felt much better but there was still work to do. I took the crucifix off the wall, wedged it between the box springs and floor and stomped. Jesus broke in half. Little white crumbs of plaster sprayed out. I looked at Dia. She had turned her back to the altar and was slumped against it. She gaped dumbfounded. I opened a window. A cool breeze slipped into the room. Lightning flashed. The thunder growled far away. I sat back down on the edge of the bed. Dia was still gaping. I waited. It began like a far away siren. It rose in pitch and intensity. She jumped up screaming, howling. She came at me throwing big roundhouse punches. At first I tried to fend off the blows then I just raised my arms to protect my head and doubled over and endured it. She hit me on the arms and head and back. It didn't hurt. She tried to kick me in the stomach but couldn't get past my elbows. She finally settled on kicking me in the shins. After about two minutes of this she stopped. I put down my arms and peeked out. She was standing over me flushed and panting. Her eyes were pure hate. She lunged again and latched onto my left arm. Her grip was strong. I gave up. It was late and I was tired. She bit me on the upper forearm. She bit down hard and fell to her knees, keeping a solid grip on my arm. I could feel her incisors penetrate the skin. I could see the muscles in her jaw straining. It didn't hurt much. The tequila had taken care of that. Her eyes were closed. She looked like she was praying again. She stayed clamped onto my arm like this for a full minute. Then she let go and fell on the bed and began flailing and thrashing.

"Goddamn you, Frank, Goddamn you!"

She ground her teeth. She clutched and bit the pillow. Finally she settled into some long hard sobbing. For the first time I felt sorry for her. For everyone.

"Well, I should go now," I said.

Dia didn't say anything. She sobbed and moaned. I got

up and left. I stood for a moment on the front steps. A light rain had started. It felt good. Dia opened the door. She'd taken off her top.

"Wait. Don't leave. Stay here with me."

I eyed her warily. I rubbed at some dried blood on my arm. It had begun to throb. She stepped out onto the porch. I moved towards her.

A noise like a shotgun going off boomed down from above. A shower of orange sparks rained from the roof of the apartment building. We both looked up. A glowing white orb like a miniature sun had appeared at the top of the downspout at the corner of the building. It wavered for a moment and then shot down the metal tube and hit the asphalt parking lot and bounced up about five feet into the air and emitted another shower of sparks and blue flame. It skittered and jumped on the asphalt like a drop of water on a hot greased skillet. It sizzled and spat hot flame and moved erratically out into the lot, bounced off a parked car, rolled into the street, and exploded with another shotgun boom over a steel sewer grate.

"Holy Moly! Did you see that?" I yelled to Dia.

She didn't answer. I turned around. She had fallen back through the front door of her apartment and was lying on her back on the floor, curled in a swoon. Her knees were pulled up to her chest and her arms were locked around them. Her eyes were closed. She shook her head from side to side and grunted and chanted in some guttural unintelligible language that I doubt had ever fallen on the ears of civilized man. I stepped inside and stood over her.

"Dia! Snap out of it for Christ's sake!"

She turned towards the sound of my voice. She opened

her eyes. They were rolled back into her head and I could only see the whites. She started wailing.

"Oh, Frank! Frank! I love you Frank. I'll never leave you. Frank! Don't leave me Frank. Don't leave me Frank. Don't leave me."

She shut her eyes and returned to her chanting. I closed the door and got in my junker and drove home. The bite became infected. I had to take antibiotics for two weeks to get rid of it. It finally healed up and left a small scar. That thing I saw was ball lightning. It is rare and usually spectacular. Spectacular enough, at any rate, to cause Dia to think the wrath of Frank had descended upon her. I never saw her again. I leave the personal ads alone.

When Jake thought back on it, which wasn't often, it seemed like his life started to fall apart when he was fifteen. About the time Mrs. Johnson next door had gotten the dog, Rasputin. His father died when Jake was sixteen. Then things went bad in high school. Fights and beatings, bad grades, a few scrapes with the police. No girlfriends. No friends. He had looked forward to getting out of there but it was worse later. Six months in the Army and booted out with a general discharge. More police trouble. Jail time. An eight month marriage. He'd moved out and back into his mother's house half a dozen times. Two dozen menial jobs. And always, like gravity, there was Rasputin. Barking, yapping, cursing him. The furry chronicler of Jake's failures. Rasputin barked when Jake left the house and barked when he returned. Drunk, sober, in a police car, fired. Yip. Yap. Yip yap yap. The dog was a demon from hell. And Jake hated the dog so deeply he was no longer conscious of it.

   At 2:00 on a Monday summer morning in his 25th year Jake and Fat Augie were parked in Jake's mother's driveway. Jake had just spent the last of his last unemployment check at a strip joint with Augie. He was drunk and mad.

   "Goddamnit. Fuckin' whores," he ranted. "I know I stuffed at least fifty dollars down those little bitches' pants and didn't even cop a good feel."

   "Screw it, Jake. Get the whiskey."

   "Shit."

   The car in the driveway had roused Rasputin. Yip yip. Yap. Yip yip yip. Jake had half a fifth of whiskey in his room which he and Augie had come to get and drink. Yip. Yap yap.

   "Can't you shut that fucking cur up?" Augie asked.

"No Augie. It's been barking at me for ten years."

"Well, get the booze then and let's get out of here."

Fat Augie was a pig and a pain in the ass. Jake looked at him. He had to be pushing 300. Big rolls of fat squirting out of him all over. Sweaty and smelly in the heat of the summer night. Jake suspected the strippers would have nothing to do with him mainly because he was with Augie. But Augie had money his parents gave him and a crummy little basement apartment where Jake could go and drink and complain about living with his mother. Jake got out of the car. Yap yap yip. He let himself into the dark house with a key and went to his room. He opened the bottom drawer of the dresser, the one he'd told his mother to stay out of. He picked up the bottle and started to walk back to the driveway. His mother had been doing some picture hanging. She'd left a hammer on a table by the door to the garage. On impulse, Jake picked it up. He went to Augie's side of the car and handed him the whiskey.

"Here," he said.

"What are you doing?"

"I'll be right back."

He went over to the gate at Mrs. Johnson's side yard. Rasputin was yapping furiously. Jake opened the gate and stepped in. He'd never been here before. The yard was planted with flowers and shrubs and carefully manicured. Rasputin reached a crescendo of barking. Jake charged at him. The barks became terror stricken. The dog was old and arthritic. It couldn't move fast. Jake cornered it against the house and swung hard with the hammer. The blow caught the dog along one side of its head. It let out a shriek like torn metal and fell over. Jake got it by the throat with his left hand and strangled it. It kicked and thrashed and then lay still. The hum of air conditioners enfolded the yard. Jake wondered if anyone had heard the commotion. Mrs. Johnson was 3/4 deaf. She wouldn't have heard anything. All the houses in the neighborhood were shut tight against the summer heat. Jake stood over the slain dog. He couldn't leave it here. He picked it up by its collar and took it to Augie's car. Augie was still sitting in the driver's seat.

"What the fuck did you do, man?" he asked.

"I killed it."

Augie looked at the limp dog in Jake's hands. "What kind a dog is it?"

"I don't know. Half poodle, half sewer rat. What difference does it make? Listen, I've got to get rid of it. Give me a ride to the country."

Augie grunted and heaved himself out of the car and opened the trunk.

"Put it in here," he said.

Jake threw the dog in and Augie closed the lid. They drove out to the edge of town. The housing tracts became sparser and ended. They stopped on a graveled county road. Augie shut off the engine and took a pull off the whiskey bottle. He handed Jake the keys.

"Throw the fucking thing in the ditch and let's get out of here."

Jake got out and went around and popped open the trunk. "Ahhhhgh!", he cried out.

Augie clamored out of the driver's seat and came back to see what Jake's problem was. Jake was standing about five feet behind the car staring into the open trunk. Rasputin was standing up. He was trembling violently and emitting a steady stream of little yelping moans.

"Jesus Christ! I thought you said it was dead!"

"I thought it was! Do something!" Jake yelled.
"What? Where's the hammer?"
"I left it at home."
"Goddamnit!"
Augie carefully reached around the dog and came up with a tire iron. He slammed it down hard on the dog's neck. It collapsed into the trunk. He picked it up by the collar and dropped it in the road. "That's what happens when you send a boy to do a man's work," he said.

They got in the car. Augie took a big slug off the bottle and handed it to Jake. Jake's eyes were huge. His hand shook a little as he drank from the whiskey.

"Run over it."
"It's dead now, Jake."
"Run over it. Just to make sure."

Augie started the car and backed up slowly. Jake thought he felt the front wheel pass over the dog. Augie pulled back until Rasputin was illuminated by the headlights. He moved forward, lining up the left front wheel on the dog. There were two distinct bumps as the front and rear tires ran over it.

"Satisfied?"
"Yeah. Let's go."

They drove slowly back to Jake's mother's house, saying nothing. The whiskey was gone. Augie pulled into the driveway.

"Hey. Sure is quiet around here, Jake. Wonder where the fuck the cur is. Ha ha."

"Yeah, Augie. Thanks for the help. Take it easy."

Jake straggled into the house and flopped on his bed. His sleep was dreamless.

Four hours later at 7:30 his mother shook him awake.

"Jake, there's a man on the phone about a job," she said.
Jake got out of bed and stumbled to the telephone.
"Hello?"
"Is this Jake Weaver?"
"Yes."
"Dick Smith at Upco General Contractors. I need some laborers at a job I've got going. You ready to work?"
"Yes, Sir."
"Then get down here as soon as you can. 19th and Mainline."
"Ok."
They hung up. Jake showered and dressed in jeans and work boots. He gobbled the breakfast his mother had prepared.
"Can you give me a ride to 19th and Mainline?" he asked her. "I've got a job."
"Of course, Jake. I'd be glad to. It's nice you've got another job. It's hard paying all the bills and buying all the food myself." His mother seldom missed a chance to remind Jake of his shortcomings.
She drove him down to the job site. It wasn't far. There was a large hole dug for the foundation of another suburban office tower. He went to the trailer that served as an office. They gave him a form to fill out. In the blank about arrests he wrote 'none'. They put him to work stripping concrete forms. After half an hour he'd broken a heavy sweat and was feeling better. By noon his hangover was gone. At five o'clock he walked home feeling better about things than he had in a long time. His approach to the house was marked by silence. The dog. The goddamn fucking flea bag was gone for good.
At dinner his mother was excited.

"Jake, Mrs. Johnson got up this morning and little Rasputin was gone!"

"Maybe a cat ate him. Ha ha."

"That's not funny, Jake. The poor dear is worried sick."

He went to bed early that night. He walked to his job the next day and worked hard. He came home exhausted and again went to bed early. The absence of the barking dog was a blessed thing. Peace reigned about the house for the first time in ten years. Walking home from work on Wednesday he was thinking about his future for the first time in a long while. This was a good paying job. He'd have enough dough on payday to move out. And not to some dump like Augie's. Tell his mother goodbye, you old hag. Get a car. Dress better. Start hanging around clubs to score some women.

As he sat down to dinner with his mother that night he could see she could hardly wait to tell him something.

"Jake! Rasputin came back today!"

When she said this Jake had a mouthful of mashed potatoes half swallowed. "Humph! Auck! What?"

"Yes! Mrs. Johnson found him on her front porch this morning. The little fellow's in terrible shape. It looks like he's been run over by a car or something. His back legs don't work. She took him to the vet who wants to put him to sleep. He doesn't think Rasputin's going to live. Mrs. Johnson is just all torn up about it."

These words fell on Jake like hammer blows. The dog had to die. He'd never have the courage to attack it again. How in the hell had the fucker survived and dragged itself home? Jake shivered. His appetite was gone.

"What's wrong Jake?"

"Nothing. She should put it to sleep."

The phone rang. His mother got up to answer it. She came back with a grimace on her face. "It's that Augie fellow."

Jake went to the phone. "Yeah?" he said.

"Jake. My man. Have I got a deal for you."

"Yeah?"

"You remember Jennifer and Diane?"

"Yeah."

Jennifer and Diane were two strippers at the club Augie went to almost nightly. They looked ok.

"Well, tomorrow's their night off. They've agreed to lay some of that sweet stuff on us at my crib."

"How much?"

"Seventy five. I figure a working man in your position can come up with that."

"I don't get paid until next week, Augie."

"Well, well, well. I guess I could front you the dough. Come on over about nine."

"Ok. Bye."

Jake sat down. Maybe a woman could get him out of this funk. He went to bed. He woke up in the middle of the night with a sensation of bugs crawling on him. It was just a dream. The next morning he was still tired. He barely got to work on time. The foreman came over to where Jake was stacking concrete forms.

"You're working out ok, Weaver," he said. "I think we've finally shaken the winos and dopers out of this crew so we can get the son of a bitch out of the ground."

"Thanks, Fred."

The day dragged by. Jake slipped once with a crow bar and banged his kneecap. It hurt like hell. He got home that night dead tired. The driveway was still silent. He walked to the sideyard and peeked through the fence. No dog. He laid on his bed for awhile then cleaned up and ate dinner with his mother.

"Can I borrow the car tonight, Mom?"

"It's almost out of gas."

"I get paid next week. Loan me a ten. I'll pay you back."

His mother dug around in her purse and came up with a ten dollar bill.

"Don't forget it's a loan," she said.

"Sure, Mom." You bitch.

Jake drove over to Augie's apartment. It looked like Augie had spent most of the day cleaning it. He'd vacuumed the carpet and washed the dishes and opened the windows to let out some of the chronic musty smell. Jake looked around. It was still a dump. Augie had a pint of gin. He mixed two drinks while Jake sat on the couch feeling like he was in a doctor's waiting room. Augie handed him a drink.

"Yes sir. Yes sir. Old Mr. Augie's gonna get his hambone boiled tonight. I've been after that Jennifer slut for a long time. You can have Diane."

There was a quick knock on the door and then it opened. The one Jake thought was Jennifer pranced into the room. She was wearing tight leather pants, high heels, and a silk blouse with a black bra. Long wavy hair dyed black. Augie beamed.

"Say momma, yer lookin' good," he said.

"Sure thing, sugardaddy."

Jake watched Jennifer do a fast professional scan of the apartment. Her face gave nothing away.

"Need a drink?" Augie asked her.

"Yeah."

"Where's Diane?"

"She'll be along in a minute. We always drive separately. In case we get split up by the action, know what I mean?"
"Yeah. I know. Say, this is Jake. Jennifer."
"Hi."
"Hi, Jake."
There were footsteps down the stairs and in walked a woman with short blonde hair wearing tight low cut jeans and a halter top. Jake checked her out. She had a hard bitten look.
"You must be Diane."
"And who are you?"
"Jake."
Augie, the host, intervened. "Need a drink?"
"Yeah. Sure."
Augie waddled around behind the bar that separated the kitchen from the living room and began mixing another drink. When he finished and Diane leaned over to pick it up Jake could see the top of her butt above her jeans. Jennifer was sitting in a chair playing distractedly with her necklace. Augie came back into the living room and turned on the stereo. "Party time, ladies. Party time," he said.

He sat down in a large overstuffed chair. Jennifer immediately got up and sat on one of his ample thighs. She began stroking the other one. "Hey, Aug. Let's can the party and get down to business," she said. Now she was stroking his crotch.

"Whatever you say, lady. Whatever you say."

They both got up and went back to Augie's bedroom and closed the door. Diane was smoking a long white cigarette and staring straight ahead. Jake moved over next to her and put his arm around her shoulder. She stubbed out the cigarette and looked at him.

"You're not bad," she said. "I figured any friend of Augie's would look like him."

Jake wasn't fat. He had muscular arms and was tanned from working outside. "I'm not exactly his friend," he said.

He leaned over and planted his mouth on hers. She responded with a lot of tongue. He worked two fingers up under the halter top. She pulled her mouth away from his.

"You got seventy five bucks?"

"Just a minute."

Jake got up and walked back to Augie's bedroom door and knocked softly. He could hear movement on the other side. Augie opened the door. He was flushed. His shirt was open and his pants were off. His big white fish belly hung out over his white briefs.

"I need the seventy five."

"Hang on."

Augie shut the door. Jake could hear more movement and a low heated argument. After about two minutes Augie opened the door again. He handed Jake a fifty dollar bill.

"A hundred and fifty is all I got and she won't take less than a hundred. Sorry, Jake. That's the way it is."

He shut the door. Jake went back to the living room.

"Say, Diane. There's a little problem."

Her face hardened instantly. "What?"

"I don't get paid until next week. Augie was gonna front me. He's only got a hundred and fifty. Your buddy back there wants a hundred. How about I owe you twenty five?"

He held up the fifty dollar bill. Diane sat back and lit another cigarette. "Well, I can't say as I blame her," she said. "I wouldn't do that slob for a hundred. But I don't work on credit. I've got better things to do than charity work."

She hopped up and grabbed her purse and headed for

the door. She opened it and turned back to him.

"But hey, when you get paid next week look me up. Club Three Deuces. Ciao."

She trotted up the stairs and was gone. Jake put the fifty in his pocket and mixed a drink and sat down on the couch. Oh well. Fuck it. He could hear the bed creak occasionally. He finished the drink and got up and turned off the stereo. There was half a pint left. He hit on it. The bed began creaking rhythmically. How could the damn thing hold up under that? He gulped the gin. When it was gone he turned off the lights and left.

He got in the car. His mother's house wasn't far. He could drive the back streets. He drove down the long apartment block and turned. A couple of blocks further down a car pulled out of a side street and followed him. A block later the red lights popped on. A cop. A fucking cop. He pulled over and quickly rolled down the windows. The cop sat in his car behind him for awhile. Probably calling one of his friends, Jake thought. Then he shut off the blinking red lights and got out and walked up to Jake's window.

"May I have your driver's license please, Sir."

"What's the problem officer?"

"You've got a tail light out."

"Well. Thanks for stopping me. I'll get it fixed tomorrow."

"Just a minute, Sir."

The cop took the license and walked back to his car. Jake was running a cold sweat. The booze was bad enough. He knew this son of a bitch. Ernie Richards. A mean, scrawny, acne pitted little shit. With big friends in high school who always backed him up and finished the fights he started with Jake. Two years out of school Jake had caught Richards in a bar without his friends and had beaten him mercilessly in the parking lot. He heard later that Richards' nose was badly broken. And now the son of a bitch was a cop. Richards came back.

"Been drinking a little?"

"No."

"Bullshit."

Richards leaned into the window. "You remember me, don't you, Jakeleg."

"No, Sir."

"Sure you do. Sure you do. I'm your own worst nightmare. Outta the car, dirtbag. It's time for your field sobriety test."

Jake got out and stood beside the car. Richards shone his flashlight in Jake's eyes as he fished a coin out of his pocket and placed it on the pavement.

"Pick it up," he said.

Jake bent over and groped around. Richards kept the light in his eyes. Jake couldn't see anything. Suddenly Richards foot shot out and caught Jake in the side. He toppled over.

"Ha ha. Well, looks like you flunked that part, dirtbag."

Jake scrambled to his feet and squared off opposite Richards. Richards unsnapped the restraint on his holster. His hand hovered over the gun butt.

"Come on, motherfucker. Come on. Go for it," he taunted.

Another police car wheeled in behind Richards'. Richards looked around nervously. He shone the light in Jake's eyes again. Jake put his hands up to block it. He never saw the kick coming. It caught him square in the groin.

"Ahhhggg!" he groaned.

He fell to his knees. Even with the gin the pain was unbelievable. The nausea came up quickly. He fell over on his side. Hot vomit poured out of his mouth. He was dimly aware of another person approaching.

"What the hell's going on, Richards!"

"Oh, this slime ball tried to jump me, Frank. Let's scrape him up and take him in."

"Bullshit. I saw the whole thing. You kicked him just for the hell of it. Get out of here. Now!"

"Ok, Frank. Ok. Cool out a little willya?"

Richards walked back to his car and peeled off. Jake still lay gasping in the warm night. The other cop helped him get up.

"Been drinking, son?"

"No," Jake sputtered weakly.

"Then why's it smell like a gin mill?"

"I don't know."

This cop was a black man about fifty years old. His sideburns were going gray. He helped Jake lean back on the car.

"That Richards is a nasty little son of a bitch," he said. "I know it. But he's still a cop. There's nothing I can do about it."

The cop thought for a moment. "Listen, how far do you live from here?" he asked.

"About five blocks."

"Can you drive it?"

"Yeah."

"Then let's make a little deal. You just drive on home like a good boy and we'll all forget about the whole thing."

"Ok."

"Ok. Take it easy. Hope you start feeling better."

The cop walked back to his car and got in. Jake eased himself into his mother's car. His groin throbbed. He started the car and drove slowly home. He somehow got inside the house without screaming and passed out on his bed.

He awoke the next morning still nauseated, his crotch aching. He slowly dressed in the baggiest pants he could find and hobbled to the kitchen to eat his breakfast. His mother wasn't up yet which was good. He didn't want any of her questions. He walked carefully to work. He got to the job site and approached the rest of the crew lounging about, getting ready to go to work.

"What the fuck happened to you, Weaver?" one of them yelled. "You're walking like you got kicked in the balls. Ha ha ha."

Jake nodded. He was told to begin stripping forms off a section of wall poured the previous day. He hobbled down and began pulling nails with a crowbar. He was weak. The nausea returned and he sat down with his head between his legs. He couldn't go on. Something was busted down there. He lit a cigarette. Maybe he should go home, tell them he was sick. He was. The foreman, Fred, came over to where Jake was sitting. His expression was serious.

"What's wrong, Weaver?"

"I don't feel so good. Must've been something I ate."

"Well, Smith wants to see you in the trailer."

"Ok."

What the hell did Smith want? Jake didn't want to talk to anyone, much less the supervisor. He went to the trailer. Smith was sitting at his desk when Jake came in. He saw Jake and stood up and handed him a check.

"Here's for four day's pay. You're fired."

"What? Why?"

"We check those applications, Weaver. Insurance. We

have to. I would anyway. I won't have a drinker and doper and liar on my job. Get your stuff and get out."

Jake hobbled out of the trailer. He picked up his lunch pail. As he walked off the construction site he heaved it into a trash bin. Goddamnit. God fucking damnit. Pricks like Smith ran everything. Owned everything. As soon as you got your head above the slime one of them would come along and push it back down. He stifled a sob. He limped home. As he approached his mother's house he was thinking maybe he could sneak in the back door and get back to his room without having to confront her. He couldn't put up with her questions and disappointment right now. He walked around the side of the house. A scuffling noise. He peeked through the fence into Mrs. Johnson's back yard. There on the porch. Something like a dirty gunnysack. Rasputin. The dog was lying on its side in the sunlight. It swiveled its head around and saw Jake looking through the fence. Yip. One eye was sutured shut. Yip yap. Its bark was the same. It raised up on its front legs and crawled to the edge of the porch dragging its useless hind legs. Yap yap yap. The good eye stared at Jake with a solid malevolence. Yip yap yap. Yap yap yap. Yap yip. Yip yip yap.

It was midnight and Joe and Matt had to piss. They were two miles south of town at the abandoned refinery. Matt pulled the old Pontiac into the entrance. Joe was in the back seat with Mary and had to reach forward to grab the door handle and get out the passenger side of the two door while Matt heaved his bulk out from under the steering wheel. Matt had said he didn't like driving around like this. He said he should probably smear shoe polish on his face and get a chauffeur's hat but he would have been more upset if Joe and Mary had both sat in front with him with Mary's bra unsnapped and Joe's hand idly cupping one of her breasts, the other hand holding a beer. Matt wandered into some weeds off to the side to leak while Joe faced the headlights and unloaded in front of the car. Big deal, thought Mary. Was this supposed to turn her on or something? Jesus, she was sick of boys. Joe and Matt came back to the car and got in the front seat. "Let's go in," said Joe.

"What for?" asked Matt.

"I don't know. Check it out. Fuck around. What are you afraid of?"

Matt pulled up to the gate. It was eight feet of chain link topped by three strands of barbed wire. Joe got out and looked at the chain and lock around the gate. He came back to the car.

"Give me a lug wrench," he said.

Matt got a lug wrench out of his trunk and handed it to Joe and stood by and watched him beat on the padlock with it. Little red sparks spat out when he hit it. Mary watched from the backseat. Four beers is enough I just want to go home, she thought. She, Joe, and Matt had split the first twelve pack and Matt and Joe had almost finished a second.

Finally the chain broke and Joe opened the gate. The sign on it said they would be arrested if found there. Matt drove the car into the refinery. Joe stuck out his arm and took a deep bow as they came past. Then he shut the gate and walked to the car parked under the looming pipes and towers.

The refinery had been closed for three years. The oil company had moved on, taking 350 jobs with it. Everybody had pissed and moaned and then got used to it. Now they said they were glad it was gone, it stunk anyway when the wind blew from the south in the summer and things were picking up again. There was a new Wal-Mart going in at the west end of the strip and several new businesses, fast food franchises and things, one being the Chik a Lik where Mary worked.

Matt and Mary got out of the car and everyone popped a new beer. Barrels and pipes and odd pieces of metal junk lay strewn about. The moon was full and bright. Joe and Mary walked over to the structure. The oil company had sawed off the ladders about eight feet above the ground to keep people from climbing up on the catwalks that ringed the cracking towers. That's what Mary thought her dad had called them. He'd left with the oil company. Libya or someplace. They hadn't heard anything from him in two years. Mary didn't know if he and her mom were even married anymore. So who cares? He was a son of a bitch anyway.

Joe dragged a barrel over to a sawed off ladder and stood on it and climbed up on the bottom rung of the ladder.

"Come on, Mare. Let's go up."

"Oh, Joe. No. I'm tired. Let's go home."

"Mare. Where's your sense of adventure?"

He held his hand out to her. Mary reluctantly climbed up on the barrel and Joe hoisted her up onto the lowest rung of the ladder. Then he scampered up to the first catwalk. Mary climbed slowly after him taking care not to spill her beer. They looked down from the catwalk. Matt was sitting on the hood of his car smoking a cigarette. He was too fat to pull himself up on the ladder. He really was the chauffeur. Joe had a car but since his second DUI he had to depend on Matt to drive Mary and him around at night when Mary got off work. Joe climbed up to the next level and Mary followed. Now they were 40 feet above the ground. Matt was scuffing around in the junk below. They could see the glow of his cigarette. The cracking towers hung over them. A spiral stairway ascended one of them. Joe started up.

"Oh Joe! Be careful!" Mary cried out.

"It's ok, baby. It's ok."

Or don't be careful, she thought. You drunken self-centered asshole. Fall off the fucking thing and kill yourself. See if I give a shit. Joe got to the top of the tower and began raving like a maniac.

"Fuck you! Fuck all of you! Fuck the world!" he screamed into the autumn night.

He threw his beer can into the void and then clunked back down the steps to Mary and pulled her to him and put his hand on her crotch. "Let's do it, babe," he said.

"Here?"

"Yeah. It'll be exciting."

"Oh Joe."

"Come on. Don't you love me?"

"I gotta take a leak."

"Well, take one."

"Here?"

"Yeah. Just do it over the side. I do it all the time."

Mary moved to the side of the catwalk and pulled down her jeans and hung her rear end out and cut loose.

"Goddamnit!"

Something was thrashing about in the weeds and trash below. It was Matt.

"You son of a bitch! You pissed on me!" he screamed up at them.

Matt thought it was Joe who'd pissed on him.

"Goddamnit! I'm leaving. You assholes can walk home."

Mary pulled up her pants and came over to Joe who was lying on his side on the catwalk doubled over with laughter.

"Joe, he's going to leave us here!"

Joe was able to talk only between bouts of laughter that shook his body.

"He's not going anywhere, babe. I've got the keys."

Now Matt was back at his car.

"Where's my keys, you assholes? Where's my fucking keys?"

Joe was unbuttoning Mary's shirt. Matt was ranting in the dark below.

"I'm going to shoot your ass!"

Bam! Blang! The bullet ricocheted off the cracking tower. Matt had taken out the .22 he kept under the seat and was firing up at the metal hulk. He couldn't see them. They were crouched behind pipes. Bam! Blang! Bam! Blang! Joe started to unzip Mary's jeans.

"No, baby," she said. "I can't do it. Not with him shooting at us. Besides, this metal will cut my back."

Joe sat and considered the situation.

"Ok, then blow me."

"Joe."

"C'mon. Do it."

"Well. Ok."

Sucking him sounded better to Mary than having her back and butt shredded by the mesh walkway while Joe humped on top of her. And if she refused he'd get mean. Joe pulled down his jeans. Mary took his dick in her mouth and set to work.

"Motherfucker!" yelled Matt.

Bam! Blang!

Mary had been fifteen, a curly haired blond, blue eyed sophomore when she met Joe. She had been much taken with the attentions of the senior star running back. Joe had quit high school when football season ended. He'd gone to work for the county. Three years later he was a Laborer, Grade II. He shoveled asphalt and set concrete forms and ran into town for beer for the crew at lunch.

Mary was having trouble. Joe had drunk too much. She could not get him fully erect. Her jaw ached. She pulled off.

"Joe, it's not going to work. Come on, hon. Let's go home."

"Oh baby, I'm almost there. Just a little bit more."

Mary sighed and bent back down. A minute later she felt him quiver. She leaned over the railing and spat.

"What'd you do that for?" Joe asked angrily.

"Joe. I'm about ready to puke. Lay off, will ya?"

Joe had told her if she loved him she'd swallow it. She usually did. But not tonight. The beer had made her queasy. Joe stood and pulled up his jeans. "Well, let's go back down," he said.

"Do you think Matt will shoot us?" Mary asked.

"Nah. He's cooled out by now."

They climbed down the ladders. Joe stood on the barrel

and helped Mary to the ground. They walked back to the car. The driver's side door was open and the interior light was on. Matt slouched behind the steering wheel with his head thrown back and his mouth open. His shirt was off. He was snoring loudly. Joe pushed at him.

"Hey, Matt. Matt. Wake up."

"Huh? Oh. You. Can't find the keys. Fucker. Why'd you piss on me?"

"Didn't know you were down there. It was an accident. Honest. I found the keys outside. Move over. I'll drive."

"No. S'my car. I drive it."

Joe handed the keys to Matt. Mary got in the back. Matt's wet shirt was wadded up and lying in the corner. Joe got in front. Matt started the car and they drove to the gate. Joe left it open. They pulled out onto the highway and headed towards town. Mary leaned back and looked up through the rear window. A tiny blinking dot was moving rapidly toward the horizon. Maybe it's a UFO, she thought.

They passed a motel. It was old and spread out along the highway. Half the neon was blinking erratically. There was one car in the parking lot. A big lighted portable sign was in front. It read: American Owned and Operated. A quarter mile down the road they came to another motel. The portable sign here read: Single 18.95 Double 19.95. There were five cars in the lot. Joe stirred in his seat.

"Merle says these sand niggers are running him out of business. Pull over."

Matt pulled onto the shoulder of the highway. Joe got out and ran over to the sign and started pulling the letters off. Idiot, thought Mary. I hope Revi doesn't see me. She slumped down in the seat. Joe stood for a moment with the letters like he was trying to think of something dirty to spell and couldn't come up with anything. Then he threw down the letters and kicked the sign and broke a large hole in the yellow plastic. He bent down and grabbed the supporting base and turned the whole thing over. It blinked once and went out. Joe ran back to the car and got in.

"Ha ha. Fuckin' sand niggers. Merle'll get a kick out of this. Let's get out of here."

Matt put the car in gear and pulled onto the highway. Mary looked through the rear window and saw two little brown faces peering out from the motel office window. They drove slowly back into town and pulled up at Mary's mother's trailer where Mary stayed. Joe leaned forward so Mary could get out of the back seat. She leaned in the window. Joe gave her a tight lipped kiss.

Mary let herself into the trailer and flopped on her bed and stared at the ceiling in the dark. Where was that little UFO headed, she wondered. She drifted off still fully clothed.

The thing with Revi had come down like this: Mary had started working at the Chik a Lik six months before under the old manager who was drunk most of the time if he was there at all. He was a laid off refinery worker who didn't think much of managing a goddamned chicken shack for some slob from Joplin. Mr. Boileau, the owner, had finally caught on to the fact that the guy was fucking things up and fired him. But not before Mary had caught on to the fact that most customers didn't count their change, being too distracted or hurried or just dumb, and began short changing them. Every once in awhile during her shift she'd estimate the amount she'd stolen and throw it into a sack she kept under the counter. The old manager never noticed. She'd be off a little every night, but not by much, so he didn't care even though the cash register told you exactly how much change to give the customer and any fool could operate it.

Revi, the sand nigger, was different. Mr. Boileau had hired him since he was the only applicant who'd graduated from high school and looked like he was capable of doing simple arithmetic and could push the right buttons on the computer to send the daily sales figures to Joplin every night. He was also a part time junior college student and had told Mr. Boileau he was interested in advancing himself in the world.

"I like ambition," Mr. Boileau had told him. "I like ambition in any man, regardless of race, creed, or color."

After about a week, Mary had noticed Revi watching her sometimes while she worked the counter. It made her nervous. Her nightly ring out was still always off by some small amount and Revi told her to be more careful when she counted out the customer's change. She said it was hard when things got busy. Three weeks after Revi had been hired he caught her. He and Mary were alone in the store after it had closed. She'd gone to the bathroom. When she came back Revi was standing at her machine holding the bag of stolen change. His face was expressionless.

"I watch you. I know what you do. Now I have proof."

There wasn't much Mary could say.

"Well, keep it then. Or put it back. I don't care. I won't do it any more."

He looked at her for a minute.

"Oh no. It not so easy. I call Mr. Boileau. You out on your butt."

"So what? You think I can't find the same shitty job down the street?"

Revi stared at her.

"I call police. This is serious crime. You go to jail. Three month, six month."

He moved to the phone and picked up the receiver and began dialing, still watching her intently. Mary was flushed and starting to sweat. She moved over to him.

"No. Please. You keep the money. Don't call the police. I'm sorry. I'm real sorry. I won't do it anymore. Fire me if you want but don't call the cops. Please?"

Revi stopped dialing. He continued to stare at her. He put the phone down.

"Ok. Maybe we make deal. You come with me."

Revi shut off the front lights. She followed him to the break room in back. There was a formica topped table with five plastic chairs around it. Revi put the money sack on the table.

"Sit down, please," he said.

Mary sat down. Revi stood next to her.

"This is deal. You give me good fuck everything ok."

Mary couldn't believe it.

"Are you crazy? That's what you want? Forget it, buddy. Go home and whack off. Leave me out of it."

"Ok. Police then."

Revi wheeled and began walking out of the room. He had her over a barrel and she knew he knew it. She played her last card.

"Revi. Wait. Come back."

He stopped and turned to look at her with the same expressionless black eyes set in his brown Asian face.

"You know that guy that comes to pick me up with his friend most nights? That big guy. He used to be a football player. That's my boyfriend. If I told him what you just said to me he'd break every bone in your body."

"I have gun make big hole in boyfriend."

"Well. Then we'd both be in jail."

Revi stared. Mary thought she detected a slight hesitation in his expression. It was a standoff. Revi shrugged and walked back to the table and sat down and dumped the money out and began counting it.

"Ok," he said. "Let's forget whole thing. You keep doing this. Don't put money in sack. Leave it in register. At end of shift we count it, subtract real amount, then we split rest. Seventy per cent for me, thirty for you. Ok?"

"No way. Fifty-fifty or I ain't doing it."

Revi considered this for a moment.

"Ok. Fifty-fifty."

"So, you wanted in on the deal. Why didn't you just say so in the first place?"

He grinned at her through slitted lizard eyes.

The operation had been running smoothly for four months. Mary had become expert at shortchanging the chicken eaters, gauging how much to cheat each one. The high school kids were easy. Sometimes they'd look at their change for a second and then look at her and then put it in their pocket. After all, the cash register had told her how much change to give back. It was right there in front of them. The grown men were easy, too. They might count the bills but the coins weren't even looked at. The women were different. The old ones usually counted every penny. Mary left them alone. About one in ten customers caught her. She'd blush and grin and give them the correct change and say she was sorry. The money added up. A quarter, a dime, a dollar when she thought she could get away with it. It averaged about eight dollars an hour. Even after splitting it with Revi she more than doubled her wage. At ten the other girls would go home. Mary cleaned up while Revi counted the money. Then he would push a button on the register and it would spit out the sum of all the entries. The difference was their nightly take.

One night when things were slack Revi opened the two video games with a key he'd made by filing slots in a knife. Mary walked over and watched him. He removed five dollars in quarters from each machine and then began fiddling with the wires.

"What're you doing?" she asked.

"Oh, just taking profits from my new business."

Mary looked into the back of the machine. There was a little gadget like a car odometer attached to some wires.

"They'll know someone's stealing. That little thing tells them how many games have been played."

Revi looked up at her.

"Listen to me, memsahib. Revi too smart for that little thing. What you think I do when you not here? While you out smoking the pot or whatever you do. I sit and think. How can Revi get more money? So I make key to game. Look at insides. Think, unhook wire to little counter, man not know how many games are played. So, I leave it hooked for five days, unhooked for two, on weekend, when most money goes in. Is good business. I be driving Mercedes-Benz when you still selling chicken."

Revi put the quarters in a chicken sack and closed the access doors on both games.

"But Revi, that's stealing."

"No. Same thing we do with chicken. That our tax on dumb people. This my tax on video game man. State put tax on everything we sell here. It all the same."

Mary thought he made sense. It was kind of all the same.

"Yes. I have other businesses, too," he continued. "The little things, they add up. Is much opportunity in the world. Most people, they can't see it. But I can. I be rich man some day. This land of opportunity."

Mary thought about this for a moment.

"What are your other businesses, Revi?" she asked.

"Ok. I tell you about one other. This dumb guy, he Indian like me. His father have much money in Bombay. He a student here, too. He take algebra and fail so he come to me. He say, 'Revi, what can you do for me?'. So I enroll this semester using his name in algebra. He pay me four hundred dollars. Is service I provide, see? The service industry. This is wave of future."

Mary had flunked math too, so she knew the kind of thing Revi's friend had gone through. She couldn't see paying someone four hundred dollars though. Fuck it. It was cheaper to drop out.

The night after Joe had broken the sign Mary could tell that Revi was in a bad mood. He was silent during the shift. When they were splitting the money at the break table Mary asked him what was wrong.

"Your boyfriend break our sign last night. My little sisters watch."

"No, Revi. Joe wouldn't do a thing like that."

"Yes. They see him. Him and fat friend in fat friend's car. You with them too?"

"Of course not."

He was silent for a minute.

"Oh well, doesn't matter. My mother sell motel soon to

her cousin. They go somewhere else. This no good place for Indian people."

"Where's your dad?"

"He in India. He send family here say he come later. He never come. Has girlfriend in Bombay."

"Is there a lot of sand in Bombay?"

"What?"

"Sand. You know. A desert. Is Bombay in a desert?"

"Oh no. Plenty rain. Trees. Beautiful. Not like here."

Mary wondered why Joe and his friends called Revi a sand nigger. Maybe Joe was dumb.

"What about you, Revi? Are you going to stay here?"

"No. I graduate juco in December then I go to university."

"What about our business?"

"We find new manager for you then, memsahib."

Fall dragged into winter. Football nights were good. The Chik a Lik would jam up after a game. Sometimes Mary would short a customer a five and get away with it. She still went out with Joe. The date usually consisted of dinner at a fast food restaurant then to the trailer Joe shared with Matt. They'd watch TV until Matt went to bed. Then they'd get in Joe's bed and make love. Mary couldn't stand doing it when Matt was there. He usually was. Joe didn't care. Other times she and Joe and Matt would just buy some beer and drive up and down the strip. There wasn't much to do in the town. She loaned Joe six hundred for part of the down payment on a new Z28. He couldn't drive it so he parked it in the ramshackle garage behind the ramshackle trailer.

In the mornings before she went to work Mary would sometimes go down to the Man Trap, the three chair beauty shop her mother owned and operated. It was located on a side street off the strip squeezed in between a dry cleaner's and an auto parts store. Mary had worked there for awhile after she'd dropped out of high school. She finally came to the point where she couldn't stand her mother or the customers or the smell of the place anymore and quit. Her mother had shrilly informed her that she was throwing away a chance at a lifetime career, careers being not too easy to come by for someone of her educational accomplishments, and what did she think she was? Too good for the place? They got along better now. Her mother seldom mentioned the possibility of Mary working there again.

Mary walked in one morning as her mother was putting the finishing touches to a ratted dyed red head. Her mother looked up.

"Been keeping kind of late hours haven't you, Mary?"

"Mom, Joe's my boyfriend. I want to spend time with him and he wants to spend time with me."

"Three o'clock, four o'clock in the morning? Listen. Merle and I were talking. Don't you think it's about time Joe made an honest woman out of you?"

"I'm already an honest woman, mom."

Except for the short changing, she thought. Anyway, that was a business.

"You know what I mean, young lady. You two been carrying on like a married couple for quite awhile now. When I was your age you were two years old."

"Well, I guess I'll probably get married one of these days."

"One of these days. I'll tell you what to do, young lady. You just quit taking those little birth control pills you're so fond of. One of these days'll come a lot quicker that way. You'll be Mrs. Joe Goodson real soon."

"Joe Goodson?" said the fake red head. She turned

around in the chair. "Why, I know that young man."

"Yeah?" said Mary.

"I don't want to be talking out of school but I've seen him lately in the evening riding around with that Laura Andersen gal in her Corvette. You know, the one that ran off to K.C. an' supposedly got married to that hop head nigger in some kind of band and then got divorced and came back here with her tail between her legs to live off daddy's money for awhile."

"I've heard of her," said Mary.

"You see?" said her mother. "That's what I'm telling you. Ain't no reason for a man to face up to his responsibilities when he's getting a free lunch."

"Ok, mom. I'll see you later."

Mary had had a suspicion that Joe was seeing somebody else on the side. It wasn't the first time. But she knew she was his real girlfriend and she loved him. Hell, he was just a man like all of them. She would probably end up married to him. It was just one of those things that was meant to be.

Joe missed picking her up from work that night. Revi gave her a ride home. She complained about Joe to him. Revi expressed his opinion.

"That guy no good, memsahib. You should get rid of him. He drunk all the time. Have dirty job. No good."

This really pissed Mary off.

"What the hell do you know, Revi? You're not even an American. I've loved Joe almost since I was a little girl. He was a football player. You couldn't do that in a million years."

They pulled up to her mother's trailer. Mary opened the door of the battered Pinto and got out.

"Well, thanks for the ride home, anyway," she said.

Revi gave her the lizard grin.

She let herself into the trailer. All the lights were off. A big color TV glowed in the center of the room. A huge wave crashed on a beach. A beautiful young woman walked through it in a skin-tight bathing suit. Her nipples poked against the fabric. She moved towards the camera. The frame split in half. The lower half of her body was replaced by the fuming open mouth of a beer bottle. The beer poured out and splashed into a frosted mug. Her mother and Merle gaped at the thing.

"Home kinda early tonight aren't you," her mother said.

"Yeah."

"Listen now Mary. Merle an I been talking. You tell her Merle."

Mary realized her mother was drunk. Merle stirred out of his lethargy.

"Yeah. Now I knew your boyfriend's dad, Mary. He was a hell of a man. Anybody give him lip he'd knock 'em on their butt. He was a man's man. I expect your boyfriend is about the same."

"What happened to Joe's dad?" Mary asked.

"Oh. Some nigger or a Mexican stuck a knife in him down in Tulsa one night. It was way before your time. But that ain't the point. What I'm tryin' to say is this: You can't do no better'n people like Joe."

"Ok. Thanks for your opinion."

Mary turned and headed for her room. She heard her mother mutter "bitch" as she walked away. Fuck her. She'd be damned if she'd end up sitting on a couch in a beat up trailer with someone like Merle.

The next morning Mary got up early. She met her mother coming out of the bathroom. She looked funny. In the kitchen her mother was kind of trying to talk without looking at her. Finally Mary walked up and looked her squarely in the face. Her mother's eye was puffed up.

"That son of a bitch hit you last night, didn't he Mom?"

Her mother didn't say anything for a moment. She sat staring into her coffee cup.

"It's life, Mary. Things don't always go the way you want them to. A person's just got to learn to put up with things."

It was a week before Christmas. Mr. Boileau showed up unexpectedly at the Chik a Lik that night about twenty minutes before closing time. He left his Mercedes parked next to the entry door. Mary and Revi were the only employees left at the store. The rest had gone home. Mr. Boileau seldom came out. This "unit" was the farthest one from Joplin. He was in an expansive mood.

"Merry Christmas. Merry Christmas. Listen. Let me tell you, Revi. This unit had the highest sales of any of 'em this year. And just to show my appreciation, I want you to give every one of your people two of these. Not one, two."

Mr. Boileau pulled out a stack of cards. Each one entitled the bearer to five dollars worth of merchandise at any Chik a Lik. He handed the stack to Revi.

"Say, Revi. I've got a hankerin' for some Chik a Lik chicken. How about givin' me a three piece. White meat, if you don't mind."

Revi went back to bag up the chicken. Mary stood at the cash register. Mr. Boileau looked at her. "How you doin', girl?" he asked.

"Just fine, Mr. Boileau. Just fine," Mary replied.

Mr. Boileau put her uptight. His gaze had a habit of drifting down to her chest.

The door opened and two late customers came in. Joe and Matt, obviously drunk. Mary wondered what they were doing here now. It was still twenty minutes until she got off work. She hoped they wouldn't cause some kind of scene. They ambled up to the counter. Joe looked at Mr. Boileau. He was a head shorter than Joe. Joe stared at him with an openly hostile expression.

"How you fellas doin' tonight?" Mr. Boileau said.

Joe said nothing and continued to stare at him. Mr. Boileau shifted nervously and cleared his throat. It didn't look good for a man to be intimidated in his own restaurant in front of his employees. Mary looked at Joe with pleading eyes. Please don't do anything stupid. This man owns the place. Fortunately Revi came back with Mr. Boileau's chicken and Joe quit staring at him and stared instead at Revi. Revi held his gaze for a moment. He didn't appear to be intimidated by Joe. Mr. Boileau broke the tension.

"Say, Revi. When you get a moment come over and chat with me for a minute, will you.?"

Revi walked to the end of the counter and let himself out through the little door and sat at a booth with Mr. Boileau. Joe leered at Mary.

"Joe, I don't get off work for another fifteen minutes. What are you doing in here drunk and all? That man you were looking at so mean owns this place. He could fire me if he wanted to."

"I don't give a shit. We got some talking to do."

"Well you'll just have to wait. Come back in twenty minutes."

"Ok. Gimme a double order of livers."

"I know you don't like livers. You said you can't stand livers. What do you want livers for?"

"I changed my mind. I love 'em. Get 'em for me. I'm the customer."

Mary went back and bagged up the livers. Anything to get Joe and Matt out of there. He could be such a pain in the ass. She handed Joe the livers and he paid her. She didn't short him though she felt like it, and he and Matt left. Revi and Mr. Boileau were having a discussion at the booth and paid no attention to her. She began wiping down the counter top. She looked up a minute later and saw Matt standing at the rear of Mr. Boileau's car. He was looking back at her with a big lopsided drunken leer. She thought at first he was pissing on the tire. She glanced at Mr. Boileau. His back was to the door so he couldn't see anything. She walked to the end of the counter to get a better look. Joe was bent over shoving the chicken livers into the gas tank. Mary quickly walked back to the other end of the counter and pretended to be engrossed in wiping it. Mr. Boileau was going to be mighty upset when his car stalled out on the way back to Joplin. She hoped he never found out Joe was her boyfriend. At least as long as she still worked there. Joe and Matt walked over to Matt's car and got in and squealed out of the lot. Mr. Boileau looked up with an expression of irritation. After a minute he and Revi got up and came over to the counter.

"Well, Martha. Revi here tells me he's leaving town at the end of the year. Sure hate to see him go. But a man's gotta do what a man's gotta do. He says you're the best employee he's got. I sure hope you stay on and help me break in a new manager. If you do I'll even give you a raise. A quarter an hour. What do you think about that?"

Mary thought it was shit. Of course she didn't say so. The son of a bitch didn't even know her name.

"Oh, that'd be fine, Mr. Boileau. Just fine," she said.

Mr. Boileau left. Mary was glad to see his car at least

make it out of the parking lot. Joe came back. He rolled up behind the Chik a Lik as she and Revi were walking out the door. Matt wasn't with him. Joe gave Revi a hard look as Mary got in the car. Revi stared back. They drove out onto the strip.

"That sand nigger ever give you any trouble?" Joe asked her.

"No. Why?"

"Cause I don't like the look of that boy. I think he's got something up his sleeve. I might have to have a talk with him one of these days."

"Oh leave him alone, Joe. He's leaving town in two weeks anyway. Why'd you put that junk in Mr. Boileau's gas tank? And what are you doing driving? You're getting your license back soon. You're going to fuck it up again."

"Listen. Just shut up a minute, willya? I don't like that Boileau character. That's why I fucked up his car. I didn't like the way he was looking at you. Now. I'm driving cause I got something important to talk to you about. I didn't want Matt along. Ok?"

"Well, what is it?"

Joe reached into the back seat and pulled up a sack and handed it to her.

"Go on. See what's in there."

Mary pulled out a bottle of perfume. Obsession. Joe pulled a little box out of his pocket and handed it to her.

"And here's something else."

Mary opened the box. It was a diamond ring.

"Mary. I want to get married. What do you say?"

She'd been waiting for this moment for three years. It left her strangely numb.

"I think we better talk about a few things first. Like what

have you been doing hanging around Laura Andersen?"

"Oh Mare. That was nothing. She's a whore. I get bored half to death with you working almost every night. Even the weekends. Shit. She's going back to K.C. in a couple of weeks anyway."

"Well, I don't want you poking her and then coming over to ask me to marry you. I'm not too smart but I ain't that big a sap."

"It's over with. What there was of it. So what's your answer? Yes or no?"

"Well. It's yes. It's always been yes."

They announced their intentions at Christmas. Mary and her mother prepared a big turkey dinner. Merle and Joe watched football games on the TV and drank beer and shots of whiskey. By dinner time Merle was passed out on the couch. The wedding was scheduled for April.

New Year's Eve came. Mary had to work. She didn't mind. She could use the money and it was Revi's last night. Mr. Boileau had brought in the new manager he'd hired to replace Revi. This guy was also a juco student. He said he planned to go to divinity school. He wore a constant expression of a painted on half smile. Sometimes it looked like pure piousness. Sometimes it looked like a smirk. The guy got on Mary's nerves. She figured she'd have to go back to a solo operation. Nothing was going to sway this dude from the straight and narrow.

The shift ended. The new guy went home. Mary and Revi split the loot for the last time. She was going to miss Revi. He'd made the operation so much easier. She'd almost forgiven him for the dirty trick he'd tried to play on her when he first caught her with the proceeds from her business. Revi was a little uneasy. He kept asking about Joe.

"This guy, Mary. You really going to marry him?"

"Yes. I've told you. I love Joe. I've loved him ever since I laid eyes on him."

"You sure? You really going to marry a man who dig ditches and break peoples' signs?"

"Goddamnit, Revi. He's not that bad. I don't suppose you've ever done anything you regretted. Huh? Is that right?"

Revi sat in silence for a full minute. He looked at her intently. He seemed to be trying to make up his mind about something. Finally he spoke.

"Well then, memsahib. I have something you should see. You will not like me. It is not nice. But I think is for the best. You wait here."

Revi left the room and went out the back door of the building. A minute later he returned carrying a large brown envelope. He sat down and looked inside it. Then he pulled out three eight by ten glossy photographs and tossed then on the table in front of Mary. Mary picked one up and studied it. It was badly out of focus. There was a double bed, a dresser, and off to one side, about two thirds of a naked blonde haired woman standing and facing the camera. It looked like Laura Andersen but the quality was too poor to make a definite judgment. What appeared to be a man's arm and shoulder intruded into the frame on the other side. Mary felt the heavy weight of nausea begin to form in her guts.

"Where'd you get this?" she said.

"The motel."

"When?"

"Last week. Sometimes I go home for lunch. Sometimes

I see things are interesting. Customers. You know. In middle of day. Have little camera like private eye. Is little hole I make in wall of unit next to office. Is very interesting business. I think once maybe is good opportunity. But no. Most people not so interested in this kind of thing. Is perhaps very dangerous, too."

Revi sat calmly watching her. She knew what was coming. She looked at the next picture. The naked woman was in the center of the photograph with her back to the camera. A man dressed in boxer shorts and black socks was embracing her. Mary could see his face over the woman's shoulder. She almost laughed. It wasn't Joe. It was Merle. The pig. Merle went to someone else's motel for his dirty little pastime. Wait'll she told her mother. Then she noticed something on the other side of the frame. It was a hand holding a cigarette. She quickly flipped to the last photo. This one was well focused and the subject matter was centered in the frame. Joe, pantless and still holding the cigarette, sat on the edge of the bed. Laura Andersen was on her hands and knees on the floor and was going down on him. Merle, still in black socks but no boxer shorts, mounted Laura from behind. Like a dog.

The nausea reared up immediately and slugged Mary hard in the stomach. The glossy photograph reflected the sick fluorescent light. The image wavered and bulged out into some kind of Salvador Dali collaboration with Heironymous Bosch. Revi had been right. Mary was furious with him.

"You slimy foreign piece of shit! Just what the hell do you think you're doing? Taking pictures of people like this."

Revi looked at her. He shrugged.

"Is business."

Before he could react Mary grabbed the brown envelope in front of him.

"Well, let's see what else you have, Mr. Sleazebag."

She pulled about eight more photos from the envelope. The first two were so blurry she wondered why he'd kept them. The next showed a young slim brown skinned girl in bed with someone Mary didn't recognize. The next one was the same girl in bed with Mr. Elwood, an assistant vice principal at the high school. The rest showed the same girl with different men. Except the last. This was of Merle again and some scaggy looking brunette Mary thought was a bar maid in a club down on the strip. Mary held up a photo with the brown skinned girl in it.

"This is your sister, isn't it? You're a pimp for your own little sister."

"It not so bad. Is good experience for her."

Mary stood up and almost fainted. The nausea was strong. She grabbed her coat and went out the back door and vomited. Joe was supposed to pick her up in a few minutes and take her to a New Year's Eve party. She had to get out of there. She walked the mile and a half to her mother's trailer. The temperature had dropped and a cold wind blew out of the north. She arrived at the trailer numb and half frozen. No one was there. Her mother and Merle were out for the evening. She turned on one light. She turned on the TV. Then she turned it off. She sat on the couch with her head in her hands and cried. Life was like walking on quicksand, she thought. Nothing was solid. Things were never like they were supposed to be. Anything could turn to shit in an instant. She smoked three cigarettes. The nausea had been replaced by a numbness that felt like it would be permanent. She went to bed and cried a little more and fell into a painful sleep.

Matt and Joe were star members of a football team. Matt threw the football to Joe and scored a touchdown. Mary's mother and father, Merle, Mr. Boileau and a host of faceless others stood on the abandoned refinery which had inexplicitly replaced the viewing stands. Revi sat at a table on the fifty yard line wearing his lizard grin and counted money out of a Chik a Lik sack. Mary surveyed the scene from the top of the highest cracking tower. She felt like jumping off. A brawl broke out on the field. The players were taking their helmets off and throwing them at each other. When the helmets hit the players they shattered. Mary stirred up into semi-consciousness. Crash!

"You lousy son of a bitch! Get the hell out of here! Don't you ever lay a hand on me again!"

This wasn't part of the dream. This was her mother and Merle going at it in the front room. It went on a while longer. Finally it stopped. They had either quit fighting or Merle had left. Mary fell asleep again. The rest of the night was dreamless.

She woke up early and looked out the window. The day was hard and cold. A new day. A new year's day. She lay in bed awhile thinking about nothing. The phone rang ten times before the caller hung up. She had figured her mother would get it. It started ringing again. On the third ring someone answered it. A minute later her mother came to her bedroom.

"It's for you, Mary."

Mary got out of bed and walked past her mother and picked up the phone in the kitchen.

"Yeah?"

"Mary. It's Matt. Listen. Sit down. I got some bad news for you."

"Yeah."

"Joe's in jail. He totaled the Z last night. He needs some bail money. You got anything?"

"I don't know."

"What do you mean you don't know? The guy's your fiance for Christ's sake."

"I don't know. Let me call you back in an hour or so."

"Well, don't take too long. How would you like to be sitting in a jail cell right now?"

"I don't know. What difference does it make? I'll call you back."

She hung up and went back and laid on her bed. Her mother came to her room.

"Who was that?"

"Nobody."

"Hell, it had to be somebody. Why'd they call so goddamned early on New Year's Day for?"

"I don't know."

Her mother looked at her with an expression of concern. Mary noticed her lip was cut and slightly puffed.

"Well listen, Mary. You seem to be in pretty good shape for a New Year's morning. I'm out of cigs. Be a doll and run down to the store and get me some, please?"

"Ok."

She dressed and put on her parka and went out into the living room. A chair lay splintered in the middle of the floor. A lamp was shattered in the corner. Merle was sprawled on the couch snoring loudly. Mary walked the two blocks to the convenience store at the corner and bought the cigarettes. She started back to the trailer. The wind was stronger now.

Little flecks of sleet skittered in front of it. The street was deserted. The people of the town were snug in their houses sleeping or nursing hangovers. A heavy cover of clouds was moving in. As she approached the trailer a lone car rattled down the street and honked. She turned. It was Revi in the beat up Pinto. He motioned for her to come over. She looked at him for a few seconds then sauntered to the car. He rolled down the window. The back seat was piled with his stuff.

"What do you want?" she asked him.

"Just to say goodbye, memsahib. No hard feelings. Ok?"

She stared at him. The guy was a snake.

"I'm going to UT now. It seventy degrees in Austin."

"Yeah? What's UT?"

"University of Texas. I study mechanical engineering. You still marry that guy?"

"No."

"Is for the best. This new guy. The manager Mr. Boileau hire. He be hard guy to work for, yes? He look like he maybe really call police he catch you."

"Yeah. He does. Guess I'll just have to be careful."

Revi shifted in his seat and looked away. Then he looked up at her.

"I really come here with business proposition for you."

"I can't wait."

"This proposition: You come to UT with me. We both get job at chicken place or some other thing. We set up new operation. Split money like before. What you think?"

"I don't know. I thought you just said you were going to go to school."

"I am. But is very expensive in Austin. I must work too. Would be better with partner in operation."

The wind began vibrating a loose piece of aluminum trim on the front of the trailer. It rose and fell in pitch and volume. A lost and grieving sound. Mary stood looking down the street, thinking.

"And look here, memsahib."

Revi picked up a metal box that was laying on the passenger seat.

"I have almost ten thousand dollar profits from businesses. No worry about money now. This I will invest. How much profits you have?"

"Oh, two, three hundred. I don't know."

"That too bad. But is okay. I have enough. So. What is answer?"

She looked down at him. He was anxiously looking up at her.

"All right. Wait here. I'll be back."

She went into the trailer. Merle was awake now and sitting morosely on the couch dressed in undershirt, boxer shorts, and his black socks. She ignored him and went to the kitchen and put the cigarettes on the table. She walked past her mother's bedroom. Her mother was sleeping again. Just as well, she thought. She went into her bedroom and threw a few pairs of jeans and some shirts and underwear into a shopping bag. She pulled out the lowest drawer of the dresser and picked up a thick brown envelope. One thousand seven hundred and twenty one dollars. The proceeds from her career at the Chik a Lik. She took one look around the room, at her stuffed animals and things, some of it left over from grade school, and left. Merle was sitting at the TV smoking a cigar.

"Where're you goin?" he asked.

"Away."

She walked out and got in the Pinto and threw her stuff in the back seat. The sleet had turned to snow. Revi put the car in gear. He was grinning at her.

"Now, memsahib. Next town we stop at motel have good fuck. Ok?"

"I don't know, Revi. Just drive the car."

DOGGED

Larry the lawyer called and told me to feed his dog for a week while he was in Vegas. I told him it was a mile from my crib and I didn't have a car and I didn't want to do it. He reminded me I still owed him two hundred dollars.

"So what?" I said.

"Then don't come crying to me next time," he replied. "It's cash on the barrel head, in advance."

I'd been in trouble before and probably would be again and in need of his dreary services. I told him I'd feed the dog. Then he told me he was taking the dog to the pound on Monday when he got back.

"Why don't you take it now and save me the trouble of feeding it all week?" I asked.

"I don't have the time. If you can find a car, you take it to the pound. Then you won't have to feed it. And you can have the dog food. Ha ha." He hung up.

I hadn't seen the mutt in over two years. It was a Great Dane. Larry used to have an MG and the dog would ride in the front seat. It was quite chic. But then Larry got a fancy German sedan and the dog was relegated to the back yard. Larry is one of those guys who likes new things. New cars, new clothes, new women. He used to put a red bandana on Bernie, the dog, when it rode in the MG. It matched the red paint. You know the type. An asshole.

I forgot about Bernie until Tuesday morning. I was sitting around. Then it hit me. Bernie. The poor fucker. Starved to death his last week on earth. I shagged up the hill to Larry's house. It's not in my neighborhood. I live in a rented basement. Larry lives in one of these renovated town houses. It has a little postage stamp back yard where Bernie was cooped up. It was late spring and getting hotter. Bernie lay on his side in the shade on the patio. The yard was covered with dog shit. The smell was horrific. There was still a little food in his bowl but the water looked slimy. I felt bad about forgetting Bernie for two days. I felt worse about the way he was kept. I've never been able to understand people who need an animal for ego reinforcement. I had a cactus once. It died.

I filled Bernie's food and water bowls. He continued to lay there. I patted his head. He slapped his tail on the ground. He looked mangy. His eyes were glazed. I looked around for some charcoal starter. I was going to kick Bernie out of the yard and set Larry's house on fire. I couldn't find any. I opened the gate and looked at Bernie.

"Bernie," I said. "Look. Freedom, Bernie."

Bernie just lay on the patio and slapped his tail. I shut the gate and left.

Wednesday, Thursday, Friday, and Saturday were the same. Bernie lay in the same spot on the patio. About half his food was gone. I guess he got up and ate it. Or else the birds did. I don't know. He didn't appear to be sick. Just beat. Everyday I'd open the gate, point outside, and say, "Ok, Bernie. Time's a'wastin'." He'd lie there and slap his tail. Fuck it. Maybe he would be better off gassed.

Sunday was like most Sundays. I began with some light Bloody Marys to take the edge off. Then I started in on a twelve pack and listened to Wagner. The heat was coming up. The Wagner reminded me of gas chambers. Gas chambers reminded me of Bernie. By three o'clock I couldn't bear the heat any longer. I walked to a fern bar a couple of blocks from my crib. It is an obnoxious place. It is dominated by two huge TV screens on which is displayed whatever inane sporting event is happening at the moment. But it's air conditioned. And Larry hangs around in there. Maybe, I thought, one of Larry's friends would give me a ride to Larry's house to feed Bernie his last meal.

The place was dead. On a hot Sunday afternoon I guess most of the clientele were off dirt biking or jet skiing or mud wrestling. What remained was just a bunch of codgers. Me in twenty years. I switched to vodka and tonic. After a while I asked the barmaid, Didi, or Bibi, or whatever her name was, what time she got off work.

"What's it to you?" she snapped.

"Just a small favor. I need a ride to Larry's house," I said.

She perked up. "Oh. Do you know Larry?"

"Yeah. Give me a ride, will you."

"Sure."

I downed a couple more. Didi, or Bibi, got off work. We got in her car. It was one of those low slung Jap rigs. I banged my head getting in. She drove me up the hill. We didn't talk. I figured she was only in it to see the fab Larry and his nifty digs. She pulled into Larry's driveway. I got out to feed Bernie. Bibi, or Didi, asked, "Where's Larry?"

"Vegas."

"Oh."

Bernie was lying on his side on the patio as usual. He flopped his tail when he saw me. I heaped up his food and changed his water. Well Bernie, old man, I guess this is it. Bernie got up and ate some dog food. It was the first time I'd seen him stand. The sucker was big. A hundred and twenty five at least. Bernie started lapping up some water. I stood by the open gate.

"Ok, Bernie," I said, "Last chance. Tomorrow's the gas chamber."

He bolted for the gate. I grabbed at him and missed. He stuck his nose in Didi's crotch.

"Oooo," she screamed, "get away from me you ugly dog!"

Bernie ran off down the driveway. I ran after him. Metaphysically speaking, it was a good idea to let Bernie loose. It was the only sane thing to do. I'd been taunting him with the idea all week. But in terms of dog shit reality, it was very stupid. Bernie could make all kinds of trouble. Trouble for Larry, trouble for me. I had to get him back.

He ran across the street and down a couple of houses and pulled up by a tulip bed in front of somebody's porch. He started sniffing. I stood on the sidewalk.

"Bernie. Here Bernie. Let's go get some more dog food, Bernie," I called.

Bernie lifted his leg and started hosing down the flowers. An ancient coot appeared in the doorway and began hissing. Bernie strode into the middle of the tulip bed and lifted his leg again. The coot teetered down the steps and started swinging a cane. Bernie ignored him.

"Bad dog," I said. "Bernie is a very bad dog."

My heart wasn't in it. Bernie finished pissing and began kicking his back legs like dogs will. Some primordial scat covering ritual. Big clots of damp earth spewed up behind him along with tulips and bulbs. The coot swelled up and turned red. Veins popped out on his forehead. An old woman ran out of the house with a green metal bottle and slapped an oxygen mask on the coot's face. Bernie loped off. He was a magnificent animal.

I ran back to Larry's driveway. Bibi was standing beside her car. "You've got to help me catch Bernie," I said. "Larry will be real happy if you help me."

"All right," she said.

We got in her car. By the time she had it backed into the street Bernie was a block away cruising down the sidewalk.

He took a right up a driveway. Didi drove down and I got out. I heard children screaming. I ran up the drive. Bernie was humping a large poodle staked to a chain in the back yard. A boy about eight threw sticks and dirt clods at him. A little girl screamed, "Bad dog hurt Fifi! Bad dog hurt Fifi! Bad dog hurt Fifi!" A woman with a dirt trowel and gardener's clothes cursed and yelled. Fifi was down in front with her paws entangled in her chain. She choked and whined. I ran over and grabbed Bernie by the scruff and tried to pull him off. He whirled and snapped at my arm. He missed by half an inch. Don't ever mess with an animal while it's having a taste.

The effort to shake me off caused Bernie to topple sideways. For a minute there was a swirling mass of dust, chain, and copulating dogs. When the animals finally got up again they were still coupled but one of Bernie's hind legs had passed over Fifi. They were welded together end to end like some insane Siamese freak show stunt. The woman ran over to me.

"You're responsible for this! I'm calling the police. You're responsible for this! I'm calling the police!" she shouted.

Little white flecks of her spittle hit me in the face. She ran inside the house. I got a water hose and began squirting Bernie and Fifi. I concentrated on the interface. Maybe something would cool off and contract. The boy kept throwing clods. I turned the hose on him. He started crying and ran up on the back porch. The girl chanted "Bad dog hurt Fifi! Bad dog hurt Fifi!". I squirted her down too. She joined the boy on the porch.

Bernie decided he'd had enough of the cold shower and ran for the driveway. He was stopped dead in his tracks by the chained Fifi. Both dogs howled piteously. Bernie pawed the ground and went nowhere. Fifi was stretched out behind him and held fast at the neck by her chain. It was an ignoble sight. Bernie deserved better. He should have been chasing bears in the Black Forest with his fellows, not immobilized in a bleak suburban backyard with his joint bent painfully backwards and wedged in a poodle.

The woman returned and stood on the porch with her brats.

"You're responsible for this! I've called the police. You're responsible for this! I've called the police!"

Bernie broke free and ran baying down the driveway. I turned the hose on the woman. I started at her crotch and worked it up to her face. She sputtered and squawked. I threw down the hose and walked down the driveway. The woman followed, cursing and threatening me.

Bibi was still in her car. I got in and banged my head. "What happened to her?" Bibi asked.

"I hosed her," I said. "Where'd Bernie go?"

"That way." She pointed down the street.

"Then onward, Bibi. This is no longer a pet hunting errand. It is a quest."

"It's Didi. Didi."

"Whatever. Let's go."

Didi started off. The squawking woman stared hard at Didi's license plate. I hoped the police had better things to do than investigate a complaint of dog rape.

Bernie was nowhere to be seen. We drove slowly down the street, peering up driveways and side yards. Two blocks away a state highway cut into town. It was divided by a medial strip and was fast and busy. I hoped Bernie would avoid it. As we approached the highway the raw sound of squealing tires followed immediately by smashing metal echoed down the street. I imagined I caught a glimpse of a leaping animal. Didi pulled to the curb.

"Look," she said. "I don't think I want to get involved any further in this. You understand, don't you? Do me a favor, ok? Don't tell Larry I gave you a ride."

"Sure thing," I said. "I understand. Maybe a few more times around the birth/death cycle and you might begin to gain a faint comprehension of these matters."

She looked at me, puzzled. I got out of the car. "Well, Fifi. Thanks for your efforts, anyway."

"It's Didi. Ass hole." She screeched off.

There I was, adrift on the sun hammered streets. The greatest drunken amateur poet extant in this shithook town. On a death mission for a soulless philistine. I walked slowly down the last block to the highway. I knew what I'd find. Bernie lying crumpled on the asphalt. Blood leaking from his mouth and ears. It's better this way Bernie. You went like a moth to the flame.

I came to the corner and beheld a wondrous sight. All four lanes of the highway were blocked. The outbound side had about twenty cars waiting but the inbound side was jammed for half a mile. The citizens were returning from their day at the lakes and sand pits and race tracks. Cars towed gaudy boats on trailers. Pickups were loaded with wheeled oriental contraptions. Lumbering motorhomes sported motorcycles and lawn chairs lashed to their fronts. Vans rocked with tired, dirty, screaming children. A cacophony of irritated horn bursts reverberated from one end of the jam to the other. The entire scene was rendered phantasmagoric by the heat rising from three hundred hot engines. A few angry curses rang out. The citizens were tired and mad, thinking now only of Monday morning and the job. Bernie, old dog, I thought, you have left in a blaze of true glory.

I approached the cause of this minor disaster. A Porsche had rear ended a station wagon and knocked it over the raised medial where it had been broadsided by a car towing a load of motorcycles. Meanwhile, the Porsche had in turn been rammed by a battered Pontiac. Bernie was not about. Trying to look like a curious pedestrian, I wended my way through the torn metal hulks. The agitated Porsche driver paced from one end of his ruined car to the other. Then he went over to a woman leaning against the station wagon and began screaming at her.

"Why didn't you run over it? Goddamnit! Why didn't you just run over it?" he raged at her.

The woman put her face in her hands and wept. Oho! Perhaps Bernie had survived. I came to the other side of the highway and scanned for Bernie. He had evaporated.

Now what. I could forget it. Go home. Tell Larry the simple truth. Bernie had run off. I was beat. Bernie could rip out every flower bed and hump every poodle from here to the Gulf. I had no intention now of arresting him and returning him to his coop to await shipment to the pound. A creature that could induce such chaos was probably not of this earth. He was an alien saboteur. I wanted to sit at his clawed feet and learn his secrets.

I plodded off down a side street. This district was unlike Larry's neighborhood. It had smaller houses and lower taxes. Smaller pretensions and lower aspirations. The yards were not well kept. Most contained an assortment of weeds. The street was lined with old and dented cars and pickups. I walked a block and stopped on the corner. No trace of Bernie. A noise that sounded like gunfire drifted in from the direction of the highway. I decided to walk one more block and quit, return to my crib and contemplate this experience, wait for Monday morning when I could stay in bed while everyone else went to work.

Halfway down the block I passed a particularly ill kept yard. It was covered with foot high dandelions gone to seed.

"Hey!"

I turned. A woman was standing in the driveway.

"You looking for a dog?" she asked.

I walked over to her. She was wearing a black bikini covered by a long sleeved cotton shirt opened at the front. She had a beautiful figure. Her face was lined and rough. She was holding a drink. Whiskey, cigarettes, and a string of bad men. She could have been anywhere between twenty five and fifty.

"Yes," I said.

"He's back here."

A hill country twang softened by twenty years gone. She turned and I followed her up her driveway. She had a nineteen year old ass. A nineteen year old ass hooked to a gnarled fifty year old head.

The back yard was enclosed by a four foot chain link fence. Bernie had cloned himself and was romping with the clone. The woman and I leaned on the fence and watched. The dogs would get down on their front legs with their butts in the air and stare at each other, tails wagging frantically. The clone would then jump up and race around the yard with Bernie in hot pursuit. Then the exercise would repeat. The only other thing in the yard was a lounge on which the woman had apparently been sunbathing when Bernie intruded. She shook the ice in her glass.

"At first I thought it was Jim come back."

"Who's Jim?"

"He's my ex-husband's dog. We had a pair of 'em. That's Sally. Harry took Jim when he left."

We watched the dogs for another minute. They seemed to be slowing a little.

"You want him?" I asked.

She didn't say anything. She continued to watch the romping dogs. Finally she turned to me with an easy grin on her face.

"Yeah. Sure. Why not?" she said.

"You think you can handle him?"

The grin broadened slightly. "You bet."

The dogs had stopped running around. Sally laid on her back with her legs parted and her forepaws folded coyly on her chest. Bernie licked her. The woman turned to me again with the same grin.

"You have any more of that?" I asked.

She saw me looking at her chest. "Anymore of what?"

"The booze. Whiskey."

"You bet."

She looked at the dogs. "Let's go inside and I'll fix you one. We ought to give these animals some privacy anyway."

We went into her kitchen. It was stark bare except for a fifth of bourbon, half gone, on the counter top. She opened a cabinet and took out a fast food giveaway tumbler and mixed me a large drink and replenished her own. We stood and sipped the drinks and looked out the kitchen window. Dusk was falling. The booze and the sun and the dog hunt had wasted me. Everything had a slightly translucent sheen. Bernie had mounted Sally. She seemed to be enjoying it more than Fifi.

The woman yawned and stretched languidly and gazed

out into the middle distance. "I think Sally likes that," she said. "She was getting real tired of those little chihuahuas and things, pissant dogs, crawling under the fence and trying to get up on her."

I slipped my hand down the bikini and squeezed her firm butt. She tilted her sand blasted face up and gave me a big wet kiss. We went into her bedroom. There wasn't a bed. I guess Harry had taken that too. She had a torn sleeping bag and some sheets on the floor. I tried some of Bernie's tricks. They worked fine.

Bill's suit coat was strangling him. It was pushing in on the sides of his neck, the carotid arteries, pinching them off and getting tighter. He reached up with both hands to prevent his death and grasped hard warm flesh. A woman's thighs. Now he could see her legs extending out before him, locked at the ankles. Silk stockings and black high heels. Squeezing down on him. Panic stricken, he beat on the legs. They were as unyielding as steel pipes. He jerked his head around, trying to see the face of this being who tormented him. Suddenly the legs parted and dissolved and Bill swam free and out and up into the fog of his life pursued by the twin horrors of his job and marriage.

MODERN PHYSICS I

The bedsheet was twisted into a rope and wrapped around his neck. He pulled it loose and lay on his side staring at a window opened two inches. The room was chilled and damp. The windows were dirty, water streaked and fly specked. The mattress was four inches thick. Bill's head was full of sludge. One eye focused, one didn't. He rolled his head slowly on the mattress. The sludge oozed painfully from one side of his skull to the other. Another wine hangover.

Bill relaxed. No hurry in getting up. Things were different now. No marriage, no job. He had to fart. He didn't like doing it under the covers. The stink lingered and would pop out five minutes later when he'd forgotten about it.

Bill eased his butt out from under the covers and squeezed off a fart. Too late he realized it wasn't only gas. He'd shit his bed. He lay rigidly now. Things always got worse by small increments. He hadn't done this since he was out of diapers, or at least as far back as he could remember. Things went down by degrees. Pimples became boils that finally drained and healed. But the healing was never complete. A slight depression always remained. Teeth became stained. The gum line receded. Joints were sprained and never completely regained their flexibility. People became familiar and monotonous.

Bill thought these things now. Minor stirrings of his semi-consciousness. The goo was cooling on his butt. It was not a comfortable feeling. Well, to hell with it, he thought. Bill relaxed another sphincter. A night's worth of wine converted to urine spread out on the mattress under him, soaking in.

Sphincters wear out. Can't focus on something twelve inches in front of your face. Can't bend the lens, like a piece of fingernail it's become hard and brittle. Can't hold it in, can't get it up. Bill relaxed the sphincters in his eyes and entered a transcendental state, a state of bliss. Bathed in warm saline equatorial waters. Floating motionless on gentle swells.

The urine was cooling, the gel was drying. Bill refocused. Both eyes were tracking now. He got off the bed and into the cramped stall shower located next to the toilet in one corner of the room. He scrubbed himself clean then held his head under the hot water for five minutes, got out, toweled off, and looked at his face in the mirror. He shaved and brushed his teeth. He pulled the covers off the bed and piled them in a corner. The mattress would dry. He dressed in wool slacks, shirt, sweater, tweed coat, cap. No tie.

The bed wetting had ruined, for the day, one of Bill's favorite pastimes. That was, lying in bed till noon or maybe one. Like Descartes, the rationalist. The father of the Cartesian coordinate system, derived from staring at the corner of his room, supposedly. Any point in space can be described by three numbers. Trouble was, it didn't work. This century had demonstrated that. World wars, rebellions, genocides, revolutions and constant terror. The three axes bend toward the center of mass.

It didn't matter now. In retrospect it never had. Marriage, job, house, car, children. Commercial real estate. Sometimes Bill wrote it like a piece of military equipment is described: Estate, real, commercial. He closed a deal on his fortieth birthday but forgot it was his birthday until he came home and saw the portable sign in his front yard. Happy Number Forty Bill. You Old Codger. It was a surprise party. He got drunk. Eighty nine days later he bagged the whole thing. Margaret was baffled, then angry, then resigned. But not with a clear understanding. He gave her everything without argument. When the divorce was settled he quit his job. His colleagues were curious and slightly envious. What would he do now? Sail the South Pacific? Be a beach bum? Mexico? A rented room in the decaying center of the city. Unemployment checks. He'd had to get a lawyer for this one, since he'd quit. Job stress. That was eighteen months ago. He hadn't talked to Margaret in six. The last time she'd given up on the detox center and was pushing the shrinks. The county mental health clinic.

Bill's room was the only one upstairs. It had been built to be used as a summer sleeping room, before air conditioning. The widow he rented it from had put in the toilet, shower, and lavatory. Bill heated soup on a hot plate. He had a small refrigerator. It was quiet.

Bill left the room. He walked down the long flight of stairs past the widow's closed sitting room. The television murmured. As the World Turns. Days of Our Lives. He was out on the sidewalk before he realized he had to think of some place to go. Well. The convenience store two blocks down. On the corner. The sidewalk was damp. This was a day in early spring. The sky was overcast. Something was going to happen. Maybe it would rain.

The last time he'd talked to Margaret, Bill had told her no, he didn't get drunk every day. Only about four times a week. That was stretching it then. Now it was clearly not true. Bill drank everyday. Deeply and methodically. Whatever he could get. The axes bend around the center of mass and finally meet.

Big drops were starting to fall when Bill got to the convenience store. The place was manned by people who spoke in a barely intelligible modern dialect. "Hihowyadoin?" "Pumpnummerthreeson." "Whatcanidoforya? Candy? Gum? Cigrets?" The prototype of a new language. A language to be used when humans lived in metal spheres buried beneath the blasted surface of the world.

Bill bought a 32 ounce Pepsi from the dispenser and a package of unfiltered cigarettes. He wandered back to the magazine rack and unwrapped the cigarettes and lit one. The video game beeped and buzzed in the corner. Two Vietnamese kids jabbered and punched at it.

Mechanix Illustrated. The magazine had always intrigued Bill. It featured a cartoon called "The Wordless Workshop." An avuncular sort and his ditsy wife, who was constantly plagued by shoes falling off racks, cats scratching furniture, towels left on the bathroom floor, were the only characters. She would complain to the husband. He would suck on his pipe and contemplate the problem. Then a light bulb would snap on above his head. He would go to his workshop and fabricate the proper configuration of wires, screws, and wooden dowels. His wife was always ecstatic when presented with the contraption. She now had another piece to add to her apparently large collection of obscure homemade gizmos.

Bill studied this thing frame by frame. Maybe, he wondered, if I was like this guy my life would be different. Maybe this man exhibits a sense of purpose that I lack. That I've always lacked. Bill browsed on to Scientific American and the Grand Unified Theory. Everything is a blob of neutrinos that explodes. Nanoseconds later it has expanded and cooled to a few trillion degrees. The physical laws of the universe are set. Gravity is inversely proportional to the square of the distance. Or maybe the cube. Everything goes downhill from there. Twenty billion years later it's dead. All sucked out into a black hole or something, a non-state of no space no time. An unstable equilibrium.

The clerk tapped Bill on the shoulder. "Hey, Buddy," he said. "Would you mind not putting your butts out on floor? It's not an ashtray, you know."

He pointed at the floor. Four or five cigarette butts were littered around Bill's feet. Bill looked at the clerk and put the magazine back on the rack and went outside. It was raining hard now. Sheets of water poured off the overhang along the front of the store. Cars with their lights on crept past in the street. Business was slow. An old broken down Chevy pulled into the lot. A scrawny white woman and two scrawny kids got out. They came out of the store a minute later, each with his own bag of potato chips.

Bill felt the comforting bulge in his coat pocket. He fingered the cap on the bottle with one hand and held the Pepsi with the other. After twenty billion years it's all rattled down to nothing. Bill set his Pepsi on a newspaper vending machine and pulled the bottle out of his pocket. A half pint of Early Times. He unscrewed the cap and took a long pull. Then another. He poured the rest of the contents into the Pepsi and put the bottle in a trash can. He walked down to one end of the overhang and sipped his drink and watched water dribble off the roof of the building.

A car made a left at the corner and then had to stop, blocking traffic behind it, before it could turn right into the store parking lot. That's a screw up, thought Bill. A thing like that could knock five or ten percent off the gross per square foot. They'd put the entry ramp too close to the corner. Bill thought about commercial real estate automatically, from habit. He didn't particularly enjoy it. All that was behind him, in another universe. He couldn't get back into it now even if he wanted to. Even if he would quit drinking and they would hire him back he couldn't do it. It was something from a previous life or the memory of a dream.

A small figure using a newspaper as a rain hat walked down the sidewalk and across the parking lot and up to the canopy. It was Dinky, who lived next to the convenience store in a house inherited from his mother. Bill sometimes drank with him in a tavern down the block. He didn't particularly like him. Dinky was a whiner and a mooch. All he had was his house and his social security checks. Not enough for an alcohol habit.

Dinky walked over to Bill and looked up. "Hey, it's rainin' cats and dogs, ain't it?" he said. Bill looked down at him and nodded.

"Hey, what're you drinking?" asked Dinky.

"Pepsi."

"Hey, loan me a dollar so I can get one. Pay you back when my check comes in."

Bill fished in his pocket and pulled out a dollar in change and gave it to Dinky.

"Thanks. Now I can buy a lotto ticket, too."

"I thought it was for a Pepsi."

"I had enough for that. But I needed a buck for the lotto."

"I wouldn't have given it to you if I'd known that. I don't believe in that swindle."

Dinky looked up, surprised. He blinked. "What do you believe in?" he asked.

Bill looked at him for a moment. "I believe you're bothering me," he said.

"Well, screw you too, buddy."

Dinky walked away and entered the store. Bill looked across the intersection at a construction site abandoned to the rain for the day. Another convenience store was going up. They'll just chew on each other's gross, now, thought Bill. Suicide.

His drink was almost gone. He had that nice morning buzz. Things were falling back into alignment. He lit another cigarette. The rain was starting to slack off. Maybe he'd walk to the bar down the street. It would open in a few minutes. But first he wanted to read about the Grand Unified Theory. Maybe something was in it that he needed to know. Maybe he'd buy the magazine and take it to the bar and study it in the gloom.

A black kid came across the parking lot. He was walking quickly with a slight limp. He was wearing a surplus army jacket a few sizes too big for him. Staring straight ahead, he passed Bill and entered the store. Bill walked to one end of the canopy and threw his cigarette out into a puddle. The two Vietnamese kids ran past him. Running hard, terror on their faces. He heard some shouting from inside the store.

Boom! Maybe, Bill thought, the kids have thrown a cherry bomb. One. Two. Three. Four. Boom! Bill walked to the entrance and reached for the door pull. The door sprung open six inches and struck his foot. For an instant Bill looked at the terrified face of the black kid. He was carrying some things in his arms held against his chest. The kid bounced back and fell to the floor on his butt and dropped his load. Bill opened the door and stood looking in. The kid sat gaping up at him. On the floor with him was a paper sack, about six packages of chocolate cupcakes, and a shotgun. The kid grabbed the paper sack and sprang up like a startled doe and hit the other door. The glass cracked but did not shatter. The kid let out a moan. Now he jerked the door inward and opened it, the way it was supposed to work. The sack tore open in his grasp. Money drifted out. The kid ran off carrying the leaking bag.

Bill walked in and looked at the stuff on the floor. The cupcakes were neatly packaged in pairs. They had little oscillatory squiggles of white icing on them. Bill picked up the shotgun. It was a double barreled twelve gauge Mossberg. Bill had hunted quail with one like this many years before with his father and great uncle. This one was ruined though. The barrels were sawed off at the stock. He opened the breach and pulled out both shells. Duck loads. They'd both been fired. Now Bill walked over and peeked behind the counter. The clerk was sprawled face up on the floor. He'd taken a load in the face. It looked like chewed meat. Blood and flecks of gore were sprayed all over the rack of cigarettes behind him. Some of them had fallen out. The clerk's name tag was still on. His name was Bill.

Bill walked to the rear of the store carrying the shotgun broken open over his forearm. Dinky was lying face down on the floor in front of the soft drink dispenser. He'd been shot in the back of the neck. Some of the pellets had missed him and had sprayed the piles of styrofoam cups stacked beside the dispenser. Blood was splattered on the wall. The coffee pot was shattered. Coffee dripped off the counter top into Dinky's hair. Dinky's left arm was thrown out away from his body. His hand clutched a lottery ticket. Bill reached down and pulled it from the dead fingers. Dinky had won the lottery. He'd won two dollars.

Bill hadn't particularly liked Dinky. Dinky had been a pest. He'd been bothering Bill five minutes before. But now he was gone. The clerk, too. The clerk who didn't like Bill's cigarette butts on the floor. Dead. Never to man a store counter again. It didn't make any sense.

The store was quiet now except for the subterranean hum of the coolers and the small tinking of the video game. The rain had almost quit. Bill lit a cigarette and walked to the magazine rack. Maybe the Grand Unified Theory would explain everything.

A car screeches to a halt in the parking lot. The car door opens and slams. Bill is standing with his back to the door. He hears this but pays no attention. He's reading, concentrating. Maybe an infinity of universes exist quasi-simultaneously, each in it's own space-time. Someone's coming in.

"Get your hands up where I can see 'em! Now! I said now, fucker! Motherfucker, get your hands up! Get your fucking hands up!"

Take 24 pounds of mass, compress it to a certain density, if you can, and it screeches off to its own space-time, its own laws of physics. You've created a universe. Bill turns absentmindedly. It's a cop. A young cop, a rookie. He's holding a .357 magnum at arm's length, pointed at Bill. His older colleagues told him this was what to get. "So they won't get back up, you hit 'em with that. That's what you need. Especially for that territory," they said. If you don't like the standard issue you've got to buy your own weapon. He's been on the force six months. His wife has to scrimp on the grocery money so that he can pay for the gun in monthly installments. She doesn't mind. She wants her husband well protected.

It's a cool day but sweat is pouring from the policeman's forehead. The gun is oscillating in his grip. Amplitude of half an inch, peak to peak. Frequency of two cycles per second. This is what Bill sees when he looks up. So this is maybe what it's all about.

The cop has seen the stuff on the floor and the blasted clerk. Now he sees the shotgun that's still hung over Bill's arm and fires his gun. The bullet traverses the fifteen feet between them and strikes Bill in the sternum which shatters. Pieces of bullet and bone rip through his chest, tearing out lung, aorta, and a chunk of spine. Bill grunts and falls back against the magazine rack. He looks down at the one in his hands. He's trying to focus. The next bullet strikes the right zygomatic arch. Bill's consciousness explodes along with his skull. He falls to the floor. The policeman runs outside, opens the car door, vomits, and grabs for the radio.

modern physics 2

some fuck in the car next to me. running his mouth, giving me the finger. a dork in a jap hot rod. going to kick my ass, put me in the hospital. must've done something he didn't like. uh oh. now he's rolled down the window. he's really going to get on me. he's had a bad day at the advertising agency. reach down. pull up the gun. twelve gauge, 18 inch barrel, pistol grip. lay the end of the barrel on the window sill. he sees it. his face turns white. he rips off through the middle of a red light. lucky for him there's no cars. maybe run him down, kick the shit out of him. fuck it. need a drink.

go in this dump. get a drink. mostly dudes a few worn out bitches. get another. just shit. people talking shit. noise, meaningless blather. just goes on and on. walking corpses, automatons. drink some more. now it's not so bad. better leave.

go to the mall. still got enough left on the card. it's horrible just walking in this place. armed guards flank the entrance, making sure the consumers remain docile. more automatons. voided entities. packs of them. hanging on to their lives like it was their sacred virginity. is it nice? is it safe? will it make be better? find this place sells tvs. look around. this one. it's ok. i need it. want to watch movies in my room at night by myself. no one to fuck with me there. tell the zit faced clerk what i need. give him the card. he puts it in the machine. it beeps, clicks. i'm sorry sir, there's not enough credit left on your card. what the fuck. the son of a bitch had five hundred left on it at least. goddamnit it. run it through again. still the same. the same. let me see that goddamned thing. let me use the phone. call these cocksuckers up, tell them not to fuck with me i've had just about enough already. sir, your credit limit is two hundred thirty eight dollars and fifty nine cents. yes, that's all sir. the latest charges? one hundred seventy dollars and three cents at Clothes by Andrea, one hundred fifty five dollars at Wild Things. yes. i'm sorry sir.

it has to be laura. that worthless little slut. i'll fucking kill her. the zit faced clerk is staring at me. hey, fuck stick, get a makeover. you snide piece of shit. got to get out of here. mash a hoard of automatons on my way out. can't fucking stand it. find the car. drive home.

margaret is in the kitchen fixing dinner when i get home. what's wrong honey? say nothing. make a double bourbon on the rocks. sit and think. drink it get another. i'll tell you what's fucking wrong, honey. that shithead daughter of yours has fucked me over good. what are you talking about? you heard me, she got to the fucking credit card, where is she? in her room. go back there. the little slut is lying on her bed, talking to some punk on the phone. pull the phone cord out of the wall. what the fuck are you doing Harold? laura, you've screwed me over good with the credit card. mama said i could. go back to margaret. what the hell is this? you gave laura the credit card? i let her buy a pair of jeans with it. a pair of jeans. a pair of fucking jeans cost three hundred plus?

go back to laura's room. she's back on the phone. jerk open the closet. three pairs of new jeans, new jackets with holes made in them. laura, what the fuck is this? jerk the shit out and throw it on the floor. fashion a good whip out of a coat hanger. mama said what, honey? hit her with it. she screams and rolls off the bed. hit her several more times. she curls up in a corner and howls. you little bitch. try to jack me around. think i work all day for your benefit? so you can hang around the mall and chew bubble gum? you're a lying little cunt. hit her with the hanger again and again. lay some welts on her.

margaret's in the room. get off her you son of a bitch. get the fuck off her. she doesn't deserve that. you can't beat the shit out of her. i'll take care of it. the hell i can't beat the shit out of her. you won't take care of shit. what are you going to do? ground her for two weeks? this is money we're talking about, margaret. my fucking sweat and blood money. i hit laura with the hanger a couple of more times.

now margaret's really pissed. she runs out of the bedroom and comes back with a pan full of frying hamburgers and throws the whole mess at me. duck and it slams into the wall. the pan leaves a big dent in the sheetrock. the grease drips off the ceiling. laura is still whimpering. go back to the living room. fix another bourbon. sit down. cool out a little. jesus this family life is a crock.

margaret and laura are scuffling about in laura's bedroom. now they're out with several suitcases. Harold, laura and i are leaving. we can't accomodate your violence anymore. my support group discussed you. you're afraid of modern women. the group leader says you're afraid of being castrated. she says your're having trouble finding the proper role to play within the context of our chosen lifestyle. i can't allow your violence into my personal space any longer. i've really been having trouble accessing you lately on any level. i'm leaving one of my crystals. meditate on it. maybe you'll realize your potential as a sentient entity.

say nothing. margaret and laura trudge out the door with their personal lifestyle shit. which car will the advanced beings take? the caddy of course, leaving me with the broken down dodge.

five years with margaret has not been good. i met her in

a honky tonk when she was pretending to be wild and free. a couple of months after marrying her i realized why old man number one had split. margaret is basically a manipulator. she affects some kind of intellectuallity by regurgitating crap she reads in cosmopolitan. she has a job but the proceeds are spent on clothes and boutique junk. then there's her daughter, laura. a margaret clone raised by malfunctioning video games. i'm a beast of burden for these harpies. a lobotomized slave chained to a treadmill. anyway, they're gone now. maybe they'll stay gone this time.

since i'm not hungry i guess i'll load some shells in the basement. press a few. press a few double ought. don't know why i think i need these. they'd shred any game you hit with them. instant chicken fajitas. instant chile sin frijoles. a car door slams outside. go up with the shotgun. look out the window and what do i see? two big policemen coming after me. it seems margaret's faith in crystal power is lacking. she's summoned the law in case the crystal doesn't work. the cops are banging loudly on the door. open up. police. we've had a domestic violence complaint. these are two irritating peckerwoods. go away. leave me alone to drink my whiskey in peace. life's a bitch, man. they won't go away. they're executing their duties under full authority of the law.

i can't take this shit. crack the window two inches aim the shotgun at the police car windshield and squeeze. the windshield turns into a spider web with a two foot hole in it. the cops aren't smart. they run back to their car and crouch behind it. could have dropped them both. easy as shooting rabbits. a titanic weight has lifted off my chest. this might be fun. one cop's got the driver's side door open. he's going for the radio. get the whiskey and while i'm at it a flare gun that's twenty five years old but maybe it's still good. the radio in the cop car crackles and spits. i'm sure they don't like what i've done to their government property. there'll be hell to pay.

the cop car is ugly. i just cut and edged the lawn and now these assholes have left this car with a busted windshield parked in my driveway. what will the neighbors think? the flare gun is not made for accuracy but the target's close. crouch down aim and pull. a flare arcs out and blows through the hole in the windshield. black smoke starts pouring out. magnesium burns hot. it'll go for five minutes. more than enough time to incinerate the car. maybe set off the gas tank. the smoke turns in to flame. a rear window shatters from the heat. got a good draft through it now. the two cops sprint off zig zagging. better arm up. this ain't over yet.

go back down to the basement. get the .308 with the scope. the ought six. these fuckers are flat to two hundred yards. plenty of ammo. more shotgun shells. the nine millimeter. a gas mask and a couple of knives. a flak jacket. drag all the shit back upstairs. lock all the doors and windows. there aren't many in this shithole. little crackerbox like all the rest on this street. a nice working class neighborhood. shit. at least it's brick. they can't shoot through the walls with anything short of a bazooka. there's sirens going off all over the place. i look out back through the kitchen window. a cop is helping the neighbors climb a fence. the little girl is clutching a doll. goddamnit, there goes the neighborhood. never know when some maniac is going to move in next door. out front they've blocked the street at each corner with police cars. can't see anyone around.

the telephone rings. answer it. it's melonhead, my boss. why'd they get this shitass to call me? just want to piss me off some more? what the fuck do you want, melonhead? you're calling to tell me i got a raise. no. that's not it. you're telling me the company health insurance will pay 50 per cent for mental health treatment. do you think i give a shit? tell you what, melon. come on over. have a beer. tell me i'm not loading shit fast enough again. tell me i don't know how to run your goddamn forklift. i'd like to shove that forklift up your ass. or a duel. name your weapon. meet me out front. we'll settle this once and for all. he's not interested. he want's to talk about my problems. hang up. a son of a bitch like that will give a person an ulcer sure as hell. the phone rings again. now it's margaret. fuck you, whore. slam down the receiver and rip the cord out of the wall. all these assholes who've plagued me for years are now concerned when i cut loose a little. fuck them all.

    down at the corner they've moved up two fire trucks and some kind of rescue vehicle and an ambulance. they're preparing for an assault. the kitchen will be my redoubt. drag the mattresses off the beds and into the kitchen and put them up over the windows. these will probably stop a tear gas cannister. drag in the tv. it's starting to get dark. leave all the lights off.

    worst i ever felt was when i nailed the old lady and the kid. shoot anything that moves. that was the order. so i did. the next morning we found them laying about 300 yards out, covered with ants. the old woman's eyes were completely clouded over with cataracts. stone blind. the little girl's head was half blown off. i puked. all these hard asses who'd cut off ears and shit were looking at me like i was some kind of criminal. then we found about 25 pounds of plastique on the old woman and some detonators in a bag the kid had been carrying. i didn't feel so bad. never could figure out what those gooks thought they were doing.

there's a screeching and squawking outside. a bullhorn is poking over the hood of one of the cop cars. some blather comes out of it then it starts screeching again. these guys are such a bunch of clowns. there's a new vehicle on the scene. it's parked back behind the rest. the TV station newswagon. oh boy. let's see if i'm on TV. flick it on. an ad. flick the channel. a preacher. in the name of God, i say to you, stop this madness now. change the channel. ken and barbie are playing catch with inanities. and now let's switch live to cynthia felcher at the gunman scene. it's barbie's cousin. cynthia felcher on the scene of the police/gunman standoff. police responding earlier this evening to a domestic violence complaint were met at the residence by a gun-wielding Viet Nam vet. the officers escaped unharmed but the police cruiser was fired on and heavily damaged by the gunman. he is identified as one Harold Smith, a former army special forces sniper and veteran of heavy combat in the Viet Nam war. his wife reports he has been despondent as of late and suffering from depression, insomnia, and nightmares. nightmares my ass. the only nightmare i've suffered from lately is living with margaret and her psychotic daughter. the scene switches. they've got the camera pointed at my house. i can see the kitchen windows. get out the .308. if they can see me i can see them. keep the barrel inside and look through the scope. it's cynthia, bigger than shit. toothy mouth, copperhead eyes. put the cross hairs on her left pupil. move them down to the gap between her front teeth. up to the middle of her forehead. she's still talking. i'm not listening. rub the trigger. caress it. i don't want to do this.

move the sights over to the back of the cameraman's head. he's holding a little portable camera while cynthia talks to the avid viewers. i won't shoot him, either. just consider the entertainment i'm providing to the citizens of this fine burg. something real. something happening in their own city. something to liven up their dead existences.

    i put down the rifle. something whispers by my cheek and splats into the refrigerator. then i hear the report. dive for the floor. turn the TV off. that was stupid, i was backlit. jesus that was close. closest anyone's ever come to taking me out. that fucker is either damn good or close. where the fuck is he? peek out. it's almost completely dark now. i can't see shit.

    larry and i enlisted together and served together and came back together. not a scratch on either one of us. we drank and ran around together back here for a few years. neither one of us gave much of a shit about the future. then the son of a bitch got run through by a kitchen knife wielded by an insane whore. the bitch had been married four times and went bananas when larry told her to take a hike. she's out of the loony bin now and married to husband number five, or so i heard. larry's still dead.

    i've suffered approximately the same fate by marrying margaret. never thought things could go to shit so quick. what is there to do now? this isn't so much fun. that rifle slug scared me sober. they've got the bullhorn working again. come out with your hands in the air. you've got thirty seconds. yeah. walk out in the dark surrounded by probably fifty scared cops with itchy trigger fingers. no thanks. i'll find some other way. they've brought out a helicopter. it's chugging away overhead. suddenly the whole house is illuminated by a brilliant light. they start firing volleys. ten, twenty, thirty rounds. from all directions. the window glass shatters and flies all over the place. i keep down and crawl to the basement stairs and go down in the dark.

    i've thought about it. there's no way out. i should have died over there and saved everyone a lot of trouble. i've written this by flashlight. my last will and testament. i'll leave it on my workbench. i pick up my trusty shotgun. pull off my shoe and sock and work my big toe into the trigger guard. lean over and give head to the barrel.

MODERN PHYSICS III

Jimmy smoke crack cocaine. He sit and wait for an angel from Heaven to come down and put her sweet lips on him. That what Roland say it like. Jimmy don't see nothin. He think maybe Roland don't know what he talkin about. Jimmy only ten.

Jimmy sittin outside the bedroom window of his crib. He climb out when his mama and Daryll started in on each other. Daryll callin his mama a dirty slut, mama tellin Daryll he's a good for nothin low down wino and bum. Jimmy sneak out when the slappin start. Little brothers sleep right through it, Jimmy can't listen no more.

He put his tube back in the cigar box and take out the peashooter. He pull the little caps out and look at them. Half dull gray and half shiny. He put em back in and spin the cylinder. He point the peashooter out at the street and go "Pow! Pow!"

Jimmy find the peashooter in some weeds over by the MacDonalds. It all rusty. He take it home and put some oil on it and shine it up real nice. Make the trigger work. Then he tell Roland he found a gun. Roland perk up real quick. "Let's see this gun," he say.

Jimmy know right then he's made a mistake. Roland see the gun he take it. Roland like that, got a mean streak five feet wide. Jimmy say, "Naw, I's just messin with you." Roland don't believe him grab him by the hair say, "Give it up, little nigger, give it up." Jimmy feel the tears come up in his eyes. This hair pullin hurt. So he go get the gun and show it to Roland. Roland look at it. He say, "Shit, this ain't no gun. This a little cap gun, little peashooter. Ain't good for nothin." Jimmy glad Roland don't like the peashooter. He won't take it now.

Roland stay next door with his auntie. He fourteen. He don't do nothin cept lay up all day and listen to some tunes after his auntie go off to work. His auntie find out Roland ain't goin to school no more. She say, "You get your hide out and get yourself a job then, boy, you wants to stay under the roof. I ain't puttin up with such foolishness."

Roland think he play the rent man. Go up to the old womens' places on check day say, "Rent man sent me." Old womens know he lyin, had this shit run on them before. They tell Roland they ain't got the rent. But Roland a big kid and he look real mean when he want. He say, "Rent man says I got to get sumpin. Come on now, what you got?" They's kinda scared now so's they give him a few dollars or a radio or sumpin just so he'll go away.

This work ok for Roland for a few days. He tell his auntie he got a job at the MacDonalds. Then Roland go to a old woman's place tell her he the rent man. She say, "Just a minute." She come back with her son or nephew or somebody. Dude look like Mr. T. He say, "What kinda shit is this?" Slap shit out of Roland. Bang him up. Roland think he better find another line of work. Find a man front him some crack cocaine. Now Roland hang around the grade school and the junior high, trade for lunch money and shit. He don't go around the high school. Get his ass kicked over there.

Day after Jimmy show Roland the peashooter Roland come to Jimmy's house when he get home from school. Roland say, "You come on over to my crib. I got sumpin for you." Jimmy go over there and Roland give him six caps for his cap gun. Then he show Jimmy how to smoke some crack cocaine and give him a tube and a little chunk of it. Jimmy don't like it all that much. Make him feel buzzy all over. Then Roland say, "Now you got's to give me sumpin." Jimmy say he ain't got nothin. Roland say well you got's to give me sumpin, you took them caps for your peashooter and smoke my crack cocaine. Jimmy tell him take em back. Didn't want it anyway. Now Roland mad. Tell Jimmy he want the bicycle. Jimmy say no, Roland say give him the bike or he tell Jimmy's mama Jimmy smoke crack cocaine and got a gun an then Roland'll kick his ass on top of it all.

So Jimmy give him the bike. Roland sell it the next day. It gone for good. This what botherin Jimmy more'n anything sittin outside the bedroom window. More'n Daryll and mama hittin at each other. Take Jimmy a whole year pickin up cans and bottles and shit buy that bike for sixty five dollar. Now Roland steal it.

Jimmy get the tube and crack cocaine back out from the cigar box and smoke the rest. He feelin all buzzy again. He get the peashooter and put the box back under the bush in it's hidin spot and walk out on the street. He walk a block up and a block over. Jimmy feelin like a bad ass dude. This a real gun, he think, shoot Roland and Daryll with it. Shoot Roland in the ass and Daryll in the head. No, shoot Daryll in the ass and Roland in the head. Jimmy swing the peashooter around go "Pow! Pow!" with his mouth. Shoot Michael Jackson and the President. Shoot He-man, take She-ra away from him.

Jimmy over by a vacant lot full of trash. He think it time to shoot a cap. He hold the cap gun up in the air and squeeze the trigger. It go "Bang!" real loud scare Jimmy. Jimmy think this one loud ass cap gun. Not worth a bike though. Jimmy kick at some trash like he always do lookin for bottles and cans. Find a bottle. Maybe start savin for another bike. Then Jimmy think shit. He feel like cryin. He miss that bike bad.

Car comin down the street. Jimmy wait till it close and throw the bottle out in front. It break all over the street. Car pull over and stop. It a police car. Jimmy hide down behind some bushes. Police get out and stand there, lookin around. Jimmy get an idea he scare the police. Point the peashooter at him and pull the trigger. Peashooter bangs and police slap his neck like he been bug bit.

Jimmy think the police foolin with him, playin cops and robbers. Police kinda walk funny and get back in his car. Jimmy hide in the bush thinkin maybe he should run off. Police car just sets there. Police ain't doin nothin. Jimmy hear the police radio. He think now he sneak up on the police scare hell out of him. Jimmy a brave dude. He creep out of the bush and sneak around back of the police car. He creep up and spy in on the police. Radio sayin "Unit twelve, repeat. Unit twelve, repeat." Police kinda settin up holdin his neck starin at the speedometer. What for, he ain't goin nowhere.

Police got his helmet off. Got blonde hair like He-man cept cut short like one of them fancy football dudes. Jimmy stick the cap gun in pull the trigger three times quick. "Bang! Bang! Bang!" Police jerk around. Jimmy jump back, think the police fixin to come after him. But the police ain't goin nowhere now. His head flop on the seat back. He starin straight up. Hand fall down from his neck. Jimmy look in. He see a trickle of blood comin out a the police's neck. He see three little blue holes side of the police's head.

Jimmy wake up now. All a sudden he know what he done. Weren't no peashooter. Was a real gun. Roland be lyin. Jimmy run like the devil was after him. He get to his crib, hide the gun, climb back in the bedroom window. He hear Daryll sawin logs. He hear the sirens goin off. He hear the whirly chopper chuggin around. All hell's busted loose. Jimmy lay real stiff in his bed lookin up. He shut his eyes tight. Maybe, he think, he stay like this till morning he wake up it all a bad dream.

APES

I'm looking at a magazine. Since the fundamentalists drove out all the smut, the supermarkets have started selling swimsuit mags. This particular item starts out at the top like a normal one piece but ends up as a g-string. It's called a thong. It leaves the model's buttocks exposed. "For swim, lounge, casual wear." Huh? The next page has a woman with gigantic breasts. They're symbolic buttocks. No other function. Cut one open. Nothing but fat, besides the nipple.

Uh-oh. The assistant manager is looking at me. He's pretending to make check marks on a clipboard but I know he's watching. I've been standing here with an empty shopping cart for over an hour. He has a little beeper or walkie-talkie hooked to his belt. "Where is he now, Joe?" "Over in meats on aisle D. Looking at skin mags." "Sell him some liver. Maybe he'll go home." I better move a little. I push the shopping cart nonchalantly down the aisle. I round the corner.

Here is a young mother in miniskirt, black fish net stockings, and high heels. I stop and fidget, pretend to look for something. She is delightful. A half asleep baby sits in the cart seat. A hyperactive brat scurries about underfoot. She's hunched over reading a box, concentrating. Her lips are pursed. Lips are symbolic vulva. Monkeys don't have them. She glances up. She looks right through me. I am invisible to most people. Now the brat has knocked some shit off the lowest shelf. She scolds him and squats down to put the shit back. The skirt rides up her thighs. The fucking assistant manager is looking at me again, tapping his clipboard against his leg. I reach out and grab something. Canned tuna. I hate canned tuna. Maybe I can mix it with D-Con and poison a cat.

Miniskirt has taken off. I find her again in produce. I survey the green peppers, the eggplant, the bananas, the miniskirt. I got all this from Desmond Morris. He was a genius. Maybe none of it's true but so what. Where else can you read that a male baboon mounts and ejaculates in eight seconds? Or that female baboons don't have orgasms. How do you think Desmond determined that? "Well, how was it? Did the earth move? Did you see God?" "Nah, none of that shit. I was just waiting for the lumox to get off so I could wander over and pick a couple of those fat lice off Junior." Now the assistant manager is not even pretending to not watch me. I'd better go. I throw in a bunch of bananas and roll to the checkout counter. The clerk rings up the tuna and bananas. I give her food stamps. Her upper lip raises a bit. She stonily counts out the change.

I go out to the parking lot and get into my pile of junk. It's a crisp, sunny Fall day. I roll down the windows and lean back, smell my fingers. I'm still a little groggy; I just got up. It's one o'clock PM. I've been sleeping too much. I've got nothing to do, nowhere to go. The sun is warm on my crotch.

Here comes miniskirt. Maybe I should proposition her. She gets the brats into a beat up old Camaro and heads out of the parking lot. I am compelled to follow. I tail her for about half a mile. She turns right at a sidestreet, goes about a block, and pulls into the driveway of a busted down bungalow. Sagging porch, no paint. I slow way down and creep by, staring at her. She looks up and recognizes me. Now I'm visible. She instinctively shields the brats. I drive home.

I carry the tuna and bananas down into my basement rat

hole. I take a knife and cut about a third off a large banana. I hollow out the larger piece with a spoon, leaving the slimy inner peel. Now I pull down my pants and look at my dick. It's half erect already after thongs, thighs, lips, eggplant. I stroke it up and insert it into the hollowed out banana. Jewish theologians say that Adam tried sexual intercourse with every animal in the Garden of Eden before God hit on the idea of Eve. God was dumb before he died. I try to get an image. Miniskirt, a thong, tits, something. The tits are cut open. All I get is baboons walking fourlegged, picking bugs off each other, nibbling them. Chimpanzees with bulging scabrous behinds. Skinny lemurs in trees. It's no good. A cockroach is crawling down the wall. I jerk the banana peel off and throw it at the roach. Got it. I pull up my pants and pace aimlessly about the room. Now it's 1:30. Eight and a half more hours and I can go to bed.

I hear people walking around upstairs. The woman is home with her brat now. She says I fucked her once. I can't remember. Her face is a blank. I don't know her name or how long she's lived there. I took a bit and brace and bored a hole from my bathroom into her bathroom. It came out against the wall under her sink. I carved out the edges with a knife so it looked like a rat or mouse had chewed it. With a small mirror I could see diagonally up and out. I looked for awhile. All I ever saw were bare legs up to about mid thigh below the sink.

The chronology of my memories is screwed up. Things that supposedly happened six months ago seem like yesterday. I can't remember yesterday. I put on some Mozart. The brat found the hole after about a week. The woman came down and asked me what I thought had done it. I told her to buy some rat traps. She didn't plug the hole.

The Mozart is soothing. A ninety minute tape. The music has stopped. I'm sitting here staring at my shoe. What time is it now? Five o'clock. The brat upstairs knocks something over. I can hear screaming, crying, stomping feet. The other inmates of the flophouse are returning. They've killed their time for the day. The music is starting up. It vibrates the structure. It oozes into my room. All of them have acquired huge high powered stereo systems. They make war with the things. I think it's Friday. It will be worse than usual tonight. Tomorrow the entry way will reek with the odor of stale smoke. There will probably be fresh vomit. Maybe some broken glass. Or blood.

I'm hungry. I go to the cupboard, the refrigerator. Bare. Now I remember. Today the project was to clean my crib and restock my larder. I have failed. My life is a constant series of distractions now. One activity interrupted by another, interrupted by another, by another. I open the can of tuna. It's packed in oil. I eat it with my fingers. The oil dribbles down my chin. I wipe my chin with the back of my hand. Then I wipe my hand on my pants. I eat a banana. Now it's 5:30.

I put on some Wagner. He is pure; he climbs and soars to the sun. But underneath is the cacophony of discordant bass notes slithering into the room. Herr Wagner sits in his marble house of reason. The floors are polished, the windows and doors are trimmed with fine woods. But tree roots are sneaking under the footings; they will crack. Termites are devouring the woodwork from within. I turn up the volume. It finishes. I start it over. It finishes. I start it over. It finishes. Now it's 9:30. I'm ready for sleep.

Someone's coming down the stairs. They knock on the door. I open it. It's the woman from upstairs.

"Hi. What're you doing?" she says.

I scratch the side of my head and look at the floor.

"Can I come in?"

"Ok."

Now I remember why her face is a blank. No features are prominent. It's the head of a fetus at six months. Her skin is clear. Her eyes are fogged and red. She comes in. She has a sack with beer in it. She offers me one. She is wearing jeanshorts cut off at the point where part of her butt sticks out. A loose blouse. Barefoot. Unlike her face her secondary sexual characteristics are normal. She sits cross legged on the couch. I sit in a chair opposite her. She pulls out a marijuana cigarette and lights it. Soon she is enveloped in a cloud of smoke.

"Where have you been all summer?" she asks.

"Here."

"You don't look very good. Your skin is white. It smells musty in here. Don't you ever open a window?"

"I stay out of the sun."

"You were happier in the spring. The night you came home drunk. The night we made love. Why didn't you ever come up and see me again? Why don't you ever party with us?"

I can't remember. I can't remember her face or her name or anything about her. She changes the subject. Her kid is driving her nuts. Her ex-husband is holding out on the child support, fucking with her. I look at my hand clutching the beer can. Little black hairs sprout between the knuckles. Hard finger nails made for digging grubs, clawing. Her nonsymbolic lips are covered by one and a half inches of material. I don't think she's wearing underwear. A few stray hairs have snuck out. She talks on. She is obviously a lonely being. What a shit hole this is. No money. Men are such turds, such self-centered assholes. I try to pay attention. I can't. I'm staring at a joint in the wallboard above her head.

"Are you ok?" she asks.

I don't respond. She sits silently for a minute.

"Well, I guess I'd better be going."

She stands up. I nod noncommittedly. She walks towards the door. My crotch is tight and aching. I get up. Her back is turned, she is about to open the door. I come up behind her and hug her with one arm. I unzip my pants with the other hand. She turns her head and looks at me, part pleased, part surprised, part wary. She can't see that my zipper is open. With both hands I quickly unsnap her shorts and pull them down around her hips. They drop to the floor. She is pretty high, or drunk. I don't know. She doesn't respond to this action. Now I grasp one of her legs behind the knee and lift it up. I push her against the door. From behind I attempt to thrust up and into her. Eight seconds is all I need. She does not like this and bucks violently backwards and throws me off. She turns and throws a roundhouse punch that catches me squarely in the left eye. Goddamn it hurts. I take a few steps back, covering my eye.

"You pig, you shithead," she screams. "I thought maybe you were different. I was wrong. You're like the rest of them, an asshole."

Now she notices her shorts are still around her ankles. She quickly pulls them up. Tears leak down her face.

"You stay away from me. And stay away from my kid, too, fucker."

She turns and races back upstairs. I sit down. She nailed me good. She's left the rest of her beer so I drink it. Maybe I can sleep. I've never been able to understand women. It seems they prefer a load of crap and lies to the truth. The beer is gone now so I go to bed.

I am awakened a couple of hours later by the beer and my eye. I have a tremendous headache. I stagger into my cramped bathroom and look in the mirror. The eye is swollen shut. It is black and purple. I pry it open and look at the orb. The white has turned blood red. I pee and gobble four aspirin. A small circle of light is on the wall above the mirror. It's the light from her bathroom. I find a small hand mirror and hold it up and look through the hole in the floor. The same. Bare legs below the sink.

Some fool is pounding on the door. Maybe it's her ex-husband, summoned to annihilate me. I'm sure he's a God fearing taxpayer eager to pulverize my ilk. Just in case, I take a loaded .38 revolver off the shelf. I go to the door and peek around the window curtain. No husband, it's Miller. I don't particularly want to see him right now. Then I notice he's holding a fifth of whiskey. I unload the revolver and drop the cartridges in a chair and cock the hammer. Then I jerk open the door and leap out and place the muzzle of the gun against Miller's forehead, yell "Freeze!", and pull the trigger. Miller yelps and jumps back, almost drops the whiskey, but he can't because I've grabbed it.

"And just what the fuck do you want, Miller?"

"I have a proposition for you," he says.

"Ok. Come in."

I get two glasses from the kitchen and fill them with whiskey. Miller paces and fidgets. He grins quickly. Now he yawns. Now he grins quickly again. I can see he's removed his chemical straightjacket today.

"Sit down, Miller. Drink the whiskey," I say. "Into self-medication tonight?"

"Yeah. That's it. Self-medication. He he he he he."

Miller is a certified looney. He's usually quite amusing.

"Why haven't you taken your pills per the good doctor's instructions?" I ask.

"It's boring, that's why. Besides, I can't get it up when I take that shit."

"Why are you interested in getting it up? Have a date tonight?"

"No. He he he he he."

Miller paces some more. He fidgets. He grimaces. He's wearing Salvation Army pants, scuffed black shoes, a dirty shirt, and a drab wornout overcoat. He finally sits down. He takes a drink of whiskey and looks at me.

"Jesus! What happened to you?" he says.

"The same thing that happened to you. I was born."

"No. Your eye. Your eye's all fucked up."

"I was bitten by a rabid skunk. No. That's not it. I was escorting an elderly lady across the street. When we got to the curb the good woman decided I was molesting her so she caned me. A pox on her, the flea ridden hag."

"You're full of shit."

"Do tell. Where's your medication?"

"Here."

He reaches into the pocket of his overcoat and throws some pills on the table top. There's two big brown capsules and four small red ones. I point to a brown one.

"What do these do?"

"They make me normal."

I point to the red ones.

"And these?"

"They help me move after I'm normal. He he he he he."

I sweep the pills off the table into my hand and throw them in my mouth and chew. They taste awful. I wash them down with whiskey. The whiskey tastes worse.

"You just took two day's worth," he says. "He he he he he."

"Why didn't you tell me?"

"You didn't ask. Haw haw. Haw."

"So what's your proposition?"

"I want you to help me hit an armored car."

"Say what?"

"Yeah. It picks up the receipts at the Burger King by my mother's house every day at 3:00."

"Now how do you propose we rob it?"

"I've got two gas masks and a cannister of tear gas. We wait until they open the door, lob in the gas, and come in behind it with guns. Drive it a couple of blocks to the get away car."

"What about the drivers?"

"They're expendable, of course."

Miller is a consummate bullshitter who doesn't work but spends his time dreaming up ridiculous schemes like this. The remark about expendability irritates me.

"So, you're going to kill two people for the day's take at a fucking Burger King?"

"Yeah. I guess so."

"You're an idiot. You woke me up in the middle of the night to listen to this crap?"

Miller is basically a meek person. He hangs his head and hunches his shoulders and stares at the floor. I guess I've hurt his feelings.

"Miller, you'd get your ass blown off trying something

like that. Why don't you grow up? Take some enjoyment in the simple pleasures of life."

He looks up. "Like what?"

"Like fucking, for instance."

"How do I do that?"

"First you have to find a woman."

"I know that. How do I find one?"

I stop. This is a problem. Miller is an unemployed part time vagrant who sleeps in cardboard boxes in alleys when his aged mother tires of his mooching and kicks him out. He's not exactly what used to be called a good catch. He gets up and goes to the can. I wish he'd leave. It's 1:00 AM now. Things are starting to get a little fuzzy. I'm having trouble moving my lips and tongue. Miller comes back from the can.

"What's that little round light on the wall above your mirror?" he asks.

"Ho! The wench is still about. Come here, I'll show you."

We go into the cramped little bathroom and I take the hand mirror and check out the hole. Still bare legs. What's she doing? Flossing? Popping zits? I give Miller the mirror. He looks for a long time. I notice he grimaces twice and yawns once.

"Who is she?" he asks.

"A hellcat, that's who."

"I'd like to meet her."

"I don't think I'm the one to present an introduction. She doesn't like me. In fact, she hates my guts. I pressed my suit tonight and this was my reward."

I point at my eye. Miller looks though the hole again.

"She sure has pretty legs," he says. "He he he he he. What made her hit you?"

"Let's skip the whole banal story."

Miller is agitated. He's grinning like a fool. I have an idea.

"Tell you what. I'll write you a letter of introduction."

"Yeah. Yeah. Do it."

I find a piece of paper and a pen. We go back to the kitchen table. I take a big slug of whiskey. The pain in my eye is gone now but I'm getting increasingly more sluggish. The drugs are starting to have an effect. I write a note:

Dear Madam—

My behaviour tonight was deplorable. I beg your pardon for my despicable actions. I have been ill lately and not of sound mind. I truly intended no harm. Please allow me to present an acquaintance of mine. Mr. Miller is a gentleman and scholar. He is short of funds presently due to his full time medical school studies. However, he is a fine chap. He has admired you from afar and pleaded for an introduction.

—Your neighbour

I give the note to Miller. He reads it.

"I'm not a medical student," he says.

"I know that. But it's your only chance."

He ponders the note a while longer.

"Well, I guess I'll go see her."

"That's the spirit. Try not to grin so much. It'll make her suspicious. Keep her off balance or she'll come at you like a ferret."

I walk him to the door. I put my hand on his shoulder.

"Goodluck and God speed, Miller."

He leaves. I hear him walk up the stairs and knock on the door. I take the whiskey and sit in a soft chair. This should be amusing. I'm betting she'll punch him back down the stairs. It's hard to disguise the fact that you're a certified lunatic. She pads to the door and opens it. I hear a muffled conversation. It's quiet for a bit. Then the door closes. Two pairs of feet are walking on the floor. The son of a bitch got in. I take another large gulp of whiskey. The bottle is half gone.

With great effort I raise my eyes to the wall clock. It's now 2:00. An hour has passed since Miller left. I am immobilized. I've been slouched here in a stupor without even realizing it. My head is bent forward and my tongue is hanging out. It feels like it's coated with sawdust. I can't retract it. I sit for a while longer in this ridiculous posture trying to decide what to do. I have to pee again. With a superhuman effort I manage to fall on my knees to the floor. With intense concentration I can crawl. My tongue is still jammed out. I can feel drool trickling off it. I make it to the kitchen table after ten minutes have passed. The sudden insane hyena cackle of Miller breaks out overhead. He's blown it now. No. The woman is giggling. She must like him. They'll make such a cute couple.

Fifteen minutes more and I get to the head. I pull myself up on the sink. I'm wobbly. My eyes don't focus very well. I finally get my dick out and aim for the bowl. Half the piss goes in the bowl and half dribbles down the front of my pants. This is an intolerable situation. I make the mistake of looking in the wall mirror. The thing looking back is not human. It's the face of a brain dead steer a second before it hits the slaughterhouse floor. No. It's not even a vertebrate. It's something scraped off the underside of a toilet seat and magnified ten thousand times. An organism that spends its life seeking little flecks of excrement.

I slump back to the floor. My bed is only ten feet away.

I slither like a salamander in muck. A vile and odious thing. Finally I manage to crawl into the bed; shoes, wet pants, smelly shirt still on. Now that I'm facing up my tongue flops back into my mouth. It feels swollen and dry, like I'm sucking on a large wad of toilet paper. The bed springs upstairs are squeaking erratically. Then they settle into a gentle rhythm. Miller has found a port in the storm.

In another part of the asylum, on the second or third floor, a violent argument breaks out. It must be very loud since I can hear it in my rat hole. I hear breaking glass as a bottle shatters outside on the driveway. Someone has thrown it through a window. Far away a police siren moans. All is well with the world.

Harry lived alone and liked it that way. Years before, he had lived with women. Harry had finally come to the conclusion that, like many other things, the expense and bother of them was, ultimately, not worth their dubious benefit. Now, in the middle of his sixth decade, he felt he had finally arrived at that plane of calm and orderly existence that had been, subconsciously at least, his lifelong aspiration. He worked in a machine shop and ran a lathe that cut metal to a tolerance measured in millionths of an inch.

THE MOWER

Each day he arrived at the job ten minutes early to drink one cup of coffee before starting time, ate his ham on rye sandwich at noon, and punched out exactly at five o'clock. In the spring and summer he mowed his lawn on the diagonal every Saturday morning. In winter his sidewalks were always shoveled as soon as the snow had quit falling. Any slight malfunction in his house, a squeaky step or leaking faucet, was fixed upon discovery. Saturday afternoon he drank his one alcoholic beverage of the week, a beer, while watching a sporting event on his television. On Sunday mornings he wrote letters to the editor. Sunday afternoons he masturbated. He had no friends and few acquaintances. His life was a scheduled sequence of procedures developed over the years to accomplish a given task with maximum efficiency. He liked it that way.

On a Saturday morning in June Harry smoked his weekly cigar in his garage and checked the amount of oil in his lawn mower. He wheeled the mower to his front yard. The weather was turning hot. He decided to cut his grass a little higher and raised the cutting height on the mower. He bent to the starter and gave the rope a steady pull. The engine spun but did not fire. He pulled again. He heard a faint snap. The engine fired once and quit. The starter rope dangled slack from Harry's hand. He jiggled it. It would not retract. Shit, said Harry.

Harry turned resolutely and wheeled the mower back to his garage. It probably just needs a slight adjustment, he thought. He took a wrench and removed the starter assembly from the mower. He laid it on his spotless work bench and flicked on an overhead fluorescent light. He found the problem immediately. A small pin that engaged a cogged wheel was sheared off. Shit. Harry closely studied the mechanism. It was made from stamped metal. Typical, he thought. A simple device, but poorly made from cheap materials. Failure was a certainty. No wonder the country was going down the drain. Harry wiped his hands on a rag and went into his house. He opened a drawer of a file cabinet in the small office he kept and in ten seconds had located the warranty card for the mower which he had purchased from a department store one year before. The store was part of a large mall on the edge of town. He would have to go there. He retrieved the starter from his work bench, shut and locked the garage door, and set off in his small fuel efficient car.

Harry usually avoided the mall. It was crowded and noisy and got on his nerves. The parking lot was always jammed with cars and a convenient spot was hard to find. Harry, however, in his methodical way, had discovered the store could be entered through a rear door that gave onto a service alley. Here is where he parked, one hundred feet from the back entrance. He got out of the car and strode purposefully forward. Halfway to the door he came to a trash dumpster. Next to it was parked a battered shopping cart which contained a half dozen flattened aluminum cans and a grotesque puppet. The puppet's paper mache head was large and crudely made. It looked like the product of a childrens' art class. The body was a piece of burlap sewed together with what appeared to be fishing line. A small dog was leashed to the cart and stood by patiently, staring up at Harry. A soft drink can hit the pavement and rattled to a stop at his feet. Another fell behind him. He heard a scuffling noise. He looked up. An old man rose from the inside of the dumpster. He was wearing baggy painters' pants and a torn work shirt. His grey hair was swept back from a high forehead. A full beaked nose jutted from his face. A scant grey stubble covered his chin. He could have been a Roman general surveying a gathering army of Huns at the Rhine. From his perch on the packed trash he stared down at Harry with faded blue eyes. Harry looked down at the dog. Its muzzle was grey like its master's. It gazed up at Harry with black obsidian eyes that reflected no light.

"Don't worry. He won't bite," the man said.

Harry said nothing and continued his march to the door. He didn't think the owners of the mall would appreciate having a derelict going through their trash. He would notify security when he was in the store. As Harry opened the entry door he glanced back towards the dumpster. The old man was still standing in it, staring at him. Harry went inside.

Cold air enveloped him. The sweat created during the brief walk from his car was chill on his brow. He made his way through the consumer electronics section. A loutish teenager slumped over a counter and murmured to a gum chewing girl clerk. A bank of TVs flashed in unison. He found the hardware department. A clerk asked if he needed help. He said no. He walked up and down the aisles until he located a duplicate of the piece he held in his hand. Yes, this was it. He took it to a sales counter and presented the warranty card. The sales clerk had to summon a floor supervisor. The floor supervisor looked at the warranty card and picked up a phone. He read a number into it, then listened for a while and hung up and dialed another number. Harry could feel the eyes of the customers waiting in line behind him. He was a trouble maker. Finally the floor supervisor hung up the phone and let Harry go with his new part. Harry walked back through consumer electronics. He remembered the derelict. He doubted the gum chewing clerk would do anything if notified of the derelict's activity. Harry thought he'd linger for a bit, maybe the man would be gone when he went back outside. He browsed through consumer electronics. The shelves were filled with sleek modular devices. Stereos pulsed lowly, TVs chattered. He rounded the end of an aisle and pulled up short in front of a crippled woman parked in her wheel chair. Her head was cocked back and held to one side. Both palsied arms were drawn up on her chest, the hands dangling limp under her chin. She regarded Harry askance through startled birdlike eyes. He watched the thin membrane of her eyelid slide down and cover one bulged orb. The lid came back up and the orb continued to stare at Harry. The bank of TVs said: It's not a car, it's your freedom. Harry turned and fled to the exit.

    The derelict had left the dumpster. Harry was glad to see this. He wanted to avoid the old man. He could be dangerous. Then he saw him. He had moved with his cart and dog to the other side of the alley. He was talking to a woman who was getting out of a car parked next to Harry's. As Harry approached, the woman turned and walked briskly away from the derelict. The old man trailed her, pushing his cart and shouting. He had taken up the puppet and set it in the child's seat of the cart. He worked the puppet and yelled at the retreating woman.

"Harlot daughter of Satan!"

The woman strode past Harry. She was tall and smartly dressed. She looked at Harry with a pained and frozen grimace. The preacher walked up and glared at Harry. He was blocking Harry's path to the car. Harry gave him a tentative nod and an uneasy grin. He only wanted to get away from the man. The preacher's faded eyes bored fiercely into him.

"Thou! Oh proud and stubborn one. Content in this world. Smug within thine ownself. Thou thinkest thou art blessed? The Pit awaits thee! Philistine! Thou writhes in thine own filth! Thy soul is wormy and maggot festered!"

Harry stood paralyzed before the preacher. The man made no attempt at ventriloquism. His gaze searched the sky as he ranted. The puppet stared straight at Harry and flung its arms about. Harry could see its details more clearly now. Its face was crudely painted with a brown skin and dark beard. Burrs and twigs had been worked into its gunny sack robe. Apparently it was supposed to represent a prophet, just in from the wilderness.

The preacher paused in his railing. Harry started to move around him. Without warning, the little dog darted forth and bit him hard on the leg, just above his ankle.

"Cletus!" yelled the derelict.

He dropped the puppet and reeled the dog away from Harry and held it dangling from the leash. Then he dumped it roughly into the shopping cart. The aluminum cans rattled. The dog scrambled up and sat and licked its lips and again stared at Harry.

"Mister, he never done that before in his life. I swear it," said the derelict.

Harry was poised between a run for his car or a retreat to the mall. He bent and pulled up his pant leg. The dog's canine teeth had penetrated the skin. Two small trickles of blood leaked into his sock. The preacher came forward.

"Did he mark ye?"

The man squatted and looked at the wound.

"Ye'll want to put a hot poultice on that. Suck the poison out. Ye'll be all right."

Harry stood and glowered at the derelict. The man looked past Harry's shoulder at something. Harry turned and followed his gaze. A security guard had emerged from the mall and was standing in the shadow of the building, watching them.

"Mister, I ain't ever had nothin' in this world. Cept trouble. I don't need no more a that."

Harry glared at the man. "You should muzzle that thing," he said. He walked around the old man and got in his car. The old man turned and trudged off down the alley. The security guard went back into the mall.

Harry sat in the hot car. He was flustered. He had to get control of himself. He pulled the new starter assembly from the bag. It was packaged on a piece of cardboard with a plastic covering sucked down tight over it. Harry looked at the part. The offspring of some infernal mechanized entity, shat forth into the world, still lodged in its birth sack. He ripped the packaging away and studied the mechanism. A bead of sweat formed on his temple and ran down the side of his head. He returned the part to the bag and started the car and drove slowly out the alley.

The old man was out on the access road with his cart, scanning the curbside for bits and pieces of his earthly sustenance. The little dog trotted behind him. Neither looked up as Harry drove past.

Harry got home and went into his kitchen and put his leg up on the sink and scrubbed the bite with dishwashing detergent and hot water. This caused a dull ache to form in his leg. He went to the garage with the new part and carefully fitted it to his mower. He wheeled the machine to his front lawn. The hot and steamy morning was turning grey. A puffy white cloud bank along the horizon was darkening. Rain, Harry thought. I'll have just enough time. He pulled the starter rope. He heard a faint snap. The engine spun but did not fire. The rope was slack in his hand. I should have had the old man arrested, thought Harry.

He pushed the mower back to the garage and left it in a corner. He did not lock the garage and went into his house. He pulled a beer from the refrigerator, three hours ahead of schedule, and went into his living room and sat down and propped his leg up on a stool. The leg was beginning to throb. The light from outside dimmed. Thunder rolled softly on the horizon.

THE MOBILE

The idea came to Doug in the last half hour of sleep, in the dawn, when dreams are clear and intense and sometimes a little frightening. He was rooting around in the dirty basement of an old house which any Jungian could have told him is a symbol for your own psyche. He awoke with a full bladder and a full erection and the idea. He thought for a minute, staring at the ceiling, and then he laughed out loud. It was absolutely brilliant. The laugh caused balls of pain to roll around in his head and he remembered he should and did have a hangover. After awhile he threw his legs over the side of the mattress and sat on the edge holding his head in his hands. The night before had been like many others. He'd ended up in the lounge at the Holiday Inn, out at the edge of town where the Interstate gnawed past. It was called 'Le Bistro' or something equally stupid. He had been with Tom, one of his old partners. Tom had been married for ten years and had slowed down. His wife let him out once a month to get drunk with Doug. They sat in the lounge. Doug knocked back his tenth or twelfth tequila and sipped his beer.

"Lissen to this, Tom, old bud, lissen to this. I had my first class of Sculpture I a couple of weeks ago. The thing is to make a head. Right?"

"Yeah," said Tom.

"Well, you got your little armature on your little stand an' you put clay on it and make a head."

"Yeah."

"Well, anyway, I went through my spiel about how to get started and how to do it and then I asked if there were any questions. You know what this little twit asks me?"

"No. What?"

"He asks, 'What is your marketing strategy?'"
"Oh, Jesus."
"Yeah. That's what he says. Can you believe it? Where do these little zombies come from? Huh? They're all like that. It's like the TV fucks the microwave oven one night and out pops one of these idiots. It's the end, Tom. The end of human culture."

"I don't know, Doug. Maybe you're overreacting a little bit."

"Shit."

Doug had brooded over his beer. Then he had begun his howling. This was a practiced howl and he was quite good at it. It sounded like some doomed beast dying in a cage. Tom had seen all this before and just watched. The place was not crowded. The bartender looked up. A table of four women found Doug quite entertaining. Doug quit howling and fell out of his chair. He lay still, like he'd passed out, for a minute, and then he got up on his hands and knees and started crawling. The women tittered nervously. Doug crawled to their table and began sniffing and grunting. He crawled around the table and then suddenly pushed his face through an opened back chair into a pair of soft buttocks. The woman jumped up. "Get away from me you weirdo!" she shrieked.

Doug had sat up on his haunches then and cut loose another long and loud howl. Tom had interpreted the look from the bartender to mean maybe that was enough and got up and came over to help Doug stand.

"Ok, Doug, buddy. I think it's about time we headed for the house. You need your beauty rest. Right?"

"Yeah. Ok."

They had stumbled out into the parking lot into the cold

crisp air and Doug had thrown up. Tom had gotten him into the passenger seat of the car and driven him home. Doug had lolled in the seat and said nothing until they got to his house.

"Oh man, help me in, ok?" he slurred. "I got some bud. Good shit. Twelve hundred an ounce stuff."

"All right."

Tom had helped him stagger into the house and up to the second floor he rented. Doug got out the marijuana and started clumsily rolling a joint. Tom stood and watched him.

"You got any coffee?" he asked.

"Yeah. Instant. I'll put it on."

"No. That's ok. I'll do it."

Tom had put on some water to boil and then they both sat at the kitchen table and smoked the joint. Tom surveyed the grungy kitchen and wondered what he was doing there at 3:00 on a Saturday morning with Doug who was obviously going to seed as a slovenly bachelor. The water had finally come to a boil and Tom had made himself a cup of coffee and drank it while Doug stood leaning against the counter top. He was nearly catatonic.

"Hey, Doug. What's wrong? What's the problem, man?"

"I'm stuck."

"You mean the commission?"

"Yeah. The commission. The fucking mobile."

"When's she want it?"

"Next week."

"And you're not finished?"

"I haven't started."

"Oh shit. Did you get an advance?"

"Yeah. A grand."

"Well, just give it back to her. Tell her you don't want to do it."

"I've already spent it. Besides, I need the rest of the money. I was going to go to Mexico for the winter."

"Well, I don't know what to tell you, man. Just do it, I guess. You've still got a few days."

"Right."

Doug left the room. Tom finished drinking the coffee. Doug didn't return. Tom got up and went looking for him. He found him asleep on a bare mattress naked and curled on his side in a fetal position. Tom had thrown a blanket over him and turned out the lights and gone home.

Now Doug sat on the mattress in the morning cradling his throbbing head. He finally got up and stumbled into the bathroom, peed, and ate four aspirin. He looked at his face in the mirror. The face of an experienced poet and rakehell. Thick black curls of hair, no sign of incipient baldness. A body like a light heavyweight. Five ten, 180 pounds. Doug had quit running but still lifted weights regularly and kept up with his karate exercise. He threw a kick at the towel rack. He misjudged and smashed his toes. He cursed and hobbled into the shower and turned up the heat.

Things hadn't always been this way. Doug had taken his MFA at the state university 200 miles away 20 years before. Then, he'd had black curls down to the middle of his back. He was the organizer and leader of a revolutionary art cell. The cell was dedicated to the eradication of all bourgeois decoration and the institution of a non-cooptable, life affirming peoples' art. Doug's specialty was mobiles. Made from machine parts, driftwood, bits of trash, whatever suited his mood. He had garnered several awards, graduated with high honors, and headed for New York. After six months he quit it, the wild man from the plains, after enduring a gloomy winter cooped in an unheated loft and rejected by every gallery he approached. He returned to the state of his youth. "It was faggots sticking pieces of shit together and calling it sculpture," was all he ever said about his N.Y. experience. Apparently, he had not forseen the latest trend and was left in its wake.

But he was more than enough for the inlanders. He applied for and obtained a position at the small college in the small town. An introductory statement was in order. He spent the summer before his first semester scouring the roads of the area in his pickup. A dog here, a squirrel there.

The showing was entitled: IN WORK: AN EXHIBIT BY NEW FACULTY. The opening night crowd was large. All of the art department, many administrators and their hangers-on, and the new college president and his new wife were there. Doug had unveiled ROADKILL. This was a mobile constructed of the animal carcasses he had collected. A large skunk was counter balanced by an opossum and several crows. A dog and domestic cat hung opposite each other. Squirrels, more birds, and various bits of flattened hubcaps and odd pieces of automobile detritus completed the piece. The unveiling was greeted with laughs, groans, and hand clapping. The college president's new wife regurgitated her champagne. The majority opinion was one of approval. Doug's work placed him among the progressive element of the faculty. It also earned the enmity of Mrs. Bond, the printmaking instructor and head of the studio arts department. She had cornered him later. "I hope you're not planning any more things like this smelly piece of trash," she had said. Doug had laughed in her face. Old bag.

An art critic from the big city newspaper had been there.

He wrote: Douglass Jones, a faculty member at Belleville State College has established himself as one of the premier avant-garde artists in the region with his piece, Roadkill. This work symbolizes the voracious and ongoing destruction of nature by the sputtering and creaking Capitalist culture. One thinks immediately of Vietnam and the burning inner cities. A masterpiece.

Of course, Doug knew this was bullshit. As Mrs. Bond had predicted the piece began to stink, despite Doug's best efforts with formaldehyde and lacquer, and had to be discarded. Nevertheless, as the art critic had predicted, Doug was established.

He settled into his new job. There was the teaching but there was also his own work, the parties, and the women. His classes were full of hiking booted young disciples eager for his instruction. There was always a woman ready to ride behind him on his Harley into the cool night stoned on LSD to some remote gathering where Doug would howl and rage and pick burning logs out of the bonfire and hurl them up to come crashing down in a shower of embers. Always a woman ready to be guided by Doug along that dangerous path to the dark and fickle god whose name is Art. A black haired sultry for the fall, a full bodied earth mother for the winter, a blond waif for spring, and a tall tan sporty type for the summer to sunbathe on his balcony reading Herman Hesse while Doug tinkered in his studio. Doug developed methods for giving them the shuck. The bored yawn. The glassy eyed stare at the ceiling.

After Doug had been on campus ten years a woman finally managed to move in with him. Her name was Marilyn. Their cohabitation lasted three months until Doug threatened suicide if she didn't leave and so she reluctantly did and got her own place and a job in a greasy spoon. Marilyn had met and married one of the greasy spoon customers, a geek who managed a chicken restaurant and salvaged broken down rental property in his spare time. Doug rarely saw her after that but when he did he scorned her husband and his money grubbing ways.

Ten years later Marilyn had contacted Doug and commissioned him to produce a mobile for a fall party she was planning. Her husband was having his third shopping mall built and was rich. He and Marilyn lived on an estate several miles from the town. Marilyn had called Doug one morning in May.

"Say, Dougieboy, how's it going?" she asked.

"Shitty, Marilyn. I haven't had a decent orgasm since 1979."

"Sure Doug. Hey, I want you to make me a mobile."

"What for?"

"Harold and I are having a party for our tenth anniversary."

"Not the Harold of Harold Smith Enterprises is it?"

"Don't get snotty, Doug. If you don't want to do it just say so."

"What do you want?"

"Something outre', of course. You'd be the first person to call for that, wouldn't you?"

"Something to shock the country club ladies?"

"Yeah. Now that you mentioned it, that's about right. Show them I'm not quite as tame as I usually appear."

"Now you're talking, Marilyn. Why don't you come over and we can discuss it in a more intimate setting. Tell Harold you're going shopping."

"Now Doug. You had your chance. I need it by the

middle of October. How much do you want?"

Doug grabbed at a ridiculous figure.

"Ten thousand."

"My. We've gotten a little greedy in our dotage, haven't we?"

"Screw it, Marilyn. You've got it, I need it. One thousand in advance. For materials."

"Ok. I'll send it to you. Bye."

This was what Doug had been waiting for. He had realized lately that he'd made a serious career mistake by staying at the college for twenty years. He'd always assumed that eventually Mrs. Bond, the old bag, would retire and he'd take her job. Now she was sixty five and had just announced her intention of staying until she was seventy. Meanwhile, things had changed. The art department classes were no longer swamped with students. A new president had been hired. He was a systems analyst from a corporation and didn't like the red ink all over the books. The studio arts department was to be merged with music, theater, and dance into something called Artistic Communications. Sculpture was out. So was Doug. This was his last semester. He had to go somewhere. Mexico sounded good enough. But he needed the dough.

Doug got out of the shower and put on a frayed bathrobe. He wandered about in his four rented rooms. The cramped living room, the cramped kitchen, the cramped bedroom, and the spacious studio. Doug had knocked out the ceiling in the studio which exposed the high rafters and made the room feel immense. Off to one side French doors let out onto the small balcony where the coeds had sunbathed years before, thinking of revolution and getting high and sex with their artist boyfriend. The boyfriend was still here paying the twentieth year's rent. He had nothing to his name. Where are you now coed? Married with children and driving around in a Volvo station wagon? Or, more likely, divorced and working some dead office job and cursing your fate? Dougieboy is still here.

Doug strolled around in the studio with his hands in the pockets of the robe. Welding torch, hand tools, drills, saws, metal, wire, wood, rope. Everything was coated with a thick layer of dust. Doug had produced nothing in five years.

He wandered into the grubby kitchen and got two hardboiled eggs and a beer and went into the living room and flicked on the TV. It was Saturday morning cartoons. What was this shit called? It had a name. Reduced animation or some shit. The cartoon was like a series of stills with only one part, like a mouth or an arm, moving. Doug sat and watched. The idea came back but it didn't seem so humorous in the sober light of day. He ate the eggs and drank the beer. He sat still for awhile then he fell to the floor on his knees and crouched down with his forehead on the floor and moaned. This wasn't the practiced howl of the night before. This was a high, keening, sobbing wail. He remained motionless in this position. The minutes ticked by on the small desk clock. He stood and shut off the television and drained his beer and walked resolutely to the studio where he found a length of rope and a hammer. He went back to his living room and sat down and calmly fashioned the rope into a hangman's noose. When he was finished he got up and pulled over a chair to stand on and took the hammer and knocked two holes through the plaster and lathe ceiling about four feet directly in front of the door. He fished the rope up and around a ceiling joist and tied it securely to itself. He got off the chair and looked at his work. It lacked something. He took the empty beer can and cinched the rope down around it, crushing it. He stood for a moment admiring the piece. Then he called Marilyn.

"Hello."

It was a man's voice.

"Is Marilyn there?"

"Who is this?"

Doug thought for a minute. Several replies went through his head. He finally said, "Doug Jones."

"Just a minute."

After a long wait Marilyn picked up the phone.

"Well, hello Doug."

"Is Harold always such a jerk?"

"Yeah. Always."

"Your mobile's ready."

"Oh, goodie. Can I pick it up today?"

"Yeah."

"Will it fit in my car?"

"Yeah. I'll help you carry it."

"Dougie, you're a doll. I'll be there in twenty minutes."

"I might be in back. Just come on in."

"Ok. Bye."

They hung up. Doug pulled another beer from the refrigerator. He turned on the TV. The cartoons were still on. A super hero was flying around. As usual, he was stiff except for an occasional movement of his mouth or cape. He got in a fight with some arthritic monster. Of course he didn't kill it. Doug got up and fetched his last can of beer. He stood by a window overlooking the street. The panes were dusty and water streaked. It was a bright sunny Fall Saturday. Sparrows flitted about trying to find some seeds in the dying grass. Some children down the street threw a miniature football around. A gleaming red BMW pulled to the curb. Marilyn got out. Doug took off his robe and got up on the chair and put the noose around his neck. The super hero was bragging to his super girl friend about how he'd vanquished the monster. Doug kicked the chair back and swung out.

I went to the professor's house at 7:00. We were supposed to go somewhere for dinner. I banged on the door of the ramshackle hut. He let me in. He was smoking a pipe and wearing slippers.

"What's up, Prof?" I said.

"I've been reading Heidegger's *Being and Time*. He thinks we perceive life as a sensation of falling from birth to death. Do you?"

AN EVENING WITH THE PROFESSOR

"Well, sometimes I wake up suddenly in the middle of the night and sort of clinch up because it feels like I was falling."

"No, no, no. That's a memory of the trauma of birth. According to Reich, anyway. A genius, until he got into that orgone energy horseshit."

"Sometimes I can't go back to sleep so I just lie there. The flophouse might creak and groan a little. I think: this is it. The termites have finally severed that one last little fiber of wood. The whole mess is going to come crashing down on me. Or I wonder about those nuclear warheads out at the airbase. Do those people really know what they're doing? What if they make a mistake and set one off? Or the water supply. Do you think the government is putting something in it to make people passive and easy to manipulate?"

"Chuck. We both know that's just your neuroses acting up. Except for the flophouse falling down. Why don't you move out of that dump?"

"I like it there."

"Huh. Well, anyway, it's apparent you don't understand what Heidegger's talking about. Game of chess?"

He already had the board set up. I did my standard Queen's Gambit opening. The professor fetched two beers from his refrigerator. We drank, smoked cigarettes, played barely decent chess. After awhile he got up to make a phone call. He'd promised to call a woman. I ruminated on our respective positions. We were both mid-thirties and divorced. He still made occasional feeble attempts at contact with women. I'd more or less given up. I studied the board awhile. Then I checked him with a knight and forked his queen. The professor came back. "Bitch wasn't home. I told her I'd call," he said.

"Maybe you waited too long."

"She should have waited for me. I'm worth the wait." He looked at the board. "Cheater," he said. "You moved my pieces while I was gone. Cheater."

"Bullshit."

He reached down and knocked the board over. I didn't care. Neither one of us liked playing much anyway. He sat down.

"Well, Chuck. Here's what I propose. We go to a clean well lighted place, have a couple of drinks, eat a decent meal, come back here and drink a glass of wine, and then I shall retire. Last Friday night I ended up doing things I didn't want to do at a place I didn't want to be with people I didn't want to be with. That cannot happen again."

"Your plan is fine with me," I said. "I can get up early tomorrow and watch cartoons."

We took the professor's pickup truck, a 1964 Chevy. We went to an Italian place along an old highway at the edge of town. It had a lounge in an adjacent room. We sat at the bar. The bartender was a young girl who looked barely old enough to serve us. We had a beer, then another. The professor began to regale the bartender and me with tales of his job.

"Listen to this. I've got this client who's charged with attempted murder of a police officer. Her husband was beating the shit out of her. He kicked her down a flight of stairs and broke one of her arms. The neighbor called the police. When the cops got there they asked her if she wanted to press charges. She said, 'Hell yes!'. As they were cuffing the guy she had a change of heart and threw a steam iron at the cop. She missed."

"I wonder why people are like that," the bartender said.

"They're poor," said the professor.

"They watch TV," I said.

The professor continued. "Anyway, I plan to argue that it can't be attempted murder because the only way the cop could have been killed was if the iron hit him in the head. However, he was wearing a helmet so that would have protected him."

"Oh that's good!" said the bartender. She leaned on the bar and batted her pretty eyelashes at the professor. She was clearly impressed with such an astute fellow. Just then I saw a grizzled head poke out from the kitchen door and give us the once over. "Janie! Get to work or hit the road!" it said.

The bartender jumped back like she'd been poked with a cattle prod and scurried away from us and began wiping down the bar. Then she took a couple of drink orders from some other customers and paid us no further attention. The professor steamed. "Can you believe a fucking prick like that? Yelling at people. Ordering them around like that."

"He's just a cook. Why doesn't she tell him to fuck off?"

"No, Chuck. He's a cook, true, but he's also the owner. I've heard he occasionally brags about being related to Mussolini or some other fascist. I believe it."

"Well, I'm hungry. Let's go somewhere else to eat."

"Hang on. They have good food here. Besides, I've got an idea."

We went into the dining room and sat down. I ordered a steak. The professor ordered spaghetti. I drank water while we waited. The professor guzzled about three glasses of cheap burgundy. The food came and we ate it. We didn't talk much. The evening had taken on a somber tone. We finished. I smoked a cigarette. The professor picked up the check. "Listen, Chuck," he said. "Give me your money for the food and get the truck and go around and wait for me in the alley by the back door."

"Why?"

"I'll pay the tab. I've got to hit the can in back on the way out. It's faster."

I didn't believe him. I gave him fifteen dollars and he handed me the keys. I went out to the parking lot and got the truck and brought it around to the alley. There was trash and junk piled around. It didn't look like the back door was used much by customers. After about a minute a light came on in a window next to the back door. The shade came up. The professor opened the window and heaved himself up. He flailed around a bit and finally got his hands on the ground. The rest of him followed. He dusted himself off and strode briskly to the truck and got in. "Make haste, my good man," he said.

I put it in gear and drove down the alley. "What did you do?" I asked.

"It's obvious, isn't it? We just stiffed that petite bourgeois Fascist for a meal."

"Then give me back my money."

"I don't have it. I gave it to Janie for a tip."

Well, shit. I turned onto a side street and came to the highway. "Hey, Chuck. Let's drop in at the Gator Club," the professor said.

"What for?"

The Gator Club was a sort of road house further out on the old highway. It had been there for years. I'd gone there infrequently for the last ten but not much lately. The crowd was younger and scruffier and either the music was louder or my nervous system was losing its tolerance.

"Janie's going up there when she gets off work in an hour."

"How about let's drive around for awhile? I'm losing my stomach for that place. You can go in and see if Janie wants to go somewhere else maybe."

"Ok."

We drove around some ratty looking neighborhoods. Mostly dirt streets. Shacks with beat out front yards on which dirty children played with plastic toys. I wondered why these houses had ever been built. Probably for railroad workers and meat packing stiffs. All that was gone now. We came to a commercial street. Pawnshops, furniture rental stores, tanning parlors.

"Chuck, how does this bullshit represent any kind of real economic activity? The whole town's like this," the professor said.

"Well, professor, I guess it's like this: the guy who owns the hamburger franchise goes to a tanning parlor and fries his butt. So he hires you to represent him in a lawsuit. You collect your fee, buy some hamburgers from him, rent some furniture, and get a tan."

"That doesn't make much sense. I think we need a new economic order."

"Yeah. You're right. Let's start a hunting, gathering tribe."

We passed a liquor store. "Pull in there. I need to do some gathering," he said. He came back with a pint of brandy. He got in, opened the bottle, and took a long pull. He offered me a hit. I declined.

I drove out to the highway and north. We pulled into the parking lot of the Gator Club. The music came through the walls and reverberated out over the dirt parking lot. We went in. The sound level was deafening, almost at the pain threshold. The acoustics were all fucked up. At the back of the place it was just white noise. The professor wandered off seeking Janie. I found a niche in the back as far from the band as I could get and ordered a beer. The beers were $1.50 a can. I gave the waitress $2.00. She kept delivering them. The sound droned on. I was dropping into a funk.

Mercifully, the band took a break. Now if the professor would return I could get out of here. A pale, thin, disheveled young man slunk over to a nearby pin ball machine and fired it up. The machine began screeching and squawking. I looked at it. A voluptuous huntress in fur bikini rode bare back on a monstrous purple headed beast. With a sword she slashed at a pack of monkey-gargoyles intent on dismounting her. The player flicked the ball out with a hip twist. Bells clanged. One of the huntress' tits lit up red. The dude got excited and flicked out another ball. More banging and clanging. The other tit lit up green. The punk began jumping up and down. He flicked out another ball and thrust his groin against the front of the machine, stroking and rocking it. The huntress' crotch began pulsing red. The dude thrashed madly, trying to keep the ball in play. Then everything went silent and dark. The player hung his head in shame and impotence. He sulked over the lifeless machine and struck it with his fist. A woman approached him and put her hand comfortingly on his shoulder. It was Lydia, my ex-wife. This was another good reason not to be here. She led the guy to the bar. I went over and tapped Lydia on the shoulder. "I forgot. At which corporation is your boyfriend the CEO?" I asked.

"None, asshole," she hissed. "Robert is an artist. And unlike you he's very sensitive and much better in bed."

Robert sniggered. I thought about taking a poke at him and then thought better. I had little taste for bar fights. I'm more the type who'll sneak back later and pour a couple pounds of sugar into someone's gas tank.

The professor was nowhere to be seen. I thought perhaps he'd become entangled in some predicament and needed rescue. I wandered around looking for him. The place was crowded and noisy. In the restroom I found his spoor; the empty brandy bottle lay shattered. I'd never find him in this mob. I returned to my niche and sat down and ordered another one. We'd been here almost two hours. If he didn't show up within the next fifteen minutes I was going to call a taxi.

The band started up again. I leaned back in my chair and looked at the ceiling. It was supported by massive concrete beams. A long span. Maybe 100 feet, clear across the joint. How old was this building? How long had rock bands vibrated it at 20 cycles per second? Or lower. Five. Somewhere around a resonant frequency. The beams could snap. The ancient steel reinforcing would finally give it up and

tons of rubble would cascade down on the revelers below.
50 KILLED, 74 INJURED WHEN ROADHOUSE ROOF COLLAPSES
STRICTER INSPECTIONS URGED

Or a disgruntled former employee could walk in with a pair of pump shotguns. Spray the crowd indiscriminately. Ruin the business. Maybe a gasoline truck would careen in off the highway and slam into the front entrance.

The dread was on me now. Crumbling buildings. Exploding gasoline trucks. Malaria. Rabies. Airplanes strewing bodies from gaping holes. Bodies in the water. Ejected through windshields. Strained through chain link fences. Riots and mayhem. Cities on fire. Chemical plants spewing burning chlorinated hydrocarbons. Nuclear installations overheating, cracking, melting. Melanoma. Car wrecks. Homicides. Suicides. Caries. Acne. Warts. Hemorrhoids. Five billion souls on earth. All yelling, cursing, stabbing, shooting, copulating.

A hand shook me out of my stupor. It was the professor. "Come up with any ideas, Chuck?" he asked.

"Yeah. Let's block the exits and fire this place."

"Oh, man. Mellow out. Ok? This is Cricket."

I noticed a woman standing behind the professor. She was short and compact and young.

"Cricket needs a ride home. I told her I'd give her one."

"Ok. Let's go."

We walked out into the parking lot. The artificial light was hard and unyielding.

"Professor," I said, "I think the man was wrong. The road of excess leads to the palace of excess."

"Oh. That's profound. Now you're redoing Blake."

I knew the professor would ridicule me if he thought it

would advance his interests with Cricket. I said nothing more. The professor was in much better shape than I'd anticipated. Surprisingly, he seemed to have sobered a little. Maybe Cricket had gotten his blood up. We got in the truck.

"Hey. You guys want to go to a party? It's close to here," said Cricket.

"No," I said.

"Come on, Chuck," said the professor. "You don't have anything better to do."

"Yes I do. Go home and go to bed. You won't mind dropping me off first will you?"

"Fuck yes I will. That's miles from here."

I gave up. There was no use in arguing. The professor was onto Cricket. I'd seen it before. Nothing ever changed. We started out. Cricket gave directions. The party house wasn't close. We wound through unpaved and unlighted back streets at the edge of town.

"How'd you get to the club, Cricket?" I asked.

"Well, I came with a guy from my shop. Keith. Keith's gay, see, and that's cool, but he met a guy there and told me he was leaving and to find my own ride home. That really pissed me off. I'm going to give him hell at the shop on Monday."

"What do you do at the shop."

"I'm a designer."

I guess that was it. It seemed like every other person you met these days was either a designer or an analyst or did something with "systems." It usually turned out to be a trumped up title for some dull and useless endeavor.

"What do you design, Cricket? Nuclear bomb triggers?"

"No, silly. Nails."

"Galvanized, 16 penny, or railroad spikes?"

"These."

She took her hands out of her lap and unfolded ten deadly looking daggers. Each one was two inches long, filed to a point, and painted with the blood of a corpse.

"Good Christ, professor. We're transporting a vampire. Do you have something to stick in her?"

Cricket giggled. The professor grunted. He hadn't said a word since we'd left the parking lot. I looked at Cricket more closely. She had hair cut severely on the sides and piled randomly on top and stuck together with hair spray. She was wearing long false eyelashes. She had about half a jar of maroon eyeliner smeared above each eye with silver glitter stuck in it.

"Cancel that. It's a Venusian cyborg."

"Oooo, you're weird," said Cricket. She moved further away from me.

"Shut up, Chuck," said the professor.

I shut up. I had nothing against Cricket. She just represented something I found discouraging. False eyelashes, false finger nails, false face. Store bought tan. Maybe she was a hologram vectored out of New York and L.A. and intersecting at this bleak point on the frozen prairie to entertain us yokels. Like M.T.V.

The professor was massaging Cricket's thigh. "My horoscope today said I'd meet a rugged stranger," she said. Things were looking good for the Prof.

We came to a freshly paved street. It meandered about for no reason. Here and there stood a newly constructed house. Poorly built with synthetic materials, they sprouted absurdly in a wind blown field. A ludicrous monument to some philistine's preening ego. We passed a machine carved wooden sign flapping in the wind. 'THE GLADE AT COLDBROOK,' it read. This was simply a lie. There was not a glade or brook within twenty miles of this God forsaken spot. I thought up some better names.

"How about this, professor: Rat Warren at Toxic Waste Dump."

He chuckled.

"Trailer Court at Abandoned Junk Yard."

Cricket didn't say anything. She was apparently not impressed with my keen wit. We pulled by some town homes or garden apartments or whatever they're called. They were ugly.

"This is it," said Cricket.

The temperature had dropped. The slush in the gutter had frozen. The truck tires crunched on the ice as we pulled to the curb. A car swung in behind us and parked. Cricket stirred in her seat. "Oh, that's Gary! Maybe he's got some toot."

We got out of the truck. The car behind us was a Corvette. The vanity license plate said 'MONEY.' A dude with a pompadour got out.

"Hi, Gary!" Cricket yelled.

"Hey. Hi, Crick," said the dude.

Cricket bounded over to Gary Corvette. I didn't think she would have much interest in the professor now. All of us walked to the door. I pulled the professor aside. "Hey. Look. This isn't going to be our kind of scene," I said. "Let's take off."

"Oh no, man. I want some stinkbait."

He was drunker than I had supposed. When he got like this he became unreasonable and difficult to handle. We went in. The place was jammed. The music was turned up loud. I didn't recognize anyone. Most of the people looked like they'd just come from a hotel cocktail party. Coats and jackets. A few ties. The professor and I didn't blend in well. He was wearing a wool flannel shirt and jeans. I was wearing old khaki pants, torn tennis shoes, and a work shirt. The work shirt had a large mustard stain on the front. I hadn't been able to get it out. We both gravitated to the kitchen and got drinks. The men stood about with arms folded, serious poses. One was touting stock in a fast food chain. Another had just bought a bra for his car. Still another was discussing the merits of various compact disc players. The professor started spewing out his standard anarchist diatribe. A Republican took exception and they began arguing. I couldn't stand such blather. I weaseled into the living room and sat down at one end of a couch. Two nice looking suburban types were conversing. I tried to sit so the mustard stain wouldn't show. One turned.

"What do you do for a living?" she asked.

"I'm usually in Mexico. I do archeological digs at pre-Columbian sites," I lied.

"Oh, really? What kind of car do you drive?"

"What?"

"What kind of car do you drive?"

"A 1967 Dodge Dart."

"Oh."

She turned back to her friend. "As I was saying, I found the darlingest Bill Blass skirt at Clothes by Andrea. I'm going to take it to Shangri-La next weekend."

Well, fuck you too, baby. Some shit was on TV. I picked up the remote control and started punching through the channels. More shit. Beer commercials, preachers, newsmen. Quacks and swindlers of all shapes and sizes. Things were closing in on me. I got up and cranked the vertical and horizontal synchs all the way to the right. Then I diddled with the color until the screen displayed ragged stripes of lime green, orange, and purple. Now you could punch through the channels and get a nice psychedelic show. The preachers and newsmen were floating multi-colored amoebae. I wished I had some peyote. A stern dude came into the room. "What're you doing?" he said.

"Uh. I don't know. The TV's not working right."

"Give me that."

He grabbed the remote control out of my hand. He went to his television and carefully readjusted it and left it on the original channel. Some rock and roll video claptrap. God Almighty life was a bore amongst such cretins. The proprietor kept the remote control. I tapped the Bill Blass woman on the shoulder.

"Say momma, what time is it?" I said.

"Are you speaking to me?"

"Yeah. What time is it?"

She looked at her watch. "It's two o'clock."

"Would you like to go home with me and look at my beetle collection?" Might as well try it one more time. It hadn't worked yet.

"I don't think so."

The pattern was holding. I nodded off. I came to smelling marijuana. The women were gone. The crowd had thinned. The remaining hipsters were passing a number around. I had to go bad. I went to the can. The door was locked. I went upstairs. Most of these pestholes had another can off the master bedroom. I went into a bedroom and opened a door. A closet. I opened the one next to it. A cramped little bathroom. Gary Corvette was taking a dump and snorting coke off a hand mirror. No. He wasn't taking a dump. The scruffy head of Cricket bobbed up and down at his crotch. He held the mirror out to me. His eyes had that preternatural sparkle. He was loaded up.

"Want some?"

"No."

He held the mirror and glass tube down for Cricket. She came up for air and greedily sucked up both lines, one in each nostril. I was mesmerized. Cricket looked up at me.

"Get the fuck out of here," she said.

I did. There was a balcony off the bedroom. I couldn't hold it any longer. I went out on the balcony and peed over the rail. It splattered all over a barbecue set on the patio below. The proprietor would have some funny tasting burgers come spring. I wandered back to the kitchen. The professor was sitting alone at a table. Beer and liquor bottles were strewn about.

"Seen Cricket?" he asked.

"Yeah. But she was headed out."

"I wanted her."

"Professor, like the old boy says, she'll never make a wife for a home lovin' man. Such as yourself. Let's get out of here."

The professor said nothing. He sat in his chair. He was leaning forward, hands on thighs, mouth slightly open, eyes unfocused, a puzzled expression on his face. I wandered back into the living room and sat down. If worse came to worse I could always call a taxi for myself and an ambulance for the professor. The party-goers had amassed a huge pile of cocaine on the coffee table and were busily inhaling it. The proprietor kept giving me dirty looks.

A coarse bellowing arose in the kitchen accompanied by a bottle being banged on a table. It was the professor. "I shall commit a revolutionary act! A criminal revolutionary act! I shall commit a criminal act! A revolutionary criminal act!" he ranted.

He lurched into the squalid room and stopped, blinking, trying to focus his eyes. He staggered forward, toppled, and smacked belly first onto the coffee table. Contrary to its appearance, the table was not solid oak but particle board covered with an imitation veneer. It disintegrated and the precious powder catapulted onto the floor. Someone shut off the stereo. Silence overwhelmed the room. One idiot fell to the floor to sniff the remnants. The professor rose to his knees with a look of quiet bewilderment. The revelers were incensed.

"Asshole!"

The professor stood up, wobbling.

"You owe me, fucker!"

The situation was going dangerously out of control. A half empty beer can missed the professor's head, bounced off the wall, and sprayed the room. The professor reached for his wallet. "Gentlemen, gentlemen. Please. I am well able to make amends. What's the damage?"

"Eight hundred, fuckwad."

The professor pulled ten one hundred dollar bills from his wallet. "Will an even thousand do?" he asked. The owner of the cocaine held out his hand and the professor counted out the ten hundreds. This wasn't good. I knew where he'd gotten the money. About a year before he'd represented an amateur counterfeiter in Federal court. He'd somehow gotten the guy off. He'd kept the grand for a souvenir. The gray side wasn't too bad but the green was much too bright and slightly smeared. I hoped the guy wouldn't notice. He didn't. He stuck the money in his pocket. I took the professor by the arm. We stumbled out the door.

"That was a brilliant performance, professor."

"Fuck 'em."

"Give me the keys. I'm driving."

"Fuck you."

He stumbled around and got in the driver's seat and started the engine. I stood for a moment in the cold morning air and got in. There was a car parked close in front of us. The professor backed up and stopped. He revved the engine up and down. Up and down. Eyes bulging, face flushed, he stared through the windshield at infinity.

"Let's get out of here," I said.

On an up rev his foot slipped off the clutch. The transmission was still in reverse. With a squeal of tires, the big steel bumper sought and found the front of the Corvette. Headlight glass tinkled in the street. The professor put the truck in low and started going through his engine revving routine again. The porch light on the condo came on. The door opened. The professor made no comment. He was still staring at infinity. "If you don't leave now we'll both be in the meat display case at Safeway," I said.

He let the clutch out. We decoupled from the Corvette. The tires dug in and then hit some ice. We went into a four wheel slide. The professor was an automaton. He finally got the truck pointed down the street and I looked out the rear window and saw the Corvette in the street light. Large splinters of fiberglass were sticking out of it at odd angles. The professor hit second gear at 40 mph as we turned left at the first side street and went into another slide. He turned right at the next street then left then right again and pulled up at a stop sign. "You drive now. There's no one following us," he said.

He got out and went around to the passenger side. I

drove the back streets slowly and carefully. Over the river and through the brown parks frozen in the late winter gloom. The moon was up. The professor slouched in the seat like a bag of laundry. He said nothing. I thought maybe he had passed out. I drove down alleys and side streets through broken down residential sections. Finally I was close to home, bed, sleep. The police had not arrested us. We were free.

As we drove past the cemetery half a mile from the professor's house he roused himself.

"Turn in there," he said.

"Why?"

"I want to see my friends."

I turned into the old cemetery and drove past some abandoned crypts. "Looks like they've all left," I said.

"No. Not here. Over there. By the trees," he slurred.

The moon was half gone but still bright and directly overhead. We rolled down the windows. Maybe you could smell some faint hint of spring in the air. It was still cold. I turned off the headlights and drove slowly on the quiet road. We pulled up under a stand of huge evergreen trees. The professor was rooting around in the glove compartment.

"So, where's your friends?"

"Up there. In the trees. The crows."

He had something in his hand. It was his Luger.

"What the fuck are you doing?"

"Itsokay. Itsokay. It's not loaded."

He pointed the gun out the window and up into the branches. A two foot blue flame erupted from the muzzle with a solid bang.

"You stupid bastard!"

I put the truck in gear and snapped on the headlights. Up

in the trees a horrible squawking arose. The birds were blind and terrified in the dark. The professor emptied the clip into the branches. The tumult increased and gathered momentum like a nuclear reaction. I could hear the birds crashing about, breaking wings and necks. I started for the exit. A huge mass of several hundred crows managed to detach itself from the trees and wheeled out over the road. I thought it was raining as the first drops of bird crap pelted the truck's hood. Then a torrent engulfed the road and truck. I couldn't see through the windshield and steered to the cemetery exit by sticking my head out the side window. The street was deserted as we made the last run for home. Through the rear view mirror I saw the blinking lights of a police car. It was far away.

    I turned and took off down a side street. We were ok. The cop was a long ways back. A few seconds later I looked in the mirror. The cop car with its red light had turned the corner behind us.

    "Oh shit, professor," I said. "You've done it now. Get rid of the gun."

    "Chuck my boy, my boy. My old man took this off a dead German officer. I'll shoot that fucking pig before I throw it away."

    I dowsed the headlights. The street curved abruptly. We went over the curb sliding on frozen slush. The truck wouldn't steer or stop and then we were going down. The truck hit something solid underneath and bottomed out. We both flew up and banged our heads on the ceiling. The truck lurched up, almost rolled over, and then settled to a stop. It was pitch black. The professor lay crumpled on the seat, moaning. I turned off the motor. I knew where we were. At the bottom of the drainage canal that bisected the city. I had missed the turn onto the bridge that spanned it.

I heard the police radio crackle as the car approached the bridge. Ice spat under its tires. The sides and bottom of the canal were lined with concrete. The sides reflected the revolving police light. The jig was up. The police car slowed and then crossed the bridge and continued on. The cop hadn't seen us. The professor quit moaning.

"You tore up my machine!" he cried. "What are we going to do now?"

"Fuck you. It's your fault. We wouldn't be here if you weren't a drunken sociopath. I'm going to walk home."

I got out. A ground fog about two feet thick covered the frozen slime. You could walk on it. Organic crap. Rotten cardboard. Turtles. Slugs.

"Chuck. Wait. You can't leave me here," said the professor. "That cop might come back. Let's try to drive out."

I got back in and started the engine. Maybe the muck wasn't deep enough to stick us. The professor was partly right. I'd gone along with his shenanigans so far. I couldn't leave him at the bottom of this ditch. We started out. The tires broke through the sludge but only sank a few inches to the concrete base. The ground fog prevented us from seeing the path we tread. Probably just as well. About three miles down, the ditch emptied into the river. Maybe we could find a place to drive out. The truck was running ok. We approached the next bridge. Junk was sticking out of the fog. Television antennae, refrigerators, old bed frames. Since the county had raised the dumping fees people took every opportunity to dispose of their trash at no charge. Free enterprise at work. It was getting lighter. We negotiated our way through the junk. The professor lamented his fate. "I'm an intellectual. A professional. A rational person. How do I get myself into these situations?"

I thought for a minute. "It's like this, Dr. Jekyll. You suit up, job ready, on Monday morning. Go downtown. Drink some coffee. Shoot the breeze with the secretaries. Go into your office. Talk on the phone. Pick your nose. Wish you were somewhere else. After five days of this Mr. Hyde is raging to get out. He's an ill kempt lout. He stinks. He has bad breath. All he wants is a bottle of whiskey and a woman. And a Luger with a full clip, if possible."

"That's absolute nonsense, Chuck. Absolute nonsense."

We lurched over the frozen slime, avoiding the larger obstacles, running over the smaller. Ahead towered the stacks of the sewage plant. Blue flames burned eternally, consuming the flatulence of the city. The concrete sides of the canal gave way to dirt. We had gained our exit. I drove up the dirt bank through a patch of weeds. The sun was breaking over the horizon. Wang wang wang wang wang screee screeee. I stopped the truck. The professor looked at me.

"What the fuck is that?" he said.

"I don't know."

The noise had stopped. I started forward. Wang wang screee screee screee. The truck was making a horrible racket. I drove over a curb and got on the street. There was an all night restaurant. We went to the alley behind it. We stopped and got out. I crawled underneath. It looked like a piece of wire fence or springs from a small bed was wrapped around the drive shaft. I crawled out.

"Do you have anything that will cut wire?" I asked the professor.

"No. But look at this."

He pointed at the left rear tire. It was half flat and losing air. "Goddamnit. Goddamnit," the professor raged.

"You have a spare, don't you? Let's put it on."

We jacked up the truck and pulled the flat tire. A cop swung into the alley. He cruised towards us, a shark sniffing blood. He stopped and rolled down his window.

"What's the problem, fellas?"

"No problem, your officer," said the professor. "My colleague and I were out for a bit of early morning bird watching. Ran into a spot of trouble."

The cop eyed the truck. It was two tone. Bird shit white on top, mud brown below. A faint smirk appeared on his face. Without further word he departed. We finished installing the spare tire. I walked around to get in on the passenger side.

"Oh, professor. Look at this."

He came around. The right rear tire was dead flat.

"Sonofabitch. Sonofafuckingbitch."

"Professor, let's fall back and regroup. Go in the restaurant and get some coffee. Then take a taxi home. Come back later and mess with this."

"No, Chuck. I'm tired. I need to go home now with my own truck and try to forget this horrible experience."

He was sweating heavily. His face was still flushed dark red and his eyes were still bulged out. "Get in," he said. "Let's make a run for it. I'm tired of this shit."

"You'll ruin the tire and probably the wheel."

"I don't care. Get in."

I got in. We started out. The noise began again, but accompanied now by a heavy vibration as the loose tire slapped around on the wheel. The professor got on a residential street and accelerated to 40 miles per hour. The truck made a noise like every demon in hell screaming in unison. The rear end was jumping and shaking. Smoke started pouring from the back. Then the shredded tire tore loose and we were down on the rim. A rooster tail of metal sparks erupted from the rear and shot twenty feet into the air. "Commander! Aircraft on fire! Abort to orbit! Prepare to eject!" I yelled. In response the professor stomped on the gas pedal and got the howling beast up to fifty. The noise increased exponentially.

The early rising burghers were about in their yards, gauging the lawn for its first mowing. They stared open mouthed as the apparition approached like a hoard of pterodactyls. A madman and his assistant at the wheel of some tortured and dying machine. Then the thing was past, leaving bits of smoking rubber and metal in its wake. The professor ignored all stop lights and signs. We grated to a halt at my crib. I got out. "Later, prof," I said. He said nothing and rattled away. The sun was unbearably bright. I staggered in and crapped out.

At noon the phone woke me from the dead. It was Lydia. "Listen, you son of a bitch," she screamed. "You ever bother me or my friends again I'll have your ass in jail faster than you can blink!"

"Fuck you!" I yelled back. I ripped the cord out of the jack, opened a window, and threw the contraption out. I went back to sleep.

At four o'clock I got up and ate two hardboiled eggs and looked at the news. A tanker was on fire in the Persian Gulf. It listed about 30 degrees, surrounded by acres of flame and thick black smoke. Two passenger trains had collided in India. Half of Lima had been knocked down by an earthquake. I shut it off and returned to bed.

Sunday morning I awoke rejuvenated. I ate breakfast and then took a walk to check on the professor. The sun was out.

The professor was in running shorts and shoes washing his truck in his driveway. It sported new rear tires and wheels. He was whistling.

"Professor, it looks like you've recovered pretty well from your quiet evening," I said.

"Well, Chuck. It's like William Blake said, 'The road of excess leads to the palace of wisdom.'"

"Ain't no fucking palace. Don't you know that by now?"

"Maybe. Maybe not. I'm headed down to the farm. Been out running. Sweated all that shit out. I'm not going to drink anymore. Going to get some of my mom's cooking, kick back, read, relax."

He shut off the water hose, got in the truck, and started it. He backed into the street. I walked along side.

"Want to have dinner next Friday?" he asked.

"I don't know. Maybe."

"Ok. See you then." He drove away.

THE ICE CREAM MAN

Howard worked at Metaltek for thirteen years and then he was laid off. Eight weeks at the outside, they told him. They wanted to install some more efficient equipment and straighten the place up. He'd be back in a cleaner, better lit, air conditioned shop in no time, they said. Howard had called them at ten weeks and was told things had not gone as smoothly as planned. They said they had decided to undertake a review of the whole organizational structure, but it was ok. They'd get back with him. Everything was still ok. Howard hadn't wasted any time sitting around moping or worrying. He'd cleaned some things up around the house and yard. Then he started a project he'd had in mind for years; turning the garage into his own private retreat.

He'd put a door in the side of the garage so you didn't have to raise the big door to get in. Then he'd cleaned everything up and thrown away a lot of junk that had been lying around in there for years. Alice had said, well, now we can park our cars in there. Hell, they hadn't parked a car in there for years, he told her, so he could do whatever he wanted. Alice just wanted to bitch a little. She didn't really care.

Howard nailed the big door down so it couldn't be opened. He insulated the inside walls and put up some paneling he got cheap at a factory seconds outlet and put a little air conditioner in the window. He bought a color TV and an old refrigerator and some used furniture at a garage sale. He installed an extension phone. Howard had an idea of poker games and beer and cigars but hardly anyone came over. He didn't know that many people anyway. The plumber next door, Al, came over one day and looked around at Howard's project and said, "Neat." He picked up a Hustler Howard had lying on a battered coffee table and thumbed through it and said, "Yeah, pretty neat." Then he put down the Hustler and went home.

One morning after he'd been off work for thirteen weeks Howard took a drive past Metaltek. The place looked like it was up and running again. The parking lot was full of cars but a lot of them Howard didn't recognize. It was about ten o'clock. He saw two long haired young guys standing outside one of the doors smoking cigarettes. On the way home, the truth of his situation suddenly knotted his gut. They weren't going to rehire him. He let out a long breath and started thinking.

Their kid, Margie, had graduated from high school that spring and moved to Dallas where she had a job at an insurance company. She also had a boyfriend. She was grown up and gone. Howard had twelve weeks of unemployment left. He received the maximum amount since his job had paid sixteen dollars an hour plus bennies. The house was almost paid off. And Alice had a job that had started out as sort of rinky-dink but had turned into a pretty good deal for her. She was a new product implementer at a Sears store at the mall. She'd started the job two years before when Margie was a sophomore and was out of the house most of the time. Howard had teased her a little bit about the crummy pay, about a middle age crisis, but he really thought her working was ok. It gave her something to do. After a year Alice had been promoted and now she worked for a new boss, Jack. At first she'd raved to Howard about what a great guy Jack was. She hadn't said much about him lately. Howard figured he'd sit around for awhile longer and then go look for a job. They'd get by. Everything was still ok.

It was that afternoon it happened. Howard was in the garage watching Family Feud. Alice had just called and told him to stick a TV dinner in the oven. She'd be working late again. She didn't know what time she'd be home. Howard popped open a beer. When he was working he'd always had a couple after he got off. Nowadays he started a little earlier and usually drank four or five.

He heard Janie, Al's wife next door, screaming. He heard a door bang and he heard Al cursing and yelling and Debbie, their little girl, crying in her small child's voice. A car door slammed and someone started the car and left the starter engaged too long until it made a shrieking metallic whine. The driver put the car in gear and backed furiously out of the driveway. Al was still out there, cursing loudly like Howard had never heard him before. Jesus, Howard thought, they must be having one terrible fight.

Al and Janie were pretty good neighbors as far as neighbors went. Their driveway and garage were right next to Howard's. Their house was a mirror image of his. If you took the floor plan of Howard's house and flipped it over the property line you'd get Al's. The whole block was like that. Sometimes Al and Janie would cook out with Howard and Alice in their backyards. Al ran a plumbing business out of his house. Janie answered the phone. They both worked hard and made good money.

Al finally quit yelling. Howard thought he'd peek out the door to see what was wrong. Al was standing in his driveway looking down at the concrete. He glanced up and saw Howard. He walked stiffly over to Howard's garage.

"Goddamn, goddamn, goddamn," Al mumbled.

"What's wrong?" said Howard. He backed out of the doorway to let Al walk into the garage. Howard had never seen Al like this. He looked like he belonged in an insane asylum.

"God fucking damnit," yelled Al. "God fucking damnit! Some fucking pervert has messed with my little girl!"

"What?" said Howard. "Who?"

"The ice cream man, she said. The fucking ice cream man."

"Well. Shit. Did you call the cops?" Howard said.

"Hell, yes. For what good it'll do. Janie took her to the hospital. I'll kill that son of a bitch. I'm going to kill that son of a bitch."

"Well, what'd he do?" Howard asked.

"She said he put his hand on her private."

"Huh?" said Howard.

"Her pussy. That's what we call her pussy. Goddamnit! Are you an idiot? Some pervert just finger fucked my little girl and you stand there and go, 'what? who? huh?' Her panties are gone too."

Some canned laughter came out of the TV. Al looked at it like he was going to kick out the picture tube. Howard edged over and clicked it off. Al paced around in Howard's garage. He saw a bag of golf clubs in one corner and went over and started rubbing his finger along the edge of the three wood. "Listen," he said. "We both know those fucking cops aren't going to do anything until they're good and fucking ready. Until they finish their donuts and coffee and take a shit down at the donut house. That fucker'll be in the next county by then. Let's go look for the son of a bitch."

"I don't know. We could get in big trouble," said Howard.

"No. We'll just hold him for the cops," said Al. "The fucker has to be around here somewhere. We'll just hold him."

"I don't know," said Howard.

"You don't know? Look, we're neighbors aren't we? We're in this together. Are we neighbors or not?"

"Yeah," said Howard. "I guess we are."

"Ok then. Let's go find him." Al pulled the three wood out of the bag. "We better take something in case he resists." Howard picked up a baseball bat. They set forth in Howard's Pontiac.

Four blocks towards the grade school they stopped to interrogate three stragglers. Howard pulled up to the curb. Al rolled down the window. "Hey," he yelled, "any you kids seen an ice cream truck?" Two of them nodded yes and one shook his head no. Two of them turned and started running away. One of the nodders gestured vaguely in a direction off to their left and then he too turned and ran. "Goofy little shits," said Al. Howard headed off in the direction the kid had indicated. Al sat rigidly, with his jaw set, holding the golf club straight up in front of him.

They drove several blocks. They came to a stop sign at an arterial street.

"Now what?" asked Howard. "Don't those guys have some kind of route? Maybe we could just call up the company and see who was driving around here today."

Al said, "Fuck that. If we don't find that bastard now he's long gone. You aren't backing out on me are you?"

"No."

"Well, get going then. We'll find him."

They crossed the street and entered another residential

section. It was early Fall. A few leaves drifted down from the maples and pin oaks that lined the street.

"Stop!" said Al. "Pull over!"

Howard pulled over to the curb and shut off the engine. There it was. The tinny rasping tune of an ice cream truck.

"Let's go," said Al.

They followed the noise. It grew louder. Then it quit. They turned a corner. The truck was parked in the middle of the block. Howard pulled up behind it. Before he had the car stopped Al jumped out with the three wood and ran for the truck. Howard parked and got out with the ball bat. He saw Al go into the truck from the curb side. Howard trotted up to the driver's side door. He heard a banging and hollering. A long haired guy with a wispy beard and a gold earring leapt out of the truck. Al tumbled out behind him and tripped and fell flat on the pavement. Howard made a motion with the bat like he was going to bunt. The man took a couple steps back and said, "What the hell is this? What's wrong with you guys?" Al got up with the three wood and took a round house swing at the man. The guy ducked and the golf club hit the side mirror on the truck. It shattered and the pieces fell into the street. The guy took a couple of more steps back. Al was getting ready with the three wood again. "You sons of bitches are crazy!" the man said and turned around and ran. Al went after him. Howard jogged behind. Al was in pretty good shape. He could almost keep up with the guy.

The man ran about half way down the block and then went up onto the front porch of a house and started pounding frantically on the door. Al was 25 yards back and closing fast. No one answered. The man jumped off the porch and ran around the side of the house. Al was in hot pursuit. "Go around the other way and head him off!" he yelled back to Howard.

Howard trotted around the other side of the house and stopped beside a redwood deck. Al was chasing the guy around a swing set in the backyard. The man kept trying to turn and reason with Al. Each time he did this Al took the opportunity to swing the three wood at him. A woman came out onto the deck. "You men!" she yelled. "You men leave that boy alone!" Al swung at the guy. He dodged under the swing set. Al lunged after him and tripped over a plastic tricycle and fell down. The man ran towards Howard. Howard made a stance like he was going to blast one over the fence. The guy stopped about six feet in front of him. Al was getting up. "Stop him, Howard! Stop him!" he yelled. The guy realized he was trapped between Howard and Al. He made for a fence along the sideyard. He jumped up and began climbing over it.

Howard took two steps and laid the bat across the man's back. Something snapped like a dowel breaking inside an upholstered chair. The man fell off the fence and laid on the ground and went, "Unhhhhh. Unhhhh." Howard stepped forward and hit him in the head. A roaring noise like a waterfall came up in Howard's ears. "Die, you goddamn pervert," he said. He hit the man again. The woman was screaming and Al was yelling and Howard kept swinging the bat. Then he stopped. It was still. His knees gave out and he sat down heavily. The woman was standing there, pale, with her hand over her mouth. "I'm going to call the police," she said. She turned and went quickly into her house and shut the door. They heard the dead bolt slide home. Howard looked up at Al. Al stood gaping at Howard. He took a half step back and dropped the golf club.

Howard looked down at his feet. His pants below his knees and his shoes were splattered with blood. There was a clot of some pinkish grey stuff stuck to one shoelace. Howard swallowed quickly to fight down a lump of nausea forming in his guts. He thought his mind was playing tricks on him. A distant melody. He looked up at some wind chimes the woman had hanging above her deck. They were slack in the calm. He heard the tune again, slightly louder. Then it stopped. Howard stood up. The melody, louder still, began again. It was no hallucination. It was the song of a cheap music box, amplified past the point of distortion, and broadcast for all to hear. An ice cream truck. Coming Howard's way.

Dave swung his car into the graveled lot of the strip joint and parked. He'd been coming here almost every day that summer on his way home from his job. It was a low paying menial job and Dave hated it and would soon quit. The sign above the door of the ramshackle building said, "Girls! Girls! Girls! Twenty Five Beautiful Showgirls For Your Viewing Pleasure!" Below it was another sign, 69FFF a portable one. This sign said, "Exclusive Engagement! Direct From Las Vegas! Ms. 69 FFF! She's Absolutely Terrifying!" This might be good, thought Dave. He got out of his car and went in.

He took his usual seat in a corner booth at the rear. He left his sunglasses on so he couldn't be recognized. Dave always sat in the rear so that he would be inconspicuous and not attract the attentions of the strippers who, when they weren't dancing, prowled through the place looking for marks to hit on. They'd forgotten about Dave by now so they left him alone. A waitress came over and he ordered a beer. All summer, stacking lumber and bags of cement in the heat, thinking about this place at the end of the day had kept him going. It was cool and dark and Dave could sip cold beers and watch the strippers from his corner. Most of them were bored and stupid young women but all of them were high breasted and pouty, with firm round asses. Dave like a mole poking his nose forth from his hole at sundown.

His shaded eyes finally adjusted to the gloom and he could see Crystal on stage, lean and tall, grinding through her routine. She was one of Dave's least favorites. She squatted down and thrust her pubes into the face of a T-shirted ball-capped lout who sat half drunk at the snack bar. He threw back his head and took a slurp from his bottle and then brayed like a jackass. Jesus Christ, thought Dave.

Crystal pulled back with an undisguised sneer of contempt, turned around, and shook her smooth ass at the grubby crew. They hooted and hollered like a tribe of apes. Crystal finished her dance and stalked off the stage.

The place was starting to fill up with the after work crowd. Construction workers, mechanics, machine operators from the factories. Most of them sat at the horseshoe shaped bar that surrounded the stage. The snack bar, they called it. Snacking was against the law. Others, guys with coats and ties, and often sunglasses like Dave's, would come in solo and sit discretely back from the stage like they were some kind of Hollywood type attending a private film screening. All of them bored with the job, bored with the grind, looking for something else, they didn't know what, in this seedy building at the edge of town.

"And now," boomed the p.a. system, "direct from Las Vegas! An exclusive two night engagement! Ms. 69 triple F! She's absolutely terrifying!" The lights dimmed. A sultry sax be-bop started up. The lights went green, then blue. A tall long haired platinum blonde sashayed onto the stage. She was wearing heels, bikini bottoms, a lace top. She strutted around, did some bumps and grinds, and then settled into a slinky jazz impression. Her breasts rolled sullenly under the lace. Stacked, thought Dave. But not abnormally so. She'd been overbilled. She seemed as bored as the rest of them. For her second number she removed the lace top and displayed the touted globes for the crowd. She really got going on this one. Cantaloupes, thought Dave. They were bigger than they'd looked covered up. They danced their own separate dance. Ms. 69 FFF leaned over. Her breasts swung as one massive pendulum. Bowling balls, thought Dave. No 69 FFF, though. Horseshit. The dance ended. The crowd clapped and whistled. Ms. 69 FFF walked off the stage.

Dave ordered another beer. Maybe he'd go home. One of the strippers, Tina, came over and sat down with him. She was a little drunk. Tina was always a little drunk. She ran her hand quickly through her bobbed blonde hair. "Did you see the udders on that cow?" she said. "I bet there's a gallon of silicone in each one of those things."

"Yeah," said Dave. "She didn't do much for me."

"Oh you're just saying that cause I'm sitting here," Tina said.

"No, it's true," said Dave. He looked at Tina. Like most of the strippers, Tina had become used to being topless in a crowd of strange men and didn't bother to cover up between dances. She also got better tips that way. Tina didn't have much up front. She was probably the flattest dancer in the whole lot. A wisp of a girl. Dave doubted she weighed more than a hundred pounds. Her little breasts didn't bother him but he knew they bothered Tina.

"It's just not fair," she said. "I work my ass off all week for a crummy hundred dollars a night and that cow comes in here for two nights and gets a thousand. Plus ten percent of the gross. It's just not fair."

"Oh come on, Tina. Lighten up, will you?" Dave said.

"All right. Sorry. I guess I've just had a shitty week. That's all. Did you know I've been thinking for a long time about quitting this place? I thought I had something lined up this week but it all turned to shit."

"Well, tell Uncle Dave about it," Dave said.

"It's not that big a deal. I met this guy in here, see, a customer. He owns some Ding Dong Taco restaurants. He said he'd make me an assistant manager at one of them. With an opportunity for advancement. I went to see him. I thought the deal was all set up, see. He just wanted to get me in bed. The only thing he had in mind was fucking me."

Tina looked like she was on the verge of crying. Dave tried to console her. "Look, Tina. You might be tired of this place but a hundred a night is nothing to sneeze at. That's almost as much as I make."

Dave was lying. It was almost twice as much as he earned. Tina sniffed a little and then got up and left. Dave saw her out in the crowd, going from table to table, working the mooches for tips. One after another the house strippers got up and did their thing and retired to scattered applause and whistling. Dave thought again about going home. He ordered another beer. Sometimes for dinner Dave would eat a Rancho Burger heated in the microwave oven behind the bar. Sometimes he'd not eat but drink instead and then drive home late, drunk to his studio apartment and lie restlessly on his mattress, waiting for the morning buzzer.

The ball-capped lout got excited about something and stood up in his seat yelling. The bouncer moved over and firmly replaced him in the chair. The crowd was getting thicker and noisier. A fight broke out up near the bar. A couple of bottles and some glasses were knocked onto the floor and shattered. The bouncers and manager worked to get the fight participants ejected. Two hours dragged by. Dave had idle thoughts and drank more beers. It was eight o'clock. Ms. 69 FFF was up again.

She came on in a dim turquoise light. Topless to start, this time, the music a primitive percussion. She began slowly swaying like a sapling in a light breeze, the breasts like huge ripe fruit quivering. The light dimmed slightly and the volume of music increased. A thin wailing melody from a wooden flute entered the song and a moment later the light strum of a crude stringed instrument. An ancient song of savannah and desert and sky, of wind and river and tree. Ms. 69 FFF stood at center stage, her voluptuous body undulating snakelike, controlled by the song. God those monsters are big, thought Dave. They appeared to him to be swelling and abating, breathing as if they possessed a separate life. The music decreased in volume and tempo. Ms. 69 quickly kicked the high heels behind her and in the same motion doffed her bikini pants. The lights went out except for a single blue one pointed up from the base of the stage. The music dropped to a whisper. The crowd was almost silent. Ms. 69 stood motionless with her head tilted back, eyes closed, hands held palms together below her chin. As the music came back up she languidly reached behind her and uncurled a small throw rug and knelt upon it and bowed down, naked and prostrate. Dave left his corner and moved to the edge of the crowd surrounding the stage. The music grew louder. The rhythm picked up.

Ms. 69 FFF slowly stretched out on the rug and rolled over onto her back. She began a slow sensuous writhing. She began caressing herself; the massive breasts, down her sides, stroking her thighs. She turned her head. Dave could see her closed eyes and swollen half parted lips. She tossed her head from side to side and continued her slow writhing. The tempo and volume increased. Ms. 69 twisted faster. A rude horn sounded from far away. The beat became urgent and demanding. Ms. 69 flailed like a madwoman. The massive tits bounced and rolled as if pummeled by some rough and invisible lover. Jesus Christ, thought Dave. Watermelons, nipples like golfballs, the aureoles as big as saucers. The horn blared loud and close. Ms. 69 jerked and moaned. She put both hands above her head, wrist on top of wrist as if pinioned there, and began arching her back and thrusting her groin into the air. Sweat ran down her sides and dripped from her face. A thin trickle of drool edged from her mouth. The music reached a climax of pounding drums and screaming horn. Ms. 69 FFF threw back her head and cried out in pain, a high lost wail. The music trailed away. The lights dimmed to almost nothing. Ms. 69 lay motionless for a full minute and then got up slowly and left the stage.

After a hushed moment the crowd broke into subdued applause. Dave, weakened, wandered back to his corner. He sat down heavily. God Almighty, he thought, she's worth a thousand dollars, She's worth ten thousand. It was like she was fucking with some kind of spirit. Partly drunk, he got another beer.

The lights went back up and Crystal came out and started doing her thing. The patrons weren't paying much attention to her. They were quieter. What they'd just seen had sucked a lot of energy out of them. Tina came over to Dave and sat quickly down in the booth. She had a bottle, it looked old, half full of some brown liquid and stoppered with a cork. "Look," she said. "Look what I found."

"What is that?" said Dave. "Where'd you get that?"

"I was watching Ms. 69 cow before her last dance. You know, peeking through a crack into her dressing room. She was drinking this shit right before she went on."

"Are you kidding?" said Dave. "Let me see that."

Tina pushed the bottle across the table to him. He picked it up and looked at it. He pulled the cork and took a whiff. "God! It smell's like cat puke," he said.

"That's not all," said Tina. "She was kneeling there in front of a candle rubbing body lotion on her udders. Then she'd take a little sip of that shit and say 'eno taerg ho gib meht ekam, eno taerg ho gib meht ekam, eno taerg ho gib meht ekam'. She did the whole bit three times like that."

"What was she saying?" asked Dave.

"'Eno taerg ho gib meht ekam' or something like that," said Tina. "I don't know what it means."

"So you stole the bottle," Dave said.

"Yeah. I thought maybe I'd try it."

"Tina, you have been working here too long. You're going nutty. I wouldn't touch that shit on a bet."

"Look. I saw her drink it. It can't hurt. Can it?" said Tina.

"I guess not. A bunch of mumbo jumbo if you ask me," said Dave.

"Let me have it," Tina said. Dave slid the bottle back across the table. Tina smelled the fluid and made a face. She took a little exploratory sip. "It's not so bad," she said. "It's kind of spicy." She took a gulp. "Eno taerg ho gib meht ekam, eno taerg ho gib meht ekam," she chanted. "Wait, I need a candle." Dave flicked his lighter and held it up. "Eno taerg ho gib meht ekam," Tina said. She guzzled some more of the fluid.

"Jesus, Tina. Don't you think you're overdoing it?" said Dave.

"You know what they say. If a little does a little good a lot'll do a lot of good. It can't hurt can it," said Tina.

Tina drank from the bottle and recited the chant three more times. Dave's arm was getting tired from holding up the lighter. Crystal's dance was ending. Tina put down the bottle of mysterious fluid and took a gulp of Dave's beer. "I'm on next," she said. "Wish me luck." She got up and went to the dressing rooms. Dave chugged the last of his beer and signalled the waitress for another. That Tina is crazier than a shit house rat, he thought.

A raucous pop tune came on, loud and driving. A modern song of factories and smoke and mechanisms, of air raids and car wrecks. A paean to the drugged and autistic. They played it often in there.

Dave waited for Tina to come out. Instead, a new girl with long auburn hair and a large bust came out topless and started jigging around. Something about her movements was familiar. Dave left his corner again and moved close to the stage. He could see her face. It was Tina in a wig. Her breasts had swelled to the size of large peaches. The potion had worked. Tina bounced her new tits and smiled uneasily. She turned and shook her rear at the crowd. They let out a collective gasp when Tina turned around again. Her breasts had expanded to the size of soccer balls. Her smile was replaced by a look of complete terror. The sudden new weight of the giant tits caused Tina to stumble forward. She reared back to keep from falling headfirst, overcompensated, and fell flat on her back. The breasts surged again. Now they were the size of beach balls. They churned and rolled as two independent and powerful entities, unconcerned with Tina, who was smothering under then.

Dave heard a scream above the noise of the crowd. He turned. Ms. 69 FFF was standing at the edge of the stage. "No! No! No!" she howled. She tore at her hair with both hands. Her once gigantic tits were gone. In their place hung two withered sacs, like huge dried chilis, extending past her waist, almost to her knees. "No! No! No!" she screamed. The skin on her face was stretched taut. Her head looked like a skull. When she opened her mouth again Dave noticed her eye teeth. They appeared half an inch longer than normal. Like a baboon's.

From then on, later, Dave was never able to determine if what had happened had been real or rather a huge and drunken hallucination. The ball-capped lout jumped up on the stage and grabbed his crotch and started in with a lewd humping action. One of Tina's tits raised up off the floor, pulled back like a cobra, and struck at him. It caught the lout full on, carried him away from the stage, and smashed him against the cinder block wall of the building. The tit retracted. The lout fell limp onto a table, which collapsed. Meanwhile, the other breast pulled back and launched itself on a trajectory towards the snack bar. It smashed into the patrons with the implacable momentum of a wrecking ball. Pandemonium broke loose. Screams, snapping chairs and bones, shattering glass. Dave jumped back and avoided being smashed by the tit. He turned and ran for his corner. A tit, now the size of a large boulder, broke free of the stage and rolled swiftly out onto the floor. Everything in its path was crushed. It hit a support post and sheared it off. With a creaking groan the ceiling of the club bulged downward. Dave grapped the bottle of potion and headed for the door. He turned once. A wall of flesh pursued him. At the threshold he tripped and fell sprawling into the gravel. He got up and looked back one more time. The doorway was filled with flesh. In the center of it, three feet in diameter, was a nipple. It stared at Dave like the eye of a sea monster. He started running.

Fifty yards from the strip joint he heard a sound like two howitzers fired in tandem. A blast of hot air knocked him down. He slowly got to his feet in a rain of debris. He saw a water heater a hundred feet in the air revolving slowly end over end on its descent back to earth. The strip joint was enveloped in smoke. A light evening breeze slowly cleared the smoke away. The strip joint was a pile of rubble. Something fluttered down and landed at Dave's feet. A long haired auburn wig. He reached down and picked it up. "Poor Tina," he said. Dave looked around. He was alone. He was the only survivor of the strip joint explosion. He heard distant sirens. They'll never believe this, he thought. They'll say it was a gas leak or something. He noticed then that he was still clutching the bottle of elixir. He started to throw it away but stopped. Instead, he walked to his car, stuffed the wig and bottle under the seat, got in, started the engine. Negotiating his way around nameless pieces of debris in the parking lot, he drove out onto the road and into the oncoming twilight.

THE CRICKET

Once, when I was a little kid, maybe six or seven years old, the water meter in front of my parents' house gave out. The city had to replace it. This was before backhoes and hydraulic machines were used. The city employed ditch diggers. There were three of them digging out the meter and I went outside to watch. I was a patient watcher. They dug all around the outer casing of the meter and then reached down and pulled the meter and casing out in one piece. All that was left was a hole in the ground with two pipes sticking into it. And three big red crickets. One of the diggers jumped into the hole and caught the crickets and put them in an empty pipe tobacco can he carried in his shirt pocket. I asked him why he did that. He said he kept the crickets for pets. He was a strong armed, simple, and gentle soul. His co-workers looked at him without expression. They evidently thought he was slightly nuts, but didn't care to remark upon it. I asked him if I could have one. He told me to find something to put it in. I got a coffee can and put some leaves and twigs in it and went back to him. He asked me if I would take good care of the cricket. I told him I would. So he gave me one. I put it in the can. I found about half a dozen sow bugs and put them in too. I thought maybe the cricket would eat them. The ditch diggers finished their work and loaded up their equipment and drove away. The cricket man waved goodbye to me. I took the can to the backyard patio and set it down and studied the insects. The sow bugs slowly crawled around on the twigs. The cricket sat by himself, motionless except for his waving antennae. I poked him with my finger. He jumped a little bit and resumed waving his antennae around. I went inside for awhile and watched television.

When I came back out the cricket was still in the same spot, waving his antennae.

The day was warm and soft. The tree leaves cast a dappled shadow on the patio bricks. I found some charcoal starter fluid and matches and set the contents of the can on fire. The burning cricket scrambled frantically in the can. His legs scraped against the side. When the fire had burned down to smoldering embers the cricket's shell exploded. It sounded like a piece of corn popping.

THE JOB:
Teresa wore a miniskirt on Friday. In the late afternoon she went to the copier and made charts for the Monday presentation. Bending and stretching, she sorted the charts into the correct order. The miniskirt began to slide up the back of her thighs and every male head in the office rotated to observe this wonder. Teresa was either unaware or unconcerned with what she was showing. Two of the office fops approached and attempted to engage her in conversation. They were rebuffed. She wasn't interested.

ANOTHER STUPID WEEKEND

I could observe Teresa from my cubicle. She did have a fine rear end. The fops were right on that account. She finished her task and left. I looked at the clock: 3:35. At this hour of the week a strange phenomenon took hold. The last sixty minutes on Friday seemed as long as the 2340 that preceded them. Maybe the whole office was being accelerated to the speed of light. Or cooled to absolute zero, where all molecular vibration ceased. It was a torture. 3:36. I turned to my box. The screen displayed columns of numbers. I punched up ONTOP.

A clever computer diddler had digitized six or eight frames of a porno movie. A well shaped set of buttocks, like Teresa's, but naked, rode female superior on a section of male torso. The standard inverted monster shot. The anonymous buttocks flexed, rose, relaxed, and settled down on the anonymous schlong again in a never ending cycle. I could leave the machine on and Monday morning the photon lovers would still be grinding futilely towards electronic orgasm. I settled back in my chair and decided to count the number of thrusts and parries executed in the 54 minutes to quitting time.

My reverie was soon interrupted by a sound like coarse sandpaper rubbed on a rusty tin can. I punched escape and the humping ONTOP was replaced by the previous columns of numbers. Billings, the supervisor, came into the cubicle. The rasping sound was Billings clearing his throat. He did it again and said, "I saw the Mongoose in here awhile ago. What did she want?"

"She wanted to know if we'd made any last minute changes," I said.

"Don't tell her anything. You understand? I'm building a file. One of these days I'm going to detonate that bitch."

Billings was having one of his fits. He kept clearing his throat. His left cheek twitched erratically. His eyes darted around the cubicle in barely disguised fear of some nameless threat. The pencil on the desk might jump up and stab him in the heart. The fluorescent light fixture might fall and crush his head. Maybe the Mongoose was at this moment putting the final edge on the knife she planned to gut him with. It was a tense situation. If I said the wrong thing he would go completely haywire. I'd seen it happen once. His eyes had unfocused and oscillated rapidly from side to side. He had stuttered and moaned and a thin leakage of white drool, white because of the antacid tablets he chewed continuously, had trickled out the side of his mouth. It had not been a pretty sight.

"Frank," I said, "it's okay. We've gone over the pitch a dozen times. You're ready. What are you worrying about?"

"I don't know. I just don't know," he said. "I don't like that bitch snooping around. That's all. Don't tell her anything." He turned around and walked out of the cubicle.

Billings was a borderline nut case. I almost felt sorry for him except he had been driven to this point by his own greed and ambition. I frequently pictured him splayed out over a barrel. One wrist was chained down by a mortgage payment on an over priced house. One ankle was held fast by an ex-wife and kid, the other by an avaricious new wife. He still had one arm free to fend off the Mongoose. She tried mightily to ream him with her knife while he tried to strangle her with one hand. They played hardball in this office.

I had nothing in it. I was a temporary employee. I'd rigged up a fake resume' and the employment service had swallowed it and sent me here on a ten month assignment. I doubted I'd last that long.

3:45. I punched up ONTOP again and considered the political situation. This was no ordinary Friday afternoon. Monday morning the big money would be in. A venture capital group out of L.A. and another from Denver. They were the small potatoes. The big fish was a Mr. Hashimoto, representing PACRIM Investments, Ltd. The company had plans for an expansion. New building, new machine tools, tax abatements, and a contingent of disgruntled low paid workers. All the company needed was money. Billing's career depended on it. So did the Mongooses'. They were locked tooth and nail in a battle to succeed the division manager.

3:56. I heard the sandpaper on tin can sound again. Punched out. Billings. "You see anyone ripping off the coffee jar this week?" he asked.

"No."

"Ok. Keep an eye out." He turned around and walked away again.

This was one of my important duties. Someone had been stealing about thirty dollars a week from the coffee money. Since I had a good view of the coffee pot, I was supposed to watch it and see if I could identify the thief. I didn't have a suspect yet but I hadn't looked very hard for one. 3:59.

I walked slowly to the water fountain and took a long drink of water. This should burn up a few minutes. Teresa sat at her desk filing a fingernail. It looked like the rash that periodically appeared on her hands had abated again. She looked brighter than I'd ever seen her.

"Have a big weekend planned, Teresa?" I asked.

She nodded vigorously. "Yes!" she said.

"What are you going to do?"

She smiled vaguely. "It's a secret," she said.

The Mongoose, aka Laura Colby, walked up and slapped a thick sheaf of papers on Teresa's desk. "I need these changes incorporated before you go home tonight," she said. Teresa made a slight grimace. The Mongoose nodded curtly to me and walked briskly back into her office. She was an odd one. She looked like someone had clamped her head in a vice and hacksawed the lower half of her face off, starting at the tip of her nose and cutting down and inwards across her lips and chin. This gave her a blunt and predatory aspect. The Mongoose did nothing to dispel the notion. She was always very formal, immaculately dressed, abrupt, and icy. She had an MBA from some Eastern business school and that was all anyone seemed to know about her. She kept a Marine survival knife mounted on the wall in her office. She had told someone it was a memento from her marriage. I thought it was a nice touch. It kept Billings anxious.

4:13. I wandered back to my cubicle. The Mongoose and Billings shared Teresa's secretarial services. They both treated her like a mongrel dog. I thought this may have been the cause of Teresa's rash. Or maybe she was allergic to the sensory deprivation and bland artificiality of the office. The office caused me to break out in a rash also. But mine was internal, on the surface of my brain, so no one could see it.

Since Teresa dodged the advances of the office fops they said things about her. The rash was a symptom of herpes or AIDS. She was 29 and never married so she must be a dyke. Or a transvestite, or even worse, a transsexual. Curiously, they were all still intent on laying her. When the fops weren't staring at her bod they made snide remarks about her, loudly.

I couldn't stand them anyway. Snots with yellow ties and suspenders, brush mustaches, apartments and Japanese sports cars. They all had degrees in business or engineering or some nonsense. In other words, not educated, but trained to grub for cash, like an organ grinder's monkey. This place was severely dragging me.

4:19. I got up and fetched my jacket and peeked out of the cubicle. No one was around. I slipped down the hall. Eleven minutes early, at the end of a dull and soundless week, I left the job and emerged into the outside world. The sun hung low on the horizon on a late Fall day. I walked across the parking lot and got into my car. I had just sold another week of my life. I started the car and pulled out into the swelling traffic.

TV NIGHT:
One hour later I dully chewed a piece of something purported to be food and stared at the chrome handle on the refrigerator. The reflection was distorted. I got up, threw the rest of the TV dinner in the trash, went into the sitting room,

began pacing. I was on a new program. This was to be an alcohol free weekend. I'd been hitting the bottle too much. Maybe it was a character defect. Maybe I was bored and frustrated. Maybe I drank just to numb myself to the spiritless nullity that was post-industrial America.

Anyway, I'd been seeing this thing. A creature. A huge lizard-like animal. The body of a lizard, with the head of a rat. The most bizarre thing about this beast was its hindquarters. Its back and legs and sides were covered with human appendages stuck on willy-nilly. Ears, fingers, noses, lips, tongues, male and female genitalia, assholes. Heironymous would have recognized it in an instant. I'd seen this creature for years in my nightmares but lately I'd seen it while awake. I'd seen it driving a car on the street and coming out of a supermarket. One day I saw it sneaking out of Billing's office. I attributed the daytime appearance of this apparition to overindulgence in alcohol and, therefore, deemed it wise to slack off.

After a half hour of mindless pacing it dawned on me that I might as well pace outside. I put on my coat and went for a walk around my neighborhood of crumbling apartment houses and dilapidated efficiency duplexes. The streets were jammed with parked cars. I walked for half a mile and saw no one. I turned and walked back on another street. Some houses were dark. From the rest, everyone of them, came the grey-green ghostlight of television. It cast a dim and eerie glow out over the bare trees and brown grass. The pestilence lay heavy on the land. I hurried along through this stricken landscape, a shade, homeless and lost in an alien netherworld. I returned to my well lit room and resumed pacing. I sat down, thought briefly of going to a liquor store or bar, discarded the idea, worked two crossword puzzles, stared at the wall. Finally, in resignation, I turned on the television.

I found an animal show. Birds twittered and squawked. A half dozen Africans and a large white man walked slowly through a dense stand of tropical trees beside a placid pond. The Africans carried coils of rope. "The hippopotamus must leave the safety of her water home to enjoy the succulent plants which grow nearby," the announcer intoned. "This is when she can most easily be captured and tagged for further study."

With a horrendous squeal of terror a hippo the size of a van bolted from the underbrush. It was followed by a baby as big as a full grown heifer. The natives made a half hearted attempt to lasso it. They missed. The hippos splashed into the pond, submerged, and disappeared. "If you leave your home will your loved ones be well protected?" the announcer asked. Now I was treated to a maudlin tale of how Mr. Citizen left his house one day and was struck dead by a hit and run driver. Oh oh, no insurance. His young wife and children were depicted moving out of their nifty tri-plex and into a cramped apartment in a rat infested slum. They weren't happy about it. After five more minutes of similar bullshit the nature show returned.

The big honky, Jim, had obtained a road grader and was revving the engine at the bank of the hippo pond. "Jim will use the grader to drive the mother and baby from the pond. Then Akim and his men will catch them in the heavy nets." A score of natives stood ready with two large nets of rope. Jim put the grader into action. Black smoke spewed from the machine, the wheels threw gouts of mud, and it plunged into the pond. A white man with a road grader running amok in the middle of Africa. This was a metaphor for a lot of things, but I was too tired to think of one.

When the grader came to the middle of the pond, the water almost up to the cab door, both hippos bolted up the opposite bank and ran straight into the nets. The natives wrestled them down to immobility. The announcer came on and talked about what a great corporation he was shilling for and all the money they'd given to various wildlife funds.

The show came back and things had taken an ugly turn. "The excitement of the chase was too much for the mother hippopotamus," said the shill. "She has expired from a heart attack." Several natives with machetes were athwart the fallen beast, hacking out great slabs of dripping meat. Others portaged the slabs away. "There will be much feasting and singing in the village tonight."

Jim and three natives were shown loading the baby hippo into the back of a truck. They forced it up a ramp, dragging it with ropes tied around its neck and jabbing it in the rear with cattle prods. "The young hippopotamus is not able to care for herself in the wilds," the shill said. "She will be taken to a modern zoo where she can live a full life, safe from predators and fed her favorite succulent plants. Have you provided for your loved ones in case of unforeseen accident or death?" I punched the remote control.

A long haired slinky in tights pulled on some kind of bungee cord contraption. "All muscles can be exercised with the Exobot 2000," I was told. Next the slinky was displayed from the rear with her knees attached to the device. She effortlessly flexed her buns and looked over her shoulder with a come hither smile. This was much better than hippos.

The scene changed. A paunchy middle aged man grunted on a treadmill. He wasn't smiling. "Or try the Exobot 5000 cardio-vascular workout system," the announcer said. "$495 plus shipping." Now the drudge was smiling as he worked the machine. An addition had been made. A rack clamped to the treadmill supported a TV set hung directly in front of the guy's face. "It's more fun with our TV mount accessory. Now you can watch National Shopping Network even while you exercise. Only $149 plus shipping." I slammed my fist down on the remote. The screen went to blissful static. The randomly moving black and white flecks were hypnotic. The hiss was soothing. I nodded off.

An Oriental voice said, "Deh ah two Rodan!" My eyes popped open. The digital clock read 1:45. A grainy black and white movie flickered on the TV screen. I sat listlessly in front of it. Two gigantic pterodactyls were ripping the shit out of downtown Tokyo. The Japanese army was firing tanks and artillery at them to no effect. One of the Rodans picked up a bus, slit it open with a claw, and started snarfing handfuls of passengers like popcorn. The other one stepped on a couple of sushi restaurants and then tore the side off a skyscraper and sucked up the terrified office workers. Like an aardvark attacking an anthill. The army was bringing up a huge gun mounted on a railroad car. Some sage once remarked that the Japs had produced these movies in subconcious mortal fear of being nuclear bombed again. It made sense to me.

The phone rang. Which fool would this be, I wondered. It was my ex-wife, Lydia.

"Hi," she said. "What are you doing?"

"Nothing."

"Robert is licking my pussy," she said. "Oh. Oh yes, Robert. Ummmmm."

A Rodan picked up the railroad gun and began squashing soldiers with it. "Lydia," I said, "what do you want?"

"I just wanted to tell you that Robert gives much better head than you ever did. Even when you were drunk. He's a much better lover than you. He's really a much better person in general than you, too. Ummmmm. Oh, yes. Oh,yes. It's so good!"

"Lydia, if you're going to pull this stunt you should wrap something around your vibrator to muffle the sound. Or is that Robert making that buzzing noise? Has he turned into an insect?"

"I really hate you," she said. "I hate you, I hate you, I hate you," she screamed and slammed down the phone. I hung up, turned off the television, went to bed.

GARAGE SALE DATE:

A miniature Rodan was chained to a treadmill by talon, wing, and neck. ONTOP played on the TV mounted in front of it. Someone was running a dentist's drill. Turning it on and off. Zeeeee! Zeeeee! Zeeeee! The noise terrified the Rodan. It strained mightily at its bonds. Zeeeee! Zeeeee! Zeeeee! The Rodan broke the chain around its neck and smashed its beak into the TV which died in a puff of smoke. It jerked around and snapped the chains holding its wings and one talon and went flapping away, the treadmill dangling below it. The dentist's drill didn't shut off. Zeeee!... Zeeee!... Zeeee!.... I flailed around and knocked the telephone awry. The drill stopped. I picked up the receiver. "Uhhh," I said.

"Hi!" it said. Please God don't let this be Lydia. "This is Janice!" It wasn't Lydia. Janice.

"Yeah?" I said.

"Ohhh. You don't remember, do you? Listen to this note

you left for me, 'Creature of the night. My blood howls for you.' And then this phone number."

"Where?"

"At that creepy place called Elmer's. You don't go in there much do you? I only went there once. With some friends from work. I drank more than I usually do. They went home and I stayed. You were there. We talked for awhile. I found this note after you left."

"When did this happen?" I mumbled.

"About two months ago."

I had no recollection of who she was or what she was talking about. That wasn't unusual though. "So," I said, "what is it you want, Janice?"

"I thought maybe we could get together. If you want to, anyway. It's ok if you don't want to."

Don't look a gift horse in the mouth. I said, "All right. When?"

"Today. My ex is coming to pick up Bobby at noon. Maybe we could get some lunch."

"That sounds ok with me. Maybe we could get something and eat it in the park."

"Terrific. Come over about 12:30, ok?"

She gave me her address. We hung up. It is a rare occurrence when strange women call. When they do, it is best to do what they propose. I wondered why she'd waited so long. Maybe she was horny today. I got out of bed.

I have masochistic tendencies. One of my habits is listening to a Saturday morning local radio call-in talkshow. The screwballs, ignoramuses, schizoids, repressed inverts, wife beaters, and anal retentives scurry out of the woodwork when they smell an open microphone. One guy had a solution for what he called the "homosexual problem." Round up all the "queers and homos" and ship them off to a deserted island. Since they wouldn't reproduce they'd just die off. Society would be permanently rid of their baleful influence. Neither the host nor any subsequent callers remarked upon the obvious absurdity of this plan. The next caller, a woman, allowed how this was a good idea but she wanted to include flag burners and pornographers in the lot. Caller number three added convicted felons, drug peddlers, and liberal politicians. Number four thought they should all be sent to one of the moons of Jupiter. "We have the technology available now," he said. It went on and on. When they were finished only one group still inhabited the land of the free and home of the brave: white, Christian, know-nothings. Given a choice, I'd rather live on one of Jupiter's moons.

I turned off the radio. It was time to visit Janice. She didn't live far. I drove over. There was a small neatly kept house. I knocked on the front door. Janice answered. I guessed she was late twenties or early thirties. Not beautiful but pretty. A sane and capable looking woman.

"Oh, hi," she said. "I've got some bad news."

"What?"

"That goddamn Frank. He called about ten minutes ago and told me he couldn't take Bobby this weekend because he's going to Las Vegas. He'd rather take his slut to Vegas than spend time with his son. I really hate that son of a bitch."

Not thinking, I said, "We can bring Bobby along."

"I was hoping you'd say that! Let me go get him."

She went to the rear of the house. I stood by the front door and waited. A video game was beeping somewhere back there. It stopped. A second later a kid about four years old going "Bweet! Bweet! Bweet! Bweet!" ran past me and banged out the door. Janice came back carrying her purse and a folded section of newspaper. She said, "Bobby's really wound up today. He's disappointed Frank didn't come to get him."

She shut the door. We went out into her front yard. Bobby was running around in circles and still making that bweeting noise. We walked over to my car parked in the street. It is a 1969 VW. It's covered with dents and corrosion. Janice looked at it doubtfully. Most people are amazed that someone would drive a ruined piece of crap like my car. It's almost un-American to own something that ugly. It's a car a welfare recipient would drive. It didn't bother me. I seldom thought about it. It ran. Today, though, I was slightly embarrassed by my car. Years of battery acid and road salt had rotted out the floor under the back seat. I'd solved that problem by removing the seat and stuffing in a couple layers of cardboard to keep the wind out.

"Uh, look," I said. "This car is definitely a two seater. I guess Bobby can sit on your lap."

"Oh, that's ok," Janice said with barely disguised relief. "We'll just take mine."

She had a small station wagon parked in the driveway. We went over to it. Bobby ran over and got in the front seat. I started to get in the back. Janice said, "No. Wait. You get in the front." She opened the driver's door and said, "Bobby, get in the back."

"No," he said.

"Bobby, get in the back or no Burger King."

Bobby mewled and whined but climbed over the front seat and got in the rear. I sat down in the front. I looked over my shoulder at Bobby and said, "Thanks, Bobby."

"Fuck you," he said.

"Oh, don't pay any attention to him," Janice said. "He gets that from that goddamn Frank." She started the car and backed out into the street.

"What's this about Burger King?" I asked.

"Oh, I'm sorry. Look, I hate to rearrange all of our plans. But I told Bobby we'd take him to Burger King and get a Happy Box. He collects these little plastic people that come in a Happy Box. You don't mind, do you? Maybe we can go to the park some other time."

"No, it's ok," I said. I couldn't stand places like that. But, as part of my new program, I'd decided to climb out of the swamp of negativity I usually lived in, be more tolerant, and try to live like a normal person, content with the pleasures of modern life. So, to Burger King we went.

The place was about two thirds full and half of them were standing in line. Janice said she'd get the food. I gave her some money and took Bobby to a booth. We sat down and waited. He was a strange little dude. He ignored my lame attempts at conversation. His eyes darted around the place, never stopping for more than a few seconds on anything. Some new movement would always divert his attention. If it wasn't moving, he wasn't interested. Something about this was eerily familiar. He held a constant dialogue with himself. He mimicked the voices of TV cartoon characters. He made video game noises and sounds like car crashes and gunfire. I decided he'd been taught to speak by a television set. I gave up on trying to talk with him.

Janice came back with the food. She gave me my blob and gave Bobby his Happy Box and sat down. Bobby flipped open the lid on the box, ignored the food, dug down to the bottom. He came up with a little plastic mermaid. His face crumpled in disappointment and anger. "I want Muscle Man!" he said. Janice said, "Bobby, you didn't get Muscle Man this time. You got a nice little mermaid. Maybe you'll get Muscle Man next time." "NO! I WANT MUSCLE MAN!" Bobby screamed out. He pushed the Happy Box over. The happy burger and happy fries fell out and the box knocked over his happy drink. "I WANT MUSCLE MAN NOW!" he screamed again, even louder.

Janice got up. I thought she was going to take Bobby outside for a sound thrashing. Instead, she went back to the food counter. There was a hurried conference with the woman behind it. Janice returned with a new Happy Box for Bobby and a rag to sop up the mess he'd made. Bobby dug into the box, pulled out a Muscle Man, nibbled on some french fries, and resumed the bizarre dialogue with himself. I chewed my grease wad and tried not to think.

I looked around the place. Saturday shoppers. A lot of kids and women, fewer men. Most of the women were anxious. They tried to keep their munchkins in line and quiet. They glanced often at Dad, trying to read him, to see if he was enjoying the outing. The men were like steers let out of a pen. They chewed their food and gazed out the windows, totally distracted. Trying to remember what time the football game started or how much booze was at the house or some excuse for slipping off for a couple hours. The American family at its leisure.

Then I saw it. The hair stood up on the back of my neck. The lizard beast. It was getting up from a booth and putting on an overcoat. I could see the fingers and tongues dangling from its haunches. It walked out the door with its tail slithering behind it. It got into a black El Dorado and drove out of the parking lot. As it came past the window it turned its head and looked directly at me.

"What's wrong?" asked Janice.

"Nothing," I said. "Just a little chill."

Janice had the section of newspaper out and was circling items with a pencil. She said, "Would you mind hitting a couple of garage sales while we're out? I really get off on them." I didn't think I liked garage sales but I couldn't remember why. The day was shot anyway. I wasn't going to seduce Janice over a bottle of wine in the park. Not with Bobby along. "That would be ok with me," I said.

We got up to leave. Bobby ran out the door ahead of us and scrambled into the front seat of the car and began honking the horn. We walked across the parking lot. "I'm thinking about taking Bobby to see a psychologist," Janice said. "I think there's something wrong with him." I wondered how she'd stumbled upon that astute observation.

Bobby pulled the same front seat routine. Janice made him get in back by threatening to curtail his TV watching. I looked over my shoulder and said, "Thanks, Bobby." He pointed both index fingers at me and went "Bang! Bang! Bang! Bang!" Nice kid.

We set off garage saleing. We came to the first place. A non-descript house in a non-descript neighborhood. We got out and walked up the driveway. About half a dozen people were picking through shit in boxes. I looked around. Polyester clothes on racks, old plastic dishes, electronic junk. All of it junk. Most of it junk when it was new. I remembered why I disliked garage sales. They made me feel like a crow or hyena or some other carrion eater. Picking through people's trash in hopes of finding a morsel. The true horror of garage sales, though, was the glimpse it gave into the sellers' lives. Especially when someone had died. The parameters of their existence were held up for all to view. A mass produced landscape painting, some lace doilies, a TV set with a broken knob. The grey drabness of the life, framed by junk. The Vietnamese have a better idea. When someone dies, just dig a big hole in the ground and throw all their shit in with them.

A short chisel-faced woman walked up. A huge man lumbered along behind her like a shaved bear. They stopped. "Do you have any Depression ware?" she asked the salesman, a weasel-like man sitting at a card table behind a money box. "No, we don't," he said. The couple turned. The man's Thorazine gaze swept over me. He lumbered away.

Janice bought some flower pots and some plastic trucks for Bobby. We went to the next place.

I was standing in the garage looking at grease spots on the floor when Bobby started whining. He was holding an object in his hands and demanding that Janice buy it for him. I went over to see what it was.

It was a human ear pickled in a jar of alcohol. "Put that thing down, Bobby!" Janice said. "I'm not going to buy it." Bobby whined and set the jar down on a table. I picked it up and studied it. It was a large ear with a few hairs growing out of it. Marks left by human teeth were clearly visible along the severed edge. The price had been ten dollars but was now discounted to five. "I'll let you have it for two dollars," said the sale conductor, a large grey haired woman. "That belonged to my sister's husband. Clarice just hated that thing." I could tell Janice was annoyed when I bought the ear for Bobby. Maybe there was hope for him after all. He exhibited a nascent appreciation of the grotesque.

The third garage sale house looked the same as the first

two except there was a "For Sale" sign stuck in the front yard with a "Sold" attached above it. The brown grass had grown high before it died. Spread along one side of the driveway were tables loaded with tools, all priced ridiculously cheap. Wrenches for ten cents, an electric drill for two dollars, a table saw for ten. Everything had a "sold" sticker stuck on it. Janice started looking through a rack of clothes. Bobby ran around in circles. I looked for an unsold tool.

"Its all been sold," said a voice from the dark recesses of the garage. I peered into it. A bald headed gnome walked halfway out into the sunlight. "Yep," he said, "it was reasonably priced so I bought it all." He came out of the garage. He looked like a leprechaun gone to seed.

"We're the neighbors, see. The widow called up from Havasu and said 'I sold the house. Sell all the stuff out of it and I'll give you 25 percent of what you get.' So that's what me and the missus are doing."

The man had taken the opportunity to steal anything he wanted from his trusting neighbor. I turned to move away. He came closer, squinting. Apparently he felt like talking and I was the designated victim.

"Now the missus and her got along fine. But me and him, we didn't see eye to eye. He was some cantankerous old fool." I took two steps back to signal I wanted to break off the conversation because I had no interest in it. He took two steps forward.

"It all started over that strip of ground between the driveways, see." The man pointed down the driveway. A three foot gap between the two identical swaths of concrete was filled in with red bricks along one side and buff down the other. "He wanted blue grass and I wanted fescue. He'd plant in some blue grass and I'd poison it out and put in fescue. Then he'd poison that and put his blue grass back in. We went along like that for several seasons. Finally, he just bricked his side in so I went ahead and did mine too, knowin' he'd poison my grass anyway. That was fifteen years ago. We never spoke another word up to the day he died."

The man squinted up at me like he expected a question. I fell for it. "When was that?" I asked.

"Why, last August. Man worked at the plants for 33 years. Retired in June. Two months later he kills hisself. You ever heard of such a thing?"

"No," I said. I really thought it was probably a fairly common occurrence. A more pertinent question was how the guy had been able to work in a factory for 33 years.

"C'mere," said the troll. He hooked his index finger at me. I didn't want to follow him but I did anyway. We stopped towards the rear at one side of the garage.

"Right here's where he did it. Put a double barreled 12 gauge under his chin. Look." He pointed up. "Blowed most of his brain pan through the roof." I looked up. There was a ragged hole about eight inches in diameter in the roof of the garage. Two sparrows pecked around the edge of it. The man stood there, looking up at me with a tight grin on his face. He was gloating over the suicide of his hated neighbor.

I walked out of the garage, down the driveway, crossed the street, and got into the front seat of Janice's car. I was garage-saled out. I stretched out and looked up through the windshield at the naked tree branches. Like bony hands, desperate, clutching for the sky. The sun was a half hour above the horizon. I tried to doze. Something was poking me in the back. I groped around in the crack in the seat and came up with Muscle Man. I studied him. He was a shirtless long haired blonde dude flexing his muscles in a body builder's pose. I flicked him into the backseat.

Janice and Bobby came back to the car. "I've had it," said Janice. "Boy, that old guy was a creep. He kept staring at me after you left. I've got a bottle of white wine at home. You want some?"

Of course I did. On the way to her house we passed a bar. There were a few battered cars and a couple of motorcycles parked in the gravel lot beside it. Beer signs glowed in the window. It looked warm and friendly. We arrived back at Janice's. Bobby ran in with the ear, bweeting, the same way he'd gone out. He went immediately to the rear of the house and turned on his video games. Janice uncorked the wine and poured two glasses. We stood in her kitchen.

For about the sixth time that day I noticed Janice looking at me, but not directly, as if there was something fascinating about the top of my head. I said, "Why do you keep looking over my head? Is someone following me?" She giggled. "No. There's no one following you. I'm just trying to see what color your aura is."

"What's that?"

"Oh, you don't know? It's an electro-magnetic energy field that surrounds every living thing. It's generated by the life force."

What bullshit. "So," I asked, "what color is mine?"

"I don't know. I haven't seen it yet."

"Maybe I don't have one."

"Oh no. Every living thing has one."

"That's what I mean."

"Silly. You've got one. Maybe it's just not fully manifested. I've got an interest in auras, see. I do color analysis for people and the first thing you have to know is the color of their aura."

"You do that for a living?" I asked.

"No. Not full time anyway. I'm a receptionist at Acme Title. I do color analysis on the side."

"People give you money for that?"

"Oh, yeah. One of my clients won the lotto right after I finished his analysis. Another one was promoted to assistant manager at Toys R Us. It's pretty complicated. I've got to know the color of your aura, your sun, moon, and rising signs, and the year you were born. Then I work it out with a calculator and some charts and tables provided by my uplink manager."

I said, "I just don't know about all that, Janice. It sounds like a lot of hocus pocus to me."

"Yeah, it does, doesn't it," she said. "I'm not all that convinced either. What I find attractive about the program, though, is the multi-level marketing configuration. I've got a downlink going with six people in it. I get 2 per cent of their gross."

I was having second thoughts about Janice. It appeared she might be a lunatic after all.

She said, "Do you think you might be interested in joining my downlink? Color analysis works great for men. Do you know anyone who might like to be analyzed?"

I said, "The people I know would become abusive and possibly violent if I tried to foist something like that off on them. Sorry. I don't think I can help you."

Janice gave a slight shrug. "Oh well, it's ok," she said. She reached across me and refilled my wine glass. Her breast brushed my arm. She put down the bottle and held up her glass. "Here's to garage sales," she said.

We clinked our glasses. Janice moved forward until both of her breasts were pushed against my chest. It was clear what she had in mind. We kissed. We gave it a lot of tongue. One thing led to another and ten minutes later we were in bed in Janice's room in the gathering twilight, making the beast with two backs.

I was a little nervous. Janice had shut the door but I didn't know if she'd locked it. Bobby was still at the video game, I could hear the muffled squawking, but perhaps he'd tire of it and come looking for us. I half expected him to burst through the door in a full Oedipal fury and bash me over the head with one of his new trucks.

The beeping video game was messing up my rhythm. Two atonal bleets pulsed in asynchronous monotony. Like two cars, a Toyota and a Cadillac maybe, far away, engaged in a honking contest. This steady electronic squawking was randomly interrupted by a mechanical farting sound. I'd finally find a groove and then the fart would go off. I kept at it.

The lack of rhythm didn't seem to bother Janice. She dug her fingernails into me. "Oh, Rick!" she said.

She said, "Oh, Rick. Oh, Rick. Oh, Rick. Oh, oh, oh, oh, yes. Oh yes, oh yes, oh yes. Yes. Yes. Yes!"

I thought of Lydia, years ago, before the wars. Waking up in the morning, tousled hair, a dreamy smile on her face. I came and rolled off Janice. We both lay staring at the blown ceiling. My name isn't Rick. I didn't know who Rick was.

After awhile Janice leaned over and gave me a little peck on the cheek and got out of bed. She had a beautiful body. She put on a bathrobe and left the room. A few minutes later I got up, slowly put my clothes back on, went looking for her.

She was in the kitchen, squeezing hamburger from a

plastic tube into a frying pan. Without looking up she said, "I'm going to make some spaghetti. You can stay and eat with us if you want." Bobby ran into the kitchen. He was making a sound like an incoming artillery shell and running at me with his head down. At the last second I realized he intended to butt me in the groin. I caught his head in my hands. His hair was soft and warm. I felt no anger towards him. He probably had not enjoyed a very easy four years of life. He pulled away from me, said "pwing, pwing, pwing," and ran away. "I think Bobby likes you," said Janice. It was dark outside. The kitchen was bright and warm. I was a loner, an intruder into the life of this remnant of a family I hardly knew. "Bobby Billings!" yelled Janice after him. "Go wash your hands and help me set the table."

"Billings?" I said. "Is your ex-husband Frank Billings?"

Janice looked up, surprised. "Yes," she said. "Do you know him?"

"Uh, no. I guess I've just heard the name," I said.

"Well you're lucky then. Because he's a real asshole."

I had to get out of there. I told Janice my father was sick and in the hospital and that I'd promised to visit him. She knew I was lying. She walked me to the door. I stood on the front stoop. "Give me a call sometime," she said, a small and faintly wistful smile on her face. I told her I would. I went to the bar we'd passed on the way to her house and started drinking.

DRUNKEN SABBATH:

"Daddy! Daddy! Daddy! Daddy!" I awoke in the stinking morning beset by a frantic homunculus jabbing grimy fingers into my face. The first conscious inspiration brought the stench of excrement with a poisonous metallic aftertaste. Seeing that I was awake, the child pranced circling into the center of the room, diaper bulging, chanting "Daddy!" like an evil omen. I sat up and ran a quick survey of my cell.

House trailer, fake panelling, dirty shag carpet, bottles, overflowing ashtrays, magazines, newspapers, TV. I did not know where I was. I stood up and walked across the disheveled room and peeked into another. A scrawny white woman snoozed in a sagging bed with a bearded fat man. The kid kept pointing at the ceiling and saying, "Daddy! Daddy! Daddy!" Fully clothed, I headed for the door.

The stoop was piled cinder blocks. I shut the door and went down to the ground. A low scud moved across the grey sky and a cold wind wheezed from the north. Next to the trailer stood a heap of broken toys, furniture, and appliances, crowned with a Harley *sans* engine and wheels. I heard a rustling noise. A rodent dog darted suddenly from under the trailer and clamped onto my pantleg. I kicked it hard upside the head. It released and ran howling to curse and threaten me from its lair. I found my car parked fifty yards down the street of trailers. It started. I drove to a corner and looked at a street sign: 66th and Conglomerate. The stink wasn't the kid; the outside air smelled the same. Sewer plant on the fritz again. I came to an arterial street and turned north to get away from it.

A vast phlegm of asphalt lay smeared to the horizon. Signs and tattered banners of commerce stood watch over trash blown streets and parking lots devoid of human purpose at that hour. I drove past blownout shopping centers, weeds, ragged car lots. Busted motels, defunct fast food restaurants. A whirlwind or a tribe of vandals had been at large in the night. Upended portasigns with skyward pointing arrows proclaimed the second coming, or some material approximation. I pulled into a Donut Hut.

Standing in line behind a man mumbling incoherently, I studied the several yellowing posters of missing children. The mumbler turned with his purchase and sloshed half of his coffee onto the floor. On the counter top was a jar rigged for money collection. The cause was a woman in need of a liver transplant. She smiled wanly from a crumpled xeroxed photo. The jar contained three cents. I bought a donut and coffee and sat down. The mumbler sat behind me. The conversation with himself went something like, "Goddamn. Goddamn. I told that son of a bitch! Goddamn. I told him. Goddamn. I told that son of a bitch! Goddamn. Goddamn. I told that son of a bitch." I tried to reconstruct the previous evening.

I'd started drinking and trading horseshit with the bearded fat man. He told me of big motorcycles and wrecking and falling off them drunk. He spoke of drinking bouts lasting weeks, and of orgies, delirious wanton women, speed, crank, ice, smack, brawls and flying teeth. He had lifted his shirt so that I could examine scars obtained from a chain whipping. Lying, I told him of a formula for methamphetamine. The drug could be manufactured with household chemicals available at any supermarket. He was interested and began calculating his profits.

When the place closed I was enticed to his house with promises of more booze and a cohort of renegade women, lean and feral, sporting leather and death's head tattoos. What we found was his wife, exhausted from her night job. She viewed my presence as she would have that of a monstrous cockroach, befriended by her errant husband at his seedy bar and brought twitching into her home. She went to bed. The evening deteriorated. The motorcyclist and I had ended it by slurring at each other over his bottle of whiskey. I hoped he wouldn't try the formula. His trailer might explode.

I sat for a minute in the donut shop and tried to imagine some idea of any meaning to the last twelve hours of my life. I could find none. I got up and went to the restroom to vomit but nothing would come up.

Back on the strip, I turned at the first cross street and wended my way through a decaying residential section. The wind in the night had stripped the trees of their remaining leaves. Winter had come, early. I stopped at a neatly kept house, out of place in that neighborhood. I knocked on the door. No one answered. As I turned to leave, the storm door popped loudly from the sudden application and release of vacuum. A woman stood in the doorway. She was dressed in a white cotton nightgown and wore no makeup. She looked as if she might have been recently crying or maybe she was only tired. She opened the storm door two inches, said, "I think he's in back," and shut it.

I left the porch and walked around the corner of the house. A new Japanese car was parked in the driveway. In front of it was an old Cadillac limousine with all tires flat. I went into the back yard. It was like the front, neatly mowed and trimmed, flower beds lining the perimeter. No one was about. Leaving, I glanced into the rear of the limousine. A body lay on the seat. It was a man, on his back, with both arms folded across his chest, eyes opened and rolled back into his head. A fat late fly worried his creased brow. I leaned over the top of the car and brought my hand down sharply on the flaking metal.

The man came bolt upright like from a coffin. He looked around for a terror stricken second and lunged for the door. It would not budge. He fell back on the seat, emitted a low howl, and commenced pounding on the door with both feet in unison. On the fourth kick it sprung open. The man lay for a minute on the seat, panting. Then he slowly crawled out of the car and stood up wobbling in the weak sunlight. Leaning forward, he vomited a thin yellow ichor onto the pavement. Long strings of it swayed from his chin. He wiped them off with the back of his hand, dry retched twice, and turned to me. "Bitch locked me out last night," he said.

He looked down at himself. His flannel shirt was spotted with food, wine, and vomit. "Go see if you can get me a shirt, ok?" he said.

I returned to the front door and knocked. The woman answered. "Paul needs a clean shirt," I said. She turned without a word. She came back with a long-sleeved shirt and a sweater. "Here," she said. I took the clothes.

"Tell him the door wasn't locked," she said and shut it. I went to the backyard.

Paul had taken off his shirt and was gasping fishlike as he ran cold water from a garden hose over his head. He turned off the water and dried himself with the dirty shirt. I handed him the clean clothes. "She said to tell you the door wasn't locked," I said.

"It doesn't make any difference at this point anyway," he said. "I must be away from here. Where are you going? Take me with you."

The place was almost identical to the dive I'd been in the night before. Dirt parking lot, cinder block walls, a strip of squat windows mounted high along one wall, like a factory, covered with dirt and grease. The neighborhood had been old residential with some commercial intrusion. Twenty years ago everything had started going downhill together. A wood frame house sat next to the parking lot. The front porch was littered with obscure chunks of greasy metal. The roof over the porch was held up by a pair of spindly two by fours. A hand lettered sign was nailed to one of them. "Motors for Sell," it said.

The proprietor was unlocking the door. We followed him inside. He turned on the lights, went behind the bar, picked up the remote control and turned on the TV in the corner, and said "Whaddya want?" I got a Bloody Mary. Paul ordered two double whiskeys. The proprietor said, "Glad to have some early business. This recession keeps up they're gonna have to start calling it a fuckin' depression." We took the drinks to a booth.

Paul drank a third of a whiskey in one gulp. He put his arms up on the back of the booth and tilted his head back and stared at the ceiling. I took a drink of Bloody Mary and chewed some crackers. We didn't talk. We were both hung over and had little to say anyway.

The TV spat a steady stream of sound bites and factoids; neutrinos and gamma rays of a decaying civilization. News of an impending financial Armageddon stuttered in from New York and Washington. Markets in uncontrolled oscillations. Massive bankruptcies and defaults. Strikes and riots in Europe and Asia. Techno-war in the fertile crescent.

The bartender smoked and fidgeted. He picked up the remote control and scanned through the cable channels. He stopped on four bikini clad women whacking a volleyball in the sand. Pseudo-sport from the blessed golden coast. "Look at them honeys," he said. "Man, I could use a dip into something like that." An unbidden image of the bartender, streaked boxers at his ankles, conjoined with one of the sun goddesses flashed into my head. The image was disjointed. These people did not inhabit the same universe. The image dissolved.

Paul brought his head off the back of the booth and looked at me. "What have you been doing?" he said.

"Not very much. Working, for a change. It's horrible."

"Yeah," he said.

The phone rang. The bartender answered it. I watched his face contract into a deep scowl as he listened. "Well hey, I got bills to pay too, goddamnit!" he said. He listened some more. "You'll get your money in due time. Things are tough all over." A moment later he shouted, "Well screw you too, you goddamned greasy old hide!" and slammed the phone down on its hook. He placed both of his hands on the bar and stared at the spot between them for a minute. Then he snapped out of his reverie and looked at Paul and me. "Fellas, let me tell you something," he said. "I'd trade my ex-wife for a hangover, the clap, and a case of the drizzlin' shits any day. Yes sir, just any ole fuckin' day." He looked like he suffered from all three conditions. I wished he'd shut up.

"So what have you been up to?" I asked Paul.

"You mean, why was I sleeping in the Cad?" he said.

"I guess."

"I met this fine young lady. She's a cocktail waitress. We went to her place when she got off work. We tried to summon a djinn but it didn't work."

"Say what?"

"Yeah. She used to be married to an Arab. He taught her

how to do it. It's supposed to be kind of dangerous. You can't predict what kind of djinn you'll get. Sometimes it's a nasty one."

"That sounds like a load of horse crap," I said.

He shrugged. "Hell, I don't know. We were just playing around. As it turned out, we couldn't summon up anything. Too much booze. She took me home and told me to come back some other time. So I crapped out in the limo."

Shafts of sunlight streamed diagonally from the row of translucent windows and cast a geometric pattern on the floor. Dust and wisps of smoke were caught in the rays and lazily ascended to expire in the upper gloom. I went to the bar and bought refills and came back and sat down. I said, "What is your wife's opinion of these activities?"

"She doesn't have one, as far as I know. And if she does, I don't care to hear it. Look, she's part of the whole rotten gestalt. I've got to get away from it."

"By summoning a djinn?"

"No. You can laugh if you want but it was interesting. She drew this triangle on the floor with a piece of chalk and put a lighted candle at each vertex. Then you put something you think the djinn might want, like money, inside the triangle and command it to appear."

I drew a triangle on the black formica table top with the condensation from the cold glasses and put twenty six cents and a matchbook that said "Learn Electronics at Home" in the middle of it. I lit two matches and held one in each hand at two of the corners. Paul lit another match and held it at the third corner and commenced with a guttural chanting. The bartender glanced up and stared at us and then shook his head and went back to his TV watching. Just two more fuck-ups on the loose.

I tried to imagine Nastassja Kinski bearing a check for a million dollars with my name on it. I decided this was a little greedy and lowered it to ten thousand. The matches started to burn my fingers. I put them out. Paul quit chanting and wiped the triangle away with the sleeve of his shirt.

The door opened. A big lank haired woman, maybe forty five years old, wearing a heavy coat and carrying a large purse came in. She ignored Paul and me and went straight to the proprietor. He was sitting at the bar watching the television. He did a double take when he saw her. She walked up to him. "I come for my money," she said. He scowled but said nothing. Then he got off the stool, walked behind the bar, opened the cash register. He pulled out a few dollars and threw them on the bar. "Here. That's all I can spare. Take it and get out of here. You'll ruin what little business I got left," he said. The woman did not pick up the money but only glared at him. I saw her removing something from her purse, below the bar, where the man could not see it. It was a hammer. She launched a roundhouse swipe at his head. He saw it coming and jerked backwards against the terraced shelves of liquor bottles behind him. The hammer cleared his nose by an inch. A couple of fifths fell from the shelves and shattered on the floor. "Aw Jesus shit, honey," the man said. The woman reared back with the hammer held overhead like she was going to throw it at him. He ducked down behind the bar. With a speed that belied his appearance, he scampered to the door, jerked it open, and was gone. His ex-wife walked down the bar, smashing each ashtray with the hammer as she passed. She came to the end of the bar and went behind it to the cash register, opened it, pulled out the bills, threw the money tray on the floor, and struck the register half a dozen times. The bell rang after each strike. Next, she turned her efforts to the bottles arrayed behind her. Each one went sailing across the room to shatter against the wall. Paul and I gaped at each other. I couldn't decide whether to stay or run for my life so I stared at the table top to avoid eye contact. The woman broke dozens of glasses hanging from racks. She opened coolers and threw bottles of beer, ripped hoses loose, pounded fixtures into scrap. Finally, she walked back to the end of the bar, studied the lithe volleyballers on the TV for a moment, and then threw the hammer through the picture tube. It imploded with a loud pop. She walked to the door, still ignoring us, and opened it. Ten seconds passed. We looked up to see if she had left. She hadn't. She was standing in the doorway, staring at us. "What're you motherfuckers looking at?" she said. Then she turned and walked out.

Neither Paul or I spoke. After a minute, he got up and went behind the bar. Shards of broken glass snapped under his feet. He came back with a pint of whiskey that had somehow survived the onslaught, sat down, opened it. He took a slug straight from the bottle. "Well," he said. "That about sums it up, doesn't it? The beginning, middle, and end of subject. All items in the proof necessary and sufficient. The fundamental relation between men is violence. Take me to see Lisa, will you?"

We left. It was midafternoon. The scud had turned into a solid overcast and the temperature had dropped. Everything was monochromatic under the dimmed light of the sun. I drove him down to the club where Lisa, his girlfriend, was working. Paul said, "Two or three months from now I'll be out of here. I'll be up in a green valley on the banks of the Bitteroot. Lisa and I will be building our own house with our own hands. I'll fly fish, read, contemplate things. Maybe Lisa can get a job in town."

I pulled into the the graveled parking lot of the place. "The Carousel Club," said the sign. It was a dump on the edge of an old industrial section. Paul got out but before he shut the door he said, "So, what do you think of my plan?"

"I think you're fucking up," I said.

He stared at me for a second and then without a word shut the door and walked away. The lizard beast in its black El Dorado wheeled into the lot as I was going out. It stared at me. I stared back. I felt no chill this time. It was like seeing an old friend.

Driving home I was struck, as always, by the seamless blight that surrounded me. A solid interlocking grid of streets, cars, power lines, signs, broken concrete and asphalt, peeling paint, buckled walls. Was this only a small glitch in the otherwise steady march to technological utopia? I thought not. I thought the future held only more ugliness, more decay, more rancor, more violence. I returned to my three room flop.

I ran a hot bath, lit a cigarette and got in. I awoke from a nightmare a few minutes later. A robed man was pounding a fire hardened stake through my chest. There was a small red spot in the middle of it. The soggy half smoked cigarette floated in the water. Someone was pounding on the door. I didn't answer it and they finally went away. I got out of the bathtub, ate some soup, listened to Mozart, and dozed off.

In the early evening I got up from my chair and went to bed. I pulled the covers over my head. Another stupid weekend was over. Another pointless week was about to begin.

THE JOB:

Monday came grey and cold. I scraped ice off the windshield and drove to the traffic jam. Waiting for a light to change, I studied the zombies in the cars alongside mine. All of them alone, semi-conscious, benumbed for the horrors of the coming work week.

The office seemed unnaturally bright, like a hothouse, after the outer gloom. Instead of the usual Monday morning somnambulance the place was buzzing with frenetic activity. This was the big day. The money men would be here soon. I got a cup of coffee and hid in my cubicle.

I was worried about the meeting but for a reason that was diametrically opposed to the reasons of Billings and the others. If the money couldn't be obtained the expansion would not happen and I would be let go. This was what I wanted. I was looking forward to a mellow winter cozied up in my flop, braving the elements only long enough to collect my unemployment checks. If, on the other hand, the expansion proceeded, I had a suspicion they would offer me permanent employment. I would refuse it. But this would create problems when I applied for unemployment benefits after turning down a job offer.

Billings poked his head into the cubicle. "You seen Teresa?" he asked. His eyes flicked around. The Las Vegas weekend had not calmed him.

"No," I said.

"Goddamnit! The bitch is late again. She's treading a thin line. A goddamn thin line." He went away. I drank coffee, stared at the wall.

Five minutes later he was back. "Listen," he said, "the meeting's going to start and I need someone to flip the charts. I want you to do it since Teresa's not here. I'm going to fire her for this. It's the end of the line for that bitch." I got up and followed him. The charts were neatly stacked on Teresa's desk. About fifty transparent reproductions of graphs, tables, and rosy predictions that Billings would use in his attempt to wheedle some dough from the money boys. I picked them up and Billings and I went into the still empty meeting room. I turned on the overhead projector, focused it on the screen, and put up the first chart. Billings picked up a pointer. "Change it when I tap like this," he said and tapped the pointer on the table top.

The group filed in and sat down. Introductions were made. There was the Mongoose, the division manager, a couple of factotums from the corporate office, and a half dozen slickers in shiny shoes and 800 dollar suits. Last but not least there was Mr. Hashimoto, a huge neckless toad of a man. He sat by himself in the rear, unsmiling, and nodded almost imperceptibly as the group was presented to him. I was not introduced. It went without saying I was only the chart flipper, a nameless flunky. Someone turned off the overhead light. We began.

Billings launched into his spiel. The growing demand for the various widgets manufactured by the company, the need for more efficient production equipment, the demonstrated ability of the company to control its labor costs. The money men sat without expression. I could not imagine how anyone could be remotely interested in this. I started to daydream. I thought about Janice. Maybe I would go back to see her. We could trade Frank Billings stories. Billings rapped hard with the pointer and brought me out of the reverie. I flipped up another chart. He glared at me for an instant and continued. A few charts later he quit talking. There was some subdued chuckling among the members of the group. I turned around and looked at the chart displayed on the screen. In large neat letters it said:

> I'VE MARRIED A WONDERFUL MAN AND
> I WON'T BE BACK.
> ALL YOU STUFFED SHIRTS CAN GO TO HELL.
>   TERESA

Hooray for Teresa. Billings quickly recovered. "Just the prank of a disgruntled former clerical employee, gentlemen," he said. I put up the next chart. Billings did not begin speaking. I turned and looked at the screen. Maybe I'd put up the wrong chart. It was a reproduction of two newspaper clippings. "Mayhem on Beacon Hill" one was titled. The other said "Husband Mutilator Released." The room was silent. I started reading. I heard a noise like someone was choking. It was the Mongoose. She was standing up and pointing at the screen in a mute fury and going "Auckkk! Auckkk! Auckkk!". Then she gave it up and ran wildly out of the room. Everyone read the clippings.

    Ten years before, when Laura Colby was an executive on the fast track in Boston and married to an equally fast track lawyer, she had been made aware of the numerous and ongoing affairs of her husband. This information had infuriated her. So, in her direct and methodical manner, she had solved the problem by using her Marine knife to amputate the offending member while hubby lay sleeping. Then she had flushed it down the toilet where it could torment her no more. The philanderer awoke, chagrined, and drove his bleeding self to the hospital. The Mongoose had been jailed, found unfit for trial, and released from a mental institution five years later. The crazy woman hadn't even bothered to change her name.

The room was silent. I looked up at Billings. He was swelled and grinning. His mortal enemy had just been struck down by a stroke of incredible luck. "Proceed please," intoned the division manager. I put up the next chart.

We still weren't back to the presentation. This was a photograph. It filled the entire screen. Frank Billings stood in the center of it. He looked anxiously over his shoulder as he poured the coffee money out of the collection jar and into a large envelope.

"Waaaaa! Ha ha ha ha. Waaaaa! Ha ha ha ha," laughed Mr. Hashimoto. He found the photograph amusing. I looked at the group. Next to Mr. Hashimoto sat the lizard beast. Its body shook with silent mirth. The tongues and genitalia quivered. The assholes winked. I looked up at Frank. He stood reddening, dumbfounded, his eyes beginning the nervous tracking that signalled the onset of a full blown fit. "For God's sake turn it off," someone said. I flicked off the projector. We sat in the dark. "Waaaaa! Ha ha ha ha."

Dick leaves work. He gets into his silver grey saab 874s (le) with full digital instrumentation, anti-lock braking system and moon roof. It is one of the perks. He drives out of the lot.

It has been a no sale day. One tire kicker in the afternoon. The guy came into the showroom, walked around a car, opened a door. Dick sat in his office with his feet on the desk, rolled a toothpick from one side of his mouth to the other, watched. The guy finally left. The sales manager came in and asked Dick why he had not sold the man. So Dick told him. It was obvious the guy was not a player. Definitely not in the market for a high performance machine. He was wearing a suit that looked like it had come from k-mart, for Christ's sake. Why waste your time? The manager shrugged his shoulders and went back to his office. Dick is his number one producer so he does not bother him much.

FUN WITH DICK AND JANE

On the street an ambulance comes up flashing behind Dick. He pulls to the side to let it pass. Further down the traffic starts to jam up. A wreck. A cop is waving one lane through. Dick slows down and looks. A corvette has left the road and collided head on with a steel light pole. The pole is cleaved into the front of the car almost to the dashboard. Two spidery hemispherical bumps, like melon halves, punctuate the windshield. The medics are loading stretchers into the ambulance. Nice car, thinks Dick. Or was. He drives home.

Someone has put some trash at the entrance to Dick's complex. It is a 24 piece from the colonel. They ate the meat off the bones and then threw everything out. The synthetic mashed potatoes are smeared along the curb. The chicken bones, plastic ware, and paper napkins are strewn ten feet down the gutter. A car has run over the cardboard bucket. There is a tire track across the colonel's little goateed face. I really hate that shit, thinks Dick. He parks and enters his condominium.

Jane is in her nurse's uniform, watching a tape of Oprah and eating fries and a strawberry shake from burger king have it your way. She tapes Oprah everyday and watches it when she gets off. Two transsexuals, male and female, have married and are describing to Oprah the bad experiences they have had in trying to adopt a child. "They just look at us like we are some kind of freaks," says the lantern jawed wife. The mousey husband nods in solemn agreement.

Dick goes into the kitchen. He notices, with some slight irritation, that Jane has purchased caffeine free coke again. It is not the real thing.

Dick puts some nachos in the microwave. When they are ready he takes them to the nintendo. He plays super mario II for four hours but can not get past the third level.

Dick goes upstairs. Jane is in panties and headphones on the nautilus in front of the three way mirror. Dick turns on leno. He flops on the bed and watches Jane exercise. She has the minimum weights on the machine but still she huffs and strains to move it. Her biceps are thin. Dick can see blue veins beneath the chalky pale skin. All of her ribs can be counted. Her breasts stare at the ceiling.

Leno is a drag so Dick flips to cheers. Jane quits exercising and goes downstairs. Dick flips through a catalog from international male. He circles the numbers on some french cut bikini underwear he wants. Jane comes back with a spoon, a tube of pillsbury super fudge cookie dough, and a box of rondos. She looks idly at cheers while she sucks on a rondo and eats spoonfuls of dough. She finishes eating the dough tube and leafs through a catalog of bleached furniture.

Dick eats Jane. He thinks of the sushi taco he had for lunch at casa de yokohama. The young waitress. The way a curl of hair came down across her forehead. Maybe next time he will try some soy sauce.

Jane eats Dick. She thinks of a budweiser commercial. The one where the girl shakes up a longneck and sprays it into her boyfriend's face.

Dick wakes up in the middle of the night. Jane is not in the bed. Dick can hear her in the bathroom, softly wretching. He goes downstairs and opens a drawer in a desk and finds his last one and a half lines of coke. He sniffs them up and feels better. He goes into the kitchen and pours himself three fingers of cold stoly. He sits in the dark and drinks it. A police siren is wailing nearby. When it stops, Dick can hear another siren in the distance. Then a third one starts up closer. They howl all night like wolves.

On Friday Dick scores big. A doctor, a plastic surgeon, half popped, comes in at closing time and Dick sells him a mercedes 450 sl. He sells him the preferred customer maintenance package. He sells him the 70,000 mile drive train package and the corrosion control package. The doctor drives off in the car with a young woman who Dick thinks is not the doctor's wife. It is time for a celebration.

Dick runs errands. He buys more nachos. He stops at a liquor store and buys a case of kirin, a quart of drambuie, and a fifth of stoly. He stops at another place and buys three grams of peruvian blue flake.

On the way home there is a car in front of Dick. It is an

ancient chevy that has been beaten almost to death. The chevy is hogging both lanes. One rear wheel has been bent so severely that it deviates six inches laterally with each rotation. This causes the chevy to wag its sagging back end as it moves down the street.

Dick tries to pass the chevy on the right. There is not enough room. Dick tries to pass the chevy on the left. It lurches sideways. Dick downshifts, screams into the oncoming lane, comes up alongside the chevy, honks his horn, and glares at the occupants. The swarthy Mexican man driving gives Dick the finger. The man's fat wife gives Dick the finger. All the man's five or six children packed into the back seat give Dick the finger.

Dick sees red. The chevy is behind him now. He reaches over and takes his stainless steel .357 magnum revolver in its black genuine eelskin holster out of his glovebox. I will kill that greasy wetback, Dick thinks. I will kill his whole dirty family. The chevy turns off on a sidestreet. Dick cools down. He puts the gun back in the glove box. He drives home.

Dick and Jane go to casa de yokohama with Tyler and Jan. Jane in halston, Dick in international male, Tyler in lauren, Jan in torn calvins and nose rings. Tyler has sushi tacos, Jan has stacked octopus enchiladas, Jane nibbles at a salad of sprouts, leeks, and capers, Dick eats Mexican hamburger. When they are finished they go to Dick and Jane's for fun.

Dick and Jane and Tyler and Jan snort peruvian blue flake. They drink kirins and stoly, they eat quaaludes Jane has lifted from work. They watch MTV.

Upstairs, Dick meets Jan coming out of the bathroom. He leads Jan into the bedroom. He pulls off Jan's torn calvins. Dick takes Jan quickly, from behind, on the nautilus in front of the three way. Jan, luded, stretches out and watches the action in the mirror, grinning.

Downstairs, in the kitchen, Tyler is talking to Jane. "I'm worried about Jan," Tyler says. "I call home from the office and no one answers. I ask him later where he was and he's real evasive." Jan has lived with Tyler since the day two weeks ago she picked him up hitch hiking on federal boulevard.

"He's so cute," she says. "Look, I know he's bi. I can live with that," she says. "It's just, you know, with AIDS, and everything."

Jane is barely listening. She is leafing through a people, looking at the pictures. She thinks maybe she has taken half a quaalude too much. A small trickle of saliva edges from the corner of her mouth.

Dick and Jan are downstairs now, watching TV. "That bitch is on my case, man," Jan says. "It's 'get a job, get a job,' man. She's starting to bust my balls. This is a bum town for an artist, man. Really. A bum town," he says. Dick doesn't pay any attention to him. Tyler and Jan finally leave.

Dick and Jane copulate in front of a video camera. The next night they watch the tape on their monitor. This time they set it up so they can watch themselves in action, Dick mounting Jane from behind, while the camera records them.

Soon they have four monitors. They can watch last week's tape, yesterday's tape, live action, letterman doing his monologue. They do it missionary style, dog style, santa fe style. Dick and Jane on the nautilus in front of the threeway. The camera is aimed at the mirrors to record an infinity of Dicks and Janes. Dick snorts coke. Jane eats

225

dough. The bank of monitors sings like a Greek chorus. It is winter and business is slow. Dick takes days off. One day Jane calls in sick. Nothing serious, just a case of the blahs. Dick is wandering in the basement of the condo. He finds the abandoned remains of an attempted hobby; he was going to refurbish an antique hand cranked telephone. He places his finger across the terminals of the generator, spins the crank, feels a small tingle in his hand. Dick has an idea.

Upstairs, Dick is on top of Jane. A wire runs from a generator terminal to Jane's anus. Another wire runs to Dick's. They copulate. Dick spins the crank. Jane feels needles sticking into her body. Dick spins the crank again. "Whoooeee!" goes Dick. "Whoooeee!" Jane sees spots. Her heart twists frantically beneath her ribs.

IN THOSE DAYS

In those days I would lie in bed until eleven when Diana came home from her morning classes. I refused to get up until she had made a pot of coffee and rolled a big Bull Durham cigarette for me. Then I would get out of bed, put on a frayed bathrobe, and sit at my writing table drinking coffee and staring out the window while Diana got ready for work. She was a waitress at a Mexican restaurant.

At first, Diana had balked at performing these simple chores for me. She told me I was lazy and that I should get up earlier and make my own coffee. So I'd tricked her. I had stayed in bed until she had gone to her job. Then I'd gotten up and had my usual day but before Diana came home late that night I took off the bathrobe and got back in bed. I told her I had been incapacitated by her lack of attention, that there was no way I could write without her support, that if she loved me she would help me in my creative efforts. She finally agreed. After all, she was going to be the wife of a famous writer.

The plan was simple. I had quit school to write a novel. Diana, my bride of two months, had agreed to support us during the six months I calculated this effort would consume. By the end of the summer, at the latest, the novel would be sold, I would have the advance, and next winter Diana and I would be in the Caribbean, lolling in the sun, and making an occasional visit to the post office to pick up my royalty checks. Often that winter, sitting at my writing table, the sky a slate grey and the wind blowing sleet outside, I would pull out the travel brochures Diana had brought home and leaf through them. They featured shots of luscious women in bikinis romping on pristine beaches of white sand and turquoise water. We had to decide between Montego Bay or Negril Beach.

I had developed a small coterie of admirers. Since I was a serious writer and they were mere college students this was only natural. Around seven o'clock they would begin to arrive. They'd roll their joints, put some rock and roll on the phono, and begin their standard tirades about what a fucked up country was the good old U.S.A. Even at that time I was not so self-deluded to believe they visited my duplex for any reason other than they had no where else to go. Most of them lived in the dorms and the rest were locals who still lived with their parents.

Sometimes I'd smoke some of their grass with them just to be sociable. I thought it was probably ok stuff if you had to dig ditches or work on an assembly line all day. But for writing, it was worthless. The muse didn't live in a reefer. She lived in bottles of dago red.

One of these guys was named Timmy. He was the richest and hippest of the bunch and also the loudest complainer. He wore his hair down to the middle of his back, had a fu manchu moustache, and carried a leather bag hooked to his belt, sort of like a hippie purse, stuffed full of reefer.

One night Timmy showed up without his purse and with a tale of police harassment and brutality. The "pigs" had collared him and "ripped off" his smoke. But they'd get theirs' one day soon. Come the revolution, the "movement" would take care of them. I thought Timmy should have considered himself lucky. Possession was still a felony then. I couldn't understand why he wasn't ensconced at the county jail, listening to the babble of the inmates all night and breathing that fine ape house air.

Two nights later Timmy was back with his leather bag

and reefer. He declined to relate the story of how he'd retrieved his purse. After he left, one of the others clued me in. Timmy had been found passed out drunk in his car near his parents' house. It wasn't the police who'd discovered him. It was a private security guard hired by the rich suburb where Timmy lived with his parents. The guard had simply taken Timmy and his reefer home to Timmy's mother and washed his hands of the matter. Timmy had brow beaten his mother for two days until she relented and gave his purse back to him.

Diana kept me on a tight budget. Needless to say, I had no compunction in cadging money from members of the club. Around nine o'clock I'd suggest a wine run. I'd take up a collection, get out of the bathrobe and dress for the first time that day, and make a solo errand to the liquor store. Here, while the Lebanese proprietor watched my every move, I'd select three bottles of rotgut and surreptitiously peel the sticker off a higher priced bottle. On the way home I'd put the sticker on one bottle and hide the other two in a bush beside the front door. At midnight, when the club disbanded for the evening, I'd fetch the hidden bottles and guzzle them in peace. I was having trouble with the writing. If I drank enough wine, I thought, the genii of the grape might come out and give me a hand.

Along with the usual pre-digested mush that passed for scholarship at the University, Diana was enrolled in a course called "Women in Society." One day, bored, I picked up the textbook for this class. It was perturbing. It appeared to have been written by a coven of hysterical Lesbians. I spent the rest of the afternoon amusing myself by erasing and rewriting sections of the book in a sneering and sarcastic fashion.

Three days later, the first day of Spring with the slush melting in the gutters, I realized there might be trouble brewing in paradise. It was Monday. The restaurant was closed so Diana usually spent the evening studying at the library. The club was in session. At eleven o'clock the door to our duplex burst open and Diana, face grey with anger, strode directly across the room and walloped me over the head with the Women in Society textbook. "That's for messing up my book, you sexist pig," she said. Then she stomped away and slammed the bedroom door shut. The members of the club were aghast to see their leader treated in such a rude manner. With hastily mumbled goodbyes, they left. Diana might be on the verge of a nervous breakdown, I thought. And what was a sexist pig? I was worried.

Things went downhill from there. The trouble was the writing. It wasn't going anywhere. I kept trying to jump start it with large amounts of wine but that didn't seem to be working. I was in an almost permanent vegetative state. Our marriage suffered. Even though I was young, twenty one, and willing, whenever Diana was home I was usually too drunk to sustain an erection. Diana got crankier and crankier.

One night she came home in an exceptionally foul humor. Mr. Mendoza, the owner of the restaurant, had placed his hand on her butt. "The Movement," Diana said, would take care of the likes of Mr. Mendoza one of these days.

Six weeks passed. Diana and I hardly spoke anymore. I continued to drink. Still, the genii refused to budge from his hidy hole. The semester was ending. It was the middle of Spring. Birds chirped in the trees, dandelions sprouted in our little front yard. One bright blue Sunday morning

Diana called me into the front room. Usually I would have ignored her and stayed in bed but some odd timbre in her voice caused me to get up. I put on the frayed bathrobe and straggled to her. She wanted to read me something she had written. I sat down, bleary eyed, hair askew, a taste like rancid cheese in my mouth, and listened. It was her term paper for the Women in Society class, the riot act, and a bill of divorcement. In accurate and exacting detail she described the sins I had committed against her and against our marriage during the six months we had been together. Everything from ridiculing her in front of other people to insulting her parents to pissing on the toilet seat and not bothering to clean it up. I sat half awake and nodded in agreement. It was true. I was a sexist pig.

Two weeks later the uncontested emergency divorce was finalized. Diana got the main asset from our marriage, a beaten up little Datsun. I packed up my clothes, some ashtrays, and my twelve pages of manuscript and moved to a room on the edge of downtown, away from the University. I took a job at the municipal sewer works and began my education. Diana packed up the Datsun and headed off to Berkeley. I never heard from her again.

After Diana left town one of her friends told me Diana had not been faithful to her matrimonial vows. For most of our marriage she'd been getting some on the side with one of her academic acquaintances. An assistant professor in the Administration of Justice department. I was angry when I heard this but eventually I came to think it was funny.

A few months later Timmy gave up on the revolution and committed suicide. That was years ago. Some of the real revolutionaries are still around. They don't work, they don't vote, they don't buy anything, and they don't pay taxes. You can see them of an evening in certain parts of town, sleeping in doorways and alleys. And as far as movements go, a bowel movement is still the best one I've found.

It was after the kids came that night about two weeks ago and broke his jaw that Arnie finally did it. That was a particularly bad night. Sometimes they leave us alone for two or three months. Then lookout, here they are, a small mob of them, throwing rocks and bricks, BUMS pieces of pipe, anything they can lay their hands on or bring with them from the towers. Tearing at the kraal we've put up, trying to get at us. Like a pack of wild dogs.

Of course, they are all young ones. They get their sex cards at fourteen and their drug cards at sixteen so then they have other things to do. But those twelve and thirteen year olds, man, they are nasty little bastards. Most of them aren't very big and they look real pale and puny. Maybe it's some kind of stuff they take, I don't know, but they're as vicious and mean as a cornered alley cat.

That particular night they managed to break a hole in the kraal and get inside the compound. Like the rest of us in there, Arnie had a piece of sheet metal he was using for a shield to keep from being pulverized by the rocks and bricks they were throwing. He said one of them, a big one, came at him with an iron rod he was using like a sword. Arnie was trying to fend the bastard off with the shield when this other little shit, he said it was a girl, swatted him upside the head with a piece of pipe. Arnie went down then and he thought they were going to kill him, but instead they just stood there and looked at him lying on the ground and then walked off.

I tell you these fuckers are weird. They never scream or yell or say anything unless you hit them pretty good and then they'll usually quit. They lose interest real fast. Sometimes they'll be coming at you with that insane glint in their eye and then stop and blink and drop their brick or rock or whatever and turn around and head back for the towers. It's like some signal only they can sense comes on or goes off in their heads. Strange creatures. I guess they're human like us but I'm not entirely convinced. Everybody always says, "Oh, don't hurt them too bad or kill them. There'll be hell to pay. The Authorities burned out a kraal two years ago after that happened." Well I say bullshit. They can kill us, right? And get away with it. After all, we're bums.

 The next morning I heard about Arnie and went over to see him. He was hurt pretty bad. Somebody'd got some tape and tried to set his jaw bone. His face was swelled up real bad on one side. He mumbled when he tried to talk but if you listened real close you could make out what he was saying. He told me he was going to get converted. I said, "Arnie, you've been saying that for a couple of years now and you still haven't done it so I don't believe even you're that big a fool. Quit talking that shit. Your jaw'll heal up." He said again he was going to do it so I got up and left.

 I know a busted jaw must hurt like hell but Arnie always was a whiner. That's probably because he's one of the few around here that just got canceled out one day. He went to his occupation and he couldn't get in. The machine told him he was dead. So he went back to his tower. He couldn't get in there either. He'd been canceled out. Some kind of computer fuck up, I guess. He hung around the complex for the rest of the day until the Authorities ran him off. He came over here and he's been here ever since. That was two years ago. He never saw his unit partner again. Or his kids. I think he said he had some. Maybe they're part of this bunch that comes over here and messes with us. Everybody has their own story. Most of them just got tired of the complex and their occupation and their unit partner and walked off one day.

I spent the rest of that day with Jane, grubbing for food and things down along the creek. We came back late in the afternoon. Arnie was gone.

Things settled back to normal, at least as normal as they ever were. More people from the towers showed up. A whole family. They said their consumption cards had been canceled. The dispensing machines had told them they were deceased. They all had a haunted grey look about them, like old pictures of war refugees I'd seen a long time ago. After a few days the couple left their kids with us and went over to the complex to see if they could get things straightened out. They didn't favor the idea of staying here. They were too used to the soft life. A few hours later they came back. The man had a broken arm, compliments of a mechoid that'd caught him trying to pry open a door into the towers.

Two weeks went by and Arnie didn't return. I started getting curious about what had become of him. I figured he was probably dead. Anyway, one afternoon I got a bad itch to go snooping so I decided to go look for Arnie, or whatever he'd become. I walked into the industrial containment zone. The place was totally deserted of people. Nothing moved anywhere except for an occasional mechoid in the distance repairing a building or carrying something or just standing stock still for minutes on end in that spooky way they have. I knew where Arnie might be because I'd been there once before with a guy who was dying and thought it was his last chance.

I finally got to the place, just another drab low slung

module. The doors were locked. I walked around the building trying the doors until I found one that opened. I went in. There was a long hall dimly lit by hundreds of overhead glowing cubes. I walked to the end of it and opened a door.

A man sat at a desk. He was the first square I'd seen in a long time. He looked up, surprised. He was pasty looking with watery pink rimmed eyes. He said, "Yes?"

I said, "I came to get converted."

He said, "Well. That's what we're here for. You'll have to fill out some forms and take some tests before we can process you, of course."

I said, "I know."

The man fidgeted around and pulled out a cigarette. He opened a drawer on his desk. He took out a form and stared at it awhile and then put it back. He said, "Stay here. I'll be back."

He got up and left. I couldn't figure what was wrong with the guy. Maybe it scared him to be alone with me. I went out the door he'd used and walked down another dimly lit corridor, trying the doors to see if they were locked.

I might as well tell you now what they did here. What they do is take out your brain and put it in a weapon. Yes, I know, you say they've got all kinds of smart computers and things for that. Had them for years. I guess it's not that simple. From little bits and pieces I've picked up there are problems with smart machines. You can make them as smart as you want but there's one thing you can't program in. They just don't fundamentally care all that much if they stay alive or not. Not like a cornered rat or a fish on the hook or a person fighting the kids. They don't have a will to live. Anyway, those smart machines aren't all that reliable and they're expensive as all get out. It's cheaper to just cut the head off a bum.

I found an unlocked door and went in. There was a huge bay dimly lighted like the halls. It was filled with these tank things. Each one had a long barrel coming out of a turret on top. One long row of them. Heavy steel tracks. Thick bundles of cable came down from the ceiling and plugged into the top of each tank. They were all sitting in the same position with the barrel pointed forward and drooped down. Nothing moved. It was quiet. All I could hear was the sound of my own footsteps. I stopped in the midst of them and hollered out, "Arnie! Hey, Arnie!"

I saw a barrel jerk up on a tank several yards down. The turret swiveled around towards me. I walked over to it. I said, "That you, Arnie?"

It said, "Yeah. How you doin'?"

I said, "Oh, ok, I guess. How do you like it here?"

It said, "Oh, fine. Just fine. I can get anything I want in here. I humped Traci Teh last night."

I said, "Well, how about that."

Traci Teh was the new star of the season. A cyborg, full modified. Hell, she was probably just a simulation. That's about the only way Arnie could've humped her. He could hump her all night. It's hard to wear out a computer program.

Arnie said, "Yeah. She was real nice."

I said, "Well, I've been with Jane down on the creek. That's pretty nice too."

Arnie said, "Jane. The creek. Shit. Old beat out hag. Dirty fuckin' creek. I'm glad I'll never see that place again. Me and Traci do it on satin sheets. And tonight I'm gonna hump Marilyn Monroe."

I said, "Well Arnie, Traci Teh, I guess you could do whatever you wanted with her. But Marilyn's a real woman. At least she was, she's been dead sixty some odd years. How are you going to hump her?"

He said, "The same way you would, goddamnit. Take her in my arms and put my dick in her."

I said, "Well, I just don't know about that, Arnie. You don't have any arms now. Much less a dick and balls."

A screeching whine penetrated out conversation. Arnie had started the tank engine. The tank jerked forward. I had to jump back to keep from getting hit. Arnie rotated the turret around. I was looking down the barrel.

"How'd you like to get blown back down to your filthy kraal?" he said.

"Well, I guess I really wouldn't, Arnie," I answered.

"Or fried with an eight KW plasma round?"

"Same thing Arnie. I really don't think I'd appreciate it."

A couple of sweat beads were rolling down the side of my face. It seemed a lot hotter in there.

"Then shut the fuck up about me and Marilyn. You unnerstand? I never liked you anyway."

"Sure Arnie. Sure. Anything you say. Just lower the barrel, ok?"

He put the barrel down and shut off the engine. I'd had no idea he had control over the machine without someone first turning it on for him.

I said, "Hey, Arnie. What about your buddies in here. Ever talk to them?"

"Nah. They don't talk," he said.

"Why not?"

"Hell, I don't know. Guess they got better things to do. Now go away. Yer startin' to bother me."

I thought for a minute.

"Say, Arnie," I asked, "how's come you can start that thing?"

"What d'you mean? It's mine now, ain't it?"

"Ever take it out for a spin?"

"Course not. I'd have to leave my umbilical."

"Well what'd they put you in it for then? Fighting a war?"

"No. There ain't no more wars. You oughta know that. Puttin down riots and things. Get outta here. I'm tired a talkin'."

"Ok," I said. "But say, if you ever get tired of just sitting around, why don't you and your buddies come down and help us out with the kids."

"Shit. Maybe I'll think about it."

"Ok then. Take it easy."

He grunted. I left. I went outside. Night was coming down. Jesus I was glad to get out of that spook house.

I walked back to the kraal through the fading twilight. Things were bothering me. Things seemed to be going a little more haywire all the time. More people showing up at the kraal, kicked out of their units or just tired of it. Rows of tanks sitting in warehouses for riots or something that haven't happened in twenty years.

The kraal fires looked friendlier than usual as I approached. Maybe I'd get up a little delegation and go back and try to talk Arnie and his friends into attacking the towers. It seemed like a good idea.

They say I did it. I guess I did. I mean, this hand pulled the trigger. I don't deny it. These eyes were looking out, telling the hand where to point it. But I'm not sure these are my hands. For a long time, ever since I was a kid, I'd sit and wiggle my fingers and try to decide what was making them move. Was it me or was it just sort of happening by itself? Or I'd look in a mirror and make all kinds of twisted faces. I'm not sure that was me doing that or looking back. Maybe it's too hard to explain.

A KILLING

The day started out shittier than most. There I was, having one awesome dream. I was about ready to ball this chick in study hall. That's what I do in study hall, mostly. Think about balling chicks. Cindy or something her name is, I don't know. Suddenly this monster grabs me and starts shaking me and saying "Honey, it's time to get up. Honey, it's time to get up." Everything turns to shit. It's the old lady. She goes away and I get down deeper in the covers, trying to bring back the dream. It's no good. It's gone. The radio man is mouthing some shit about the weather. I lay there. The old lady comes back in awhile and says "Get up now! You're going to be late for school again!" This really pisses me off. I rear up in the bed and yell "Shut the fuck up, bitch!" She screams and runs out of the room.

I can hear her in the kitchen, cursing and throwing shit around. She comes back in a few minutes and starts pounding me with a broom. I'm down under the covers so it doesn't hurt. She's really mad. "Get up you worthless little ungrateful bastard!" she screams. "I wish to God I'd had an abortion! I've had enough! I want you out of here. Tonight! Move back in with your father. You bastards can live together!"

She stomps out of the room again screaming. She's

having a fit. She starts breaking dishes in the kitchen and yelling and cursing me and the old man and about everyone else. I don't think she likes her job, either. She's a secretary for some asshole somewhere. She finally leaves the house. I stay in bed and sleep some more.

    A couple hours later the phone rings. I get up and answer it. It's Itchy. He says he's got a line on some dust if I can come up with fifty. Good stuff he says. The dork's at school. I tell him I'll pick him up at 11:30 lunch break. I get some cereal and flip on the tube. I sit there and munch and watch these poor schmucks from Anytown, USA make asses of themselves just so they can win a new washing machine. The host makes all kinds of snide remarks and really puts the shit on them. They don't get it. I'd like to go there and sit in the front row. Wait till the host and the schmucks get going. Then jump up on the stage with an automatic rifle. Unload on all those idiots right on national TV. It'd be hilarious.

    I've got to find some money. I go into the old lady's bedroom and root around in the dresser drawers. Here it is. Right next to a vibrator and under a bottle of vodka. A nice one hundred. I take the money and the booze.

    Sometimes I feel sorry for the old lady. She hasn't done so well since dad left. Like these clowns she drags home. I can always tell when she's got a date with one of them. She gives me some money and says stay out as late as you want. What she means is: don't come home at all. She'd rather the clowns didn't know she had a seventeen year old son. But sometimes I do come home late. There's usually an Olds or Caddy parked in the drive. I get up in the morning and here's some dude sitting there with a cup of coffee and a mean hangover. Fucking loafers and slacks and a polyester shirt and a permanent. Smelling like a French whorehouse.

Poseurs and phonies. They glare at me and I glare back. Most of them I never see again.

It's time to get Itchy. I go out and get in my car. The old man left me the boat when he split. About the only thing he ever gave me. He's dead as far as I'm concerned. He doesn't exist. But the boat's a good one. Full power, air. I fire it up and take off.

Itchy's standing on the curb in front of Metro. He gets in.

"What's up, chump?" I say.

"Oh man, it's a drag," he says.

"Yeah it is. Why bother?"

"You know."

"Shit."

We drive down the street. "So? Where's the dust?" I say.

"This guy goes to Reagan Prep. I called him. He's home. Way out on the westside."

We go out there. It's a long way. The houses out there are like mansions. Dumb poor kids like me and Itchy go to Metro. Dumb rich kids go to Reagan Prep. We pull into this big circular driveway at one of the mansions. We get out and ring the doorbell. This black woman opens the door. "Daniel here?" says Itchy. She doesn't say anything, just shuts the door. A minute later this guy wearing mirrored shades opens the door a crack. Itch says, "Hey, Daniel. I brought my partner." Daniel doesn't say anything. He looks at me and kind of nods. He opens the door wider and we follow him inside. We go up to his room. Daniel says, "Whose got the bread?"

"I got it," I say. "You got the change?"

This Daniel guy just stands there and stares at me through his mirrored shades. "You come with me," he says to Itchy. "You stay here," he says to me. They leave. I don't like this Daniel prick. I look around his room. It's like as big as our living room with its own bathroom and everything. And it's stuffed full of shit. Fucking guitars and amplifiers all over the place. A huge stereo with gigantic speakers. Head banger posters and cuntbook centerfolds on the walls. Two TVs. I sit down in a chair next to Daniel's bed. I hope we don't get ripped off.

Then I see it. The stock of a gun sticking out from under the bed. I reach down and pull it out. It's not a gun it's this bitchin fucking crossbow. It's got a steel bow and a steel cable string. There's a metal cannister hooked underneath. I open it up and it's full of these nasty looking little aluminum arrows. The thing's got a lever built in for cocking it. I crank back the string and put an arrow in the slot. I'm sitting facing the door. This fucking Daniel's going to freak when he comes in and sees a loaded crossbow pointed at his balls. I want this thing. It's the only thing worth a shit in this whole fucking room. I get a window open, I get the screen pushed off, I throw the crossbow out.

Itchy and Daniel come back. Itchy's sniffing and rubbing his nose. "It's good shit," he says.

"How much?" I say.

"Sixty," says Daniel.

"Itchy said fifty."

"Take it or leave it," he says.

I give him the hundred. He pulls out a wallet and hands me two twenties. Me and Itchy walk down the stairs. Daniel stays in his room. When we get outside I make a quick detour around the side of the house. The crossbow's lying in a bed of tulips. I hold it in front of me so nobody can see

it from the house and walk to the car. We get in and I put it in the backseat.
"You steal that from Daniel?" Itchy says.
"Oh no, man. I just found it lying there."
"Daniel's going to be pissed."
"So fuck Daniel. You don't know anything, right?"
"Yeah. Ok. Let's go get some .45."
We cruise back into town. Itch taps out some dust and we both huff a load. I put in an Anthrax tape. We pull up behind this greasy spoon. This friend of Itchy's brother eats lunch there. He buys us booze for a fee. Itch goes in. A while later he comes out and gets back in the car. "He'll do it as soon as he's done eating," he says. The guy comes out, goes in the liquor store next door, and comes out with a sack and comes over to Itchy's side. "Two six packs of Colt .45," he says. "Fifteen dollars."
"Hey, man. It used to be ten," says Itchy.
"The price went up."
Itchy looks at me. I dig out a twenty. The guy takes it and hands back a five. He turns and walks back into the greasy spoon.
"That son of a bitch," Itchy says.
"Let's put him down," I say.
"Huh?"
"The crossbow. Let's wait here and nail him with it when he comes out."
"You're a crazy motherfucker. Let's go."
I put in some AC/DC. We drive down to the normal high school. There's this fine looking bitch strutting on the sidewalk. Itchy takes a big slurp of .45 and leans out and asks her if she'd like to sit on his face. She starts walking faster.

He asks her if she's ever been fucked dog style. She turns around and walks the other way. I throw out an empty can. He hands me another one. He takes his empty and stomps it flat and tells me to drive real close to this line of parked cars. He leans out and uses a sharp edge on the can to scratch each car as we drive past. He really gets them good, clear down to bare metal. We go a couple blocks like this. Somebody's yelling at us. Itchy says he needs some cigarettes. We go to a 7-11. We go into the restroom. The toilet lid is down and Itchy doesn't want to lift it up so he just pisses on it. I piss in the sink. Itchy pisses on the roll of toilet paper. I piss all over the soap dispenser then we both piss on the floor and leave. I lift a couple handfuls of gum and candy while Itchy buys some cigarettes. We go back out and get in the car.

"Oh fuck man, I gotta go back to the joint now," Itchy says.

"What're you talking about?" I say. "I thought you were splitting for the rest of the day."

"No way. My p.o. calls those fuckers up every week and gets my attendance record. It's the straight and narrow now for me, he says. Any more fuck ups, like another dirty U.A., and it's back to the industrial detention center."

"You pussy. What a fucking drag."

I drive him back to Metro. I pull up in front. We both huff a little more dust. For a second I think I might go to my woodworking class. I kind of like it there. But then I think, fuck it, what's the use. I've got better things to do. Itch gets out. "Later," he says. I drive away. I'm all set. I've got the rest of the dust and a six pack of .45 and the vodka. I drive around on the streets. I don't know where I'm going. I've got this job washing dishes at a seafood restaurant but it doesn't start for an hour and a half so there's plenty of time to waste. I get on this one street and just keep going in one direction. I get to a freeway. I take the entrance ramp and get on it. It's busy.

When I was about twelve they gave me this hamster for my birthday. I don't remember if I asked for it or what. Maybe it was part of the old lady's improvement program. You know, I'd get to feed the hamster and clean its cage and all that rot. Teach me some responsibility. I played with it for a couple of weeks. Mostly what it did was sleep and eat. The only other thing it did was get on this wheel in its cage and run for hours on end. Then it would quit and go back to sleep.

One day after it'd been on the wheel for awhile I bent down and looked at its face. Beady black little pig eyes staring straight ahead. I sat and watched it some more. Then I opened the window and threw the cage and the hamster out. Nothing that stupid, I thought, should be allowed to live.

That summer the old man found the cage in the bushes while he was mowing. The hamster was just this little dried up scrap of fur by then. He asked me what had happened. I told him I couldn't remember. He looked at me for a long time. I think that was the same summer he started banging his new twat.

Goddamnit! That's exactly what these people in their cars on this freeway remind me of. That fucking hamster on its wheel in its cage. I reach back and get the crossbow. I steer with my knees and cock it and load it with one of the arrows. There's a guy right next to me in a little sport coupe piece of shit. He's talking on his car phone. I honk the horn. He looks up. I give him the finger. He scowls and gives it back. I zip down the power window, slide over, steer with my left hand, put the crossbow on the window sill, point it at him.

It's so fine. The terror on his face right before I pull the trigger. But it misses him and breaks a hole in the little window behind him. He's scared shitless and weaves all over his lane and almost smashes into the guard rail. Then he stomps on it and pulls away, fast. Ha ha. Ha ha ha ha ha. I get off at the next exit. I'll bet that fucker shit his pants.

I crack another .45 and cruise along. This is niggertown. Black people stand on the corners and sit on their sagging porches and stare at me as I drive past. Cross an intersection. Now it's white niggertown. People stand in front of their broken houses and look at the busted old cars in their driveways. They're waiting for something to happen. Anything. All of them.

I go like this on the side streets all the way to the mall where I work. Employees are supposed to park in back but it's still an hour until I have to start so I park up front by the street. I'll just sit here and huff some more dust and drink the .45 and watch people go by. I've got a lot of time to kill.

I put in an old Black Sabbath tape. It's one of my favorites. I sniff the rest of the dust. I'm really loaded. I get the crossbow and play with it and start thinking about that Daniel. It's not Dan or Danny, it's fucking Daniel. Rich fag boy. Cocksucker. It just really pisses me off to think about that asshole. I think I'll take his crossbow back to him and shoot him between the eyes with it.

Cars go by in herds. Some of them turn into the mall. Some of them pull into the fast food joints that are all over the place. It's all so fucking useless. Bust open another beer. Take a hit of vodka. Can't go home now. Can't go to the old man's either. He won't have me. Besides, I hate the fucker.

There's a school crossing on the street right in front of me. These yard apes are starting to drift up and punch the button and wait for the light to change so they can cross. They shove at each other and run around while they wait. They're just happy to be out of the joint for the day. Sorry kids, but it just gets worse.

There's one crumb muncher that's a mean little shit. He's taken off his jacket and he's whipping a little girl with it. She screams and runs away from him but he follows her and keeps whipping her and laughing. He quits and struts around. He'll probably be a supervisor in a factory someday. He's got this lunch box with that E.T. thing on it. I really hate that thing. It's everywhere. Everyone thinks it's just great. Some rubber toy is going to come down in a big spaceship and fix everything for them.

The kid starts whipping the girl again. I'm going to teach him a lesson and shoot an arrow through his E.T. lunch box. I point the crossbow out the window and squeeze one off. Uh-oh. I hit the little girl. It's like one of those mechanical ducks you shoot at in a carnival game. One second she's standing there, the next she's down on the ground with an arrow sticking out of her head. The other kids start screaming and running around in circles. Some of them are pointing at me.

About a week ago me and Itchy were fucked up and had this contest to see who could hold a lit cigarette on their hand the longest. I guess I won. I've got this big scab on the back of my hand. I pick at it. The new skin is pink around the edge of the scab. I pick at it some more.

I've seen things spraying for bugs that you wouldn't believe. Like that woman. The company's got these steady contracts with some of the big landlords around town. Guys that own fifty or sixty junky houses, slumlords really. People move in and out of those places all the time and the bugs move in and out with them. I went to that woman's house about two o'clock or two thirty. She answered the door in a tattered old bathrobe. She wasn't wearing makeup and her hair was hanging out all over the place. She let me in and then sat back down in front of the TV and picked up a drink she was working on. Middle of winter and hotter than Hell in there. Just a regular piece of bad news she was. I did the kitchen and bathroom. That's all we're supposed to do. You'll find 90 per cent of your roaches in the kitchen but people do hate to see a bug while they're taking a bath. Worse than while they're eating. I came back out into her living room to leave by the front door and she asked me if I'd hit the bedroom. Said she'd seen a couple roaches back there. It doesn't make any difference to me. Five minutes and five cents worth of spray. I went back there to do it but I noticed this crib with a baby lying in it. I was going to go tell her that maybe she ought to take the baby out of there before I sprayed but then I thought it looked strange. It looked kind of blue and its arms were bent up under its chin. I went back out to the living room and told her maybe there was something wrong with her kid. She said, "Yeah, there's something wrong with him. He's dead. He's been dead for two days." She said she'd been meaning to get down to the ADC office and tell them about it but she hadn't gotten around to it yet. I opened the door and stood there with one hand on the door knob and the can of bug juice in the other. Somebody won something on the game

BUGMAN

show she was watching and they started clanging a bell. She sat there on the couch and gave me the up and down. I noticed she was pretty drunk. She had that squirrely glazed over look. Her bathrobe was opened so that about half her tits was showing. She asked me if I'd been getting it nice and regular.

I didn't tell Marie about the baby. I figured it would just upset her. She's pretty upset most of the time already. Sometimes I wake up in the middle of the night and she's lying there crying. She won't tell me why. She wants me to quit. She says the spray will kill me. I don't see how I can do that. It's all I know.

ABOUT THE AUTHOR

Purnell Christian is an electrical engineer. *Modern Physics* is his first published work. He lives in Wichita, Kansas.

A NOTE ON THE TYPE

Modern Physics is composed in a computerized version of Weiss, a typeface originally designed for the Bauer type foundry of Germany by Emil Rudolph Weiss in 1925. Formerly a poet, Weiss turned his attention to lettering and type designing after receiving admiration from his editors for his beautifully rendered handwritten poems.

Many typographers consider Weiss to be an uncommonly distinctive, original face, and point to the capital and lower-case S as evidence. Both letters have an inverted appearance, with the weight focused on the top, rather than the bottom, half.